Dear Readers,

Many years ago, when I was a kid, my father said to me, "Bill, it doesn't really matter what you do in life. What's important is to be the *best* William Johnstone you can be."

I've never forgotten those words. And now, many years and almost two hundred books later, I like to think that I am still trying to be the best William Johnstone I can be. Whether it's Ben Raines in the Ashes series, or Frank Morgan, the last gunfighter, or Smoke Jensen, our intrepid mountain man, or John Barrone and his hardworking crew keeping America safe from terrorist lowlifes in the Code Name series, I want to make each new book better than the last and deliver powerful storytelling.

Equally important, I try to create the kinds of believable characters that we can all identify with, real people who face tough challenges. When one of my creations blasts an enemy into the middle of next week, you can be damn sure he had a good reason.

As a storyteller, my job is to entertain you, my readers, and to make sure that you get plenty of enjoyment from my books for your hard-earned money. This is not a job I take lightly. And I greatly appreciate your feedback—you are my gold, and your opinions *do* count. So please keep the letters and e-mails coming.

Respectfully yours,

William W. Johnstone

BOOK YOUR PLACE ON OUR WEBSITE AND MAKE THE READING CONNECTION!

We've created a customized website just for our very special readers, where you can get the inside scoop on everything that's going on with Zebra, Pinnacle and Kensington books.

When you come online, you'll have the exciting opportunity to:

- View covers of upcoming books
- Read sample chapters
- Learn about our future publishing schedule (listed by publication month *and author*)
- Find out when your favorite authors will be visiting a city near you
- Search for and order backlist books from our online catalog
- Check out author bios and background information
- Send e-mail to your favorite authors
- Meet the Kensington staff online
- Join us in weekly chats with authors, readers and other guests
- Get writing guidelines
- AND MUCH MORE!

Visit our website at
http://www.kensingtonbooks.com

WILLIAM W. JOHNSTONE

WITH FRED AUSTIN

REVENGE
OF
EAGLES

PINNACLE BOOKS
Kensington Publishing Corp.
http://www.kensingtonbooks.com

CHAPTER 1

Falcon MacCallister stood on the depot platform at Glenwood Springs, Colorado. Behind him, the train popped and snapped as the bearings and gearboxes cooled. The relief valve vented steam in puffs that made it sound as if the mighty engine was trying to recover its breath after a difficult run.

Standing slightly over six feet tall, Falcon had shoulders so wide and muscular, and a waist so flat and thin, that his suits had to be custom-made for him. His eyes were pale blue, staring out from a chiseled face. He had wheat-colored hair, which he wore short and neat under a black hat decorated with a turquoise-encrusted silver band. Right now he was wearing a black suit with a crisp white shirt and a black string tie.

He had come to Glenwood Springs because an old friend was here. Walking across the depot platform, he threw his grip in the back of a hack.

"The Glenwood Springs Hotel," he said.

The driver snapped the reins over his horse and the Light Brett carriage pulled away.

"You moving to our fair city, or are you just here for a visit?" the driver asked over the clip-clop of the horses' hooves.

"Visiting."

"Ah. And will you be taking our waters? The sulphur springs are good for what ails you."

"No."

"Well, you certainly picked a good time to visit us. We are having a beautiful spring," the driver said. Realizing then that his passenger wasn't much of a talker, the driver stopped trying to make conversation, and concentrated on his driving.

The Hotel Glenwood sat in such a way as to allow its front door to open onto the corner of Fifth Street and Colorado Avenue. It was a large, imposing edifice that could compete with just about any hotel Falcon had ever seen, including those in New York. It was three stories high, with dormer windows in the roof that made the attic usable as well. A roofed balcony wrapped around the second floor, providing an arched roof for the ground-level porch.

Falcon paid the fare, then stepped into the hotel. The lobby was large, with overstuffed sofas and chairs, highly polished brass spittoons, and a few potted plants. The carpet was light brown, decorated with a pattern of roses.

"Yes, sir," the clerk behind the desk said brightly. "Come to take the waters?"

"No. I need a room."

The clerk turned the registration book toward him, and Falcon signed in.

By the time Falcon finished signing, the clerk was holding a room key. "Very good, sir, you'll be in Room 307, Mister. . . ." He looked at the registration; then his eyes grew wide and he swallowed. "MacCallister? You are Falcon MacCallister?"

"I am."

"Oh, uh, Mr. MacCallister, I beg your pardon," he said. Turning, he hung the key back up on the board, then got another one. "Three-oh-seven would not be an appropriate room for you. I'm sure you will find this one much more to your liking. It is three-oh-one, it's our corner room, and as you'll see when you go up there, it has cupola windows, which will provide you with an excellent view of our fair city."

"Thanks."

"Is there anything else I can do for you?"

"Yes. I believe John Henry Holliday is staying in this hotel."

"John Henry?"

"Dr. Holliday."

"Doctor . . ." The hotel clerk gasped. "Good Lord, sir, do you mean Doc Holliday?"

"Yes."

"Well, yes, yes, as a matter of fact he is a guest in our hotel. He is here in Glenwood Springs, taking the cure for his tuberculosis."

"What room?"

The clerk smiled. "He is in three-oh-three, which, as it turns out, is right next to your own room. But you won't find him there now. He is down at the springs. He generally returns to the hotel around suppertime, though."

"Thanks."

Falcon went to his room. His name often elicited the kind of response he got from the hotel clerk. There were those who said that he was one of the most accomplished men with a six-gun to ever roam the West. Stories about him were told and retold until they reached legendary proportions, and Falcon MacCallister seemed larger than life.

But the truth was, and Falcon understood and accepted this . . . many of the stories told about him had actually happened to his father, Jamie Ian MacCallister.

From the War for Texas Independence to the Colorado Rockies, to the goldfields of California, to the battlefields of the Civil War, Jamie MacCallister had made a name for himself, raised a family, and amassed a fortune. If some of

Jamie's exploits were confused with some of Falcon's, it was understandable. On the other hand, Falcon's own exploits had put his name in the history books, alongside that of his storied father.

The corner of Falcon's hotel room was circular and surrounded by bay windows that, as the clerk had promised, afforded excellent views of both streets. A settee and an easy chair converted the corner into a sitting area. Falcon stepped up to the windows and looked out over the town, and into the mountains beyond. He recalled his first meeting with Doc Holliday.

After Falcon's wife, Mary, was killed by renegade Indians, Falcon started moving. He had no particular place to go, and nothing he had to do when he got there. But somehow moving around seemed to help him get over the pain of his loss.

He found himself in Tombstone, Arizona Territory, during one such sojourn, and as he stood at the bar in the Oriental Café, two star-packers stepped up beside him. One of the deputies was very short, but with a prominent belly rise. The other, who was younger, was reed-thin and gawky.

"Mister, Your name wouldn't be Falcon MacCallister now, would it?" the short, fat one asked.

"It is."

"You're under arrest."

"For what?"

"For murder, or so the wanted posters say."

"Deputy, if you've got paper on me, it's no good," Falcon said. "All the dodgers have been recalled."

"I don't remember no recall notice," the short one said, his hand moving toward his pistol. "I'm Deputy Stillwell, and I'm puttin' you under arrest."

"I told you, the papers have been recalled. Check with the sheriff."

Stillwell shook his head. "Can't do that," he said. "Seein' as how

Sheriff Behan's outta town, why, that makes me'n Jimmy here in charge."

By now the confrontation between Falcon and the deputies had caught the attention of everyone in the saloon, and all other conversation came to a halt. Over in the corner, Falcon saw a well-dressed man sitting by himself. He had a deck of cards spread out in front of him, and was playing solitaire. He continued to play, but it was clear that he was monitoring everything that was going on.

"All right, if you insist, I'll go to the sheriff's office with you, and find the recall notices," Falcon said.

"We ain't goin' nowhere till your hands is up and your holsters is empty," Stillwell said, starting for his gun.

As quick as thought, Falcon drew both guns. He had them cocked and aimed before either of the deputies could clear leather.

The two deputies slowly raised their hands, their eyes wide with naked fear.

"What . . . what're you goin' to do with us, mister?" the one named Jimmy asked.

Falcon let out a long sigh. "Well, I'll be damned if I know," he said. "I just came into town for a drink, meal, and bath. I guess we can go on over to the jail, like we were going to, and I'll prove to you that I'm not a wanted man."

At that moment, Falcon noticed that the man in the dark suit, the one who had been playing cards, got up from his corner table and approached them.

"Good afternoon, Mr. MacCallister. My name's John Henry Holliday."

"Holliday?" Falcon asked. Then something about the man matched a description he had heard once. "Would you be Doc Holliday?"

"That's what they call me," Doc Holliday replied.

Falcon had heard of Doc Holliday, and he wondered why he was stepping in to take a hand in the situation.

"Perhaps I can be of some assistance here," Doc said, answering Falcon's unasked question. He nodded toward the two deputies. *"These two misguided gentlemen lack the intelligence of a cow turd. But I'm sure they thought they were just doing their job."*

Falcon nodded. *"As slow as they are, maybe they should start thinking about some other form of employment."*

Doc chuckled. *"I imagine that thought is going through their little pea-sized minds right now."*

Doc turned toward Deputy Stillwell. *"Suppose I take Mr. MacCallister over to the city marshal's office and have Wyatt check him out. Would that satisfy you boys?"*

Both nodded their heads. *"Yes, sir, Doc,"* Stillwell answered.

Doc glanced back toward Falcon.

"That all right with you?"

"Sure, fine, just so I get something to eat before much longer." Falcon holstered his pistols, but so quickly had he drawn them that Stillwell and Jimmy knew they were in as much danger from him now as they had been when he had the guns in his hands. They kept their hands up.

Oh, for cryin' out loud, will you two idiots put your hands down?" Doc said to them. Then, turning back to Falcon, he said, "It is all right for them to put their hands down, isn't it?"

"Yes, of course," Falcon replied.

With a sigh of relief, both Stillwell and Jimmy lowered their hands.

"I tell you what, Mr. MacCallister," Doc began.

"Falcon," Falcon corrected.

"All right, Falcon it is. Right after we see Wyatt and get this straightened out, we'll go to Campbell and Hatch's saloon. They've got the best food, and what's more important, the best whiskey in town."

Falcon's reverie was interrupted by the sudden out-break of a deep hacking cough, coming from the hall just outside his room. Falcon moved to his door and opened it, just as Doc Holliday was using the key to his own room.

"Damn. I'm going to have to write a letter to the governor," Falcon said. "It appears that they will let just anyone into the state now."

Doc looked up with a quick flash of anger. Then, as he recognized Falcon, the anger left his face to be replaced by a broad smile.

"Well, as I live and breathe . . . barely . . . if it isn't Falcon MacCallister!"

"In the flesh," Falcon said.

Doc stepped toward him with his hand extended. "Damn, Falcon, I can't tell you how pleased I am to see you."

"Hello, Doc," Falcon replied, extending his own hand. "What's new?"

"I'm dying," Doc replied. He laughed. "But then there is nothing new about that, is there? I've been dying for the last fifteen years. I tried to get someone to shoot me along the way, but I kept running into idiots who couldn't shoot their way out of a paper bag. What are you doing in Colorado?"

"I live here, remember?" Falcon said.

"Oh, yes, you have your own town, as I seem to recall. MacCallister, Colorado."

"Not my town," Falcon said. "It's just a town with my father's name."

"Well, come on in and have a drink. I've got whiskey in my room."

"Sounds good to me," Falcon said.

Doc returned to his door and started to unlock it, but before he could do so, he broke out into another spasmodic round of coughing. He pulled a handkerchief from his pocket, and Falcon saw that it was already discolored with flecks of blood.

After the coughing spell, Doc put the handkerchief away and smiled wanly at Falcon.

"I beg your pardon for that outbreak," he said.

Falcon didn't answer, because he knew no answer was required. Doc managed to get the door unlocked; then he pushed it open and made a gesture of invitation with his hand.

Doc's room was obviously a residential rather than a transient room, for it had, in addition to the hotel furniture, a few things that were Doc's personal property. Next to a chair, there was a table on which lay a deck of cards spread out in an ongoing game of solitaire. There was also a cabinet, which Falcon did not have in his room.

Doc reached into the cabinet to pull out a bottle and two glasses. He poured the whiskey, then handed one of the glasses over to Falcon.

"Here's to old times," Doc said, lifting his glass.

Falcon returned the salute. Then, stepping over to the cabinet, he examined Doc's collection of photographs.

"That was my mother," Doc said, pointing to the photograph of an attractive woman who was sitting with the stiffness so necessary for photographs.

"And that one is . . . ?" Falcon asked, pointing to the photo of a younger woman.

"Big Nose Kate," Doc said.

"Oh, yes, I thought I recognized her. Whatever happened to her?"

Doc picked up the picture and looked at it for a while, then put it down.

"She went back to whorin'," he said dismissively.

"Sorry."

"Hell, it don't matter none to me. If she can still sell her ass, more power to her, I say."

"Here's one of Wyatt, I see."

"Yes."

"You ever hear from Wyatt?"

"From time to time," Doc said. "I think he's out in California, or maybe up in Alaska now. You know how he moves around."

"Yes," Falcon said.

Part of Wyatt's moving around, Falcon knew, had to do with the fact that he had revenged the murder of one brother and the crippling of another by going on a killing rampage that didn't end until every one of his adversaries were dead.

"So, do you stay in MacCallister all the time now, or do you still move around a bit?" Doc asked.

"I move around."

"Do you ever get back down to Arizona?"

"I haven't been there for a while."

"Would you like to go back?"

"I don't know. Maybe I would someday. If I had a reason to go."

"What if you owned a silver mine? I mean one that actually had silver. Would that be reason enough for you to go back to Arizona?"

"I don't know. Perhaps it would. Why do you ask? Do you have something in mind?"

"It just so happens that I own a silver mine down there in the Cababi Mountains, near Oro Blanco."

"Do you now?" Falcon said, smiling. "How is it doing?"

"I can answer that in two words," Doc said. "It isn't."

"I thought you said it actually had silver."

"It does, and that's the hell of it. Truth is, I think there's probably ten times more silver still there than has been taken out. But I can't get anyone I trust to run it."

"That can be a problem."

"How would you like to own the mine?"

"I beg your pardon?"

"I'll sell it to you for five thousand dollars."

"Doc, if, as you say, there is still a lot of silver in the

mine, you know it is worth more than five thousand dollars. Why would you sell it so cheaply?"

"What good is a lot of money to me now?" Doc asked. "Look, I figure I've got no more than six months left to live . . . a year at the absolute most." He took in the room with a wave of his arm. "I'm running out of money, and when I can no longer pay for this room, I'm going to be kicked out. I'll wind up in the poorhouse."

For the first time since he had known Doc, Falcon saw a little bit of fear in Doc's eyes.

"I don't want to wind up in a poorhouse, Falcon," he said. "Five thousand dollars would keep me in comfort, here in this room, for the rest of my life."

Falcon stroked his chin. He had more money now than he would ever spend. He did not need a silver mine. He would rather just give Doc five thousand dollars and be done with it, but he knew that Doc wouldn't take a handout from him.

Falcon smiled.

"Sure, why not?" he said. "I've been looking for a reason to go back down there anyway."

"Thank you, Falcon," Doc said in genuine appreciation. "Thank you more than I can say."

"I'll go to the bank tomorrow and cash a draft, then bring you the money."

"No hurry, I'm not dying tonight. Oh, by the way, speaking of dying . . . you do remember your run-in with the Apaches last time you were down there, don't you?"

"Oh, yes," Falcon said. "I remember."

"Good, because you damn well better believe that the Apaches remember. So, look out for yourself while you are down there, okay?"

"I will," Falcon promised.

In his room that night, Falcon recalled his encounter with Naiche, the last chief of the free Chiricahuas. Falcon and Mickey Free had fought the Apache in the

Apache way, scalping those they killed, poking out their eyes, and carving out their hearts. Falcon had sent fear into the hearts of the Indians. They had never encountered such savagery from white men before. They were accustomed to being the ones who struck terror into the hearts of their enemies; now that terror was being returned, many times over.

At first, even the whites were put off by the ferocity of Falcon's campaign. But when he tracked down the Indian butchers and killed them, one by one, the raids on white ranches, farms, and travelers stopped, and Falcon brought peace back to southern Arizona.

As he drifted off to sleep that night, he wondered if anyone in Arizona would remember him.

CHAPTER 2

The dancers were making their own music to accompany their dances. Bells were attached to a strap of leather at their ankles and as they danced about, the bells jingled. They also had bells strapped to their knees and elbows. The dancers moved to and fro around the sitting council, accompanied in their dancing by the singing of children.

Ha-nam-a yo-o ya hai huh-wurt . . .
Far on the desert ridges stands the cactus
Ka-na-hu-va muh-muhk
lo the blossoms swaying
Ka-cho-wuch-chi ka-no-ya ki-moi
to and fro the blossoms swaying, swaying.

When the dancers, and the young Apache children, were finished, Keytano stood from his position at the head of the council and smiled at them.

"You dance and sing well," he said to them. "And you have brought joy to the hearts of all who heard you."

After the surrender of Geronimo most of the Chiricahua, who were deemed the most aggressive and war-like of all the Apache, were removed from Arizona. What remained were the Western Apache, Mescalero, Jicarilla, and Lipan. The Apache occupied some two million acres of reservation and designated land.

They were not required to stay with their particular band, but could move around freely within the area designated for them. As a result, many of the subgroups began to blend, and the Cababi Mountain settlement was, in fact, a mixture of Western Apache, Jicarilla, and what few remained of the Chiricahua.

Keytano was the leader of the Cababi Mountain settlement. He was a nephew of the great Indian leader Cochise and first cousin to both Geronimo and Nachie.

Since the capture of Geronimo, a condition of relative peace had existed. But now that peace was being strained by the steady encroachment of the white man. More and more white men were wandering into land that had been promised to the Apache by treaty. And most damaging of all, a tributary from the Santa Cruz River had been dammed up by some of the white settlers, thus depriving the Cababi settlement of its water. The lack of water was having disastrous effects.

Then, recently, three white prospectors who were trespassing on Indian land had been killed, and that had raised the tension between the whites and the Apache. The situation had reached the point where it was necessary for Keytano to call a council to discuss what should be done.

"They put their cattle on our land, and they roam our mountains looking for the white and yellow metal," Chetopa said. Chetopa was several years younger than Keytano and, lately, had been challenging the older chief for leadership.

"Chetopa, I know that it was you and some of your followers who killed the white men," Keytano said. "By your foolishness, you have brought danger to all of our people."

"You say it is foolishness, I say it is courage," Chetopa said defiantly. He struck his breast with his fist. "I do not fear the white man. I do not tremble before his army."

"It is not only his army we must fight. Do you not

remember Dlo Binanta, the tall white man with hair the color of wheat? The man who brought fear and sorrow to so many of our wickiups?"

"I do not fear Dlo Binanta."

"You do not fear him because he has gone to the mountains far to the north," Ketano said. "But if there is one white man like Dlo Binanta, then there may be more."

"You have become an old woman," Chetopa said, scoffing in derision. "It is clear to all who have eyes to see what should be done. We must take up the fight and run the whites off our land."

Several of the young warriors grunted and nodded in agreement with Chetopa.

"And how would we do this, Chetopa?" another asked. This was Nincha, brother to Keytano. "We are very few now."

"Do you lose your courage when you grow old?" Chetopa asked. "Those with Geronimo were very few, but he fought the white man for many years, killing many, and bringing terror into their hearts."

"And I ask you, Chetopa, where is Geronimo now?" Nincha said.

There were others who spoke like Chetopa, saying that the path of war was the only way, but there were more who agreed with Nincha. Finally, after listening to the council, Keytano raised his hands to call for silence.

"Hear me, my brothers," he said. "We will not make war now. We will send word to the white soldier chief and ask him to use his soldiers to keep the white men from our lands."

Chetopa made a scoffing sound. "That will do nothing," he said.

"Perhaps it will do nothing, but we must try."

"And if it does nothing?"

"Then we will meet in council again," Keytano said.

After the council broke up, Keytano went to the wickiup of his sister. "May I enter?" he called.

Tolietha stood quickly, the flour of the flat bread she was making still on her hands.

"Yes, my brother," she answered.

In the war with the whites, many Apache were killed, and many others were captured and sent away. Keytano never thought that he would be chief, but the duty had fallen to him and he tried, always, to do what was best for his people.

When the white government said that all the young ones would have to go away to school, some protested, and said they would flee to Mexico. But Keytano had held them together, and told them that it would be good for their people to learn some of the ways of the whites, especially how to read and write.

Keytano's own daughter had gone away to school, and just this morning, the trading post had given him a letter that came from her. He had not had time to do anything with it before the council met, but now, Keytano held the letter before him, showing it to his sister.

"I have received this from my daughter," he said. "I would like one of the young ones to tell me the words."

Tolietha signaled to one of her children who was being educated in the mission school.

"Read this to your uncle," she ordered.

The boy, who was about twelve, took the letter from Keytano, opened it, and began to read.

Father,

I have completed my schooling and will be coming home soon. I miss you and my mother, and I miss our home and the mountains.

I have learned much while I was here. Some of the things I learned will be very good, and I believe I can use what I have learned to help our people.

*But I think it would be good if the whites could learn
some things from us. They do not understand the air, the
water, the land, and the mountains. They do not understand the animals and the plants. They do not understand
that all people, all animals, all plants, the sky, the water,
the land, are all a part of the whole.*
They do not understand how to live with life.
They know only how to live without life.

Finishing the letter, the young boy gave it back to
Keytano.

"It is good that she is coming home," Keytano said. "I
will tell her mother this good news."

Falcon MacCallister was tired. He had been traveling for
nearly two weeks now, riding on a combination of stagecoach and train. He was on a train now, having connected
with the Southern Pacific at Sweetwater. He had boarded
the train late last night, and as it had come south through
the Sonora Desert, Falcon had been unable to get comfortable in the hard seats of the day coach. He was in a day
coach because there was neither a Wagner nor Pullman
parlor car attached to this train, it being considered a
local. He had just sat back down after walking around to
stretch out the kinks, when the front door opened and the
conductor started through the car.

"Calabasas! This is Calabasas!" the conductor called,
passing down the aisle. Falcon, who was sitting on the right
side of the car, stared through the window as the train
began to slow, then finally squeal to a stop. He saw a low-
lying adobe building with a white sign hanging from the
roof. The sign read CALABASAS, ELEVATION 4000 FEET.

Falcon stood up, reached into the overhead rack, and
pulled down a canvas grip, his only luggage. When he
stepped down from the train a moment later, he saw a

man with a badge, holding a shotgun, standing by the express car. The agent in the express car was handing down a canvas bag to another man; then he and the armed lawman started up the street. Falcon had obviously just witnessed the transfer of a money shipment, and he wondered idly how much might be in the little canvas bag that they were guarding so carefully.

Right across the street from the depot was the Railroad Hotel. Falcon walked toward it, picking his way through the horse droppings. A dog slept on the front stoop of the hotel, so secure in its right to be there that it didn't even open an eye as Falcon stepped up onto the porch.

Falcon pushed open the door and a small, attached bell jangled as he stepped inside. There was nobody behind the desk, but the jingling bell summoned the clerk from a room that was adjacent to the desk.

"Yes, sir?"

"I need a room," Falcon said.

"Very good, sir," the clerk said, turning the registration book around for Falcon to sign.

The clerk handed Falcon a key.

"That'll be fifty cents a night," the clerk said. "Three dollars if you stay an entire week. That saves you fifty cents."

"I'll take it one night at a time," Falcon said, handing the clerk half a dollar. "Does a bath come with it?"

"Indeed it does, sir," the clerk said. "We have bathing rooms on every floor."

"Sounds good," Falcon said, picking up his grip and heading for the stairs.

The bathing room the clerk spoke of was at the far end of the upstairs hallway. Water came from a tank overhead, heated by the sun and brought to the room by turning a spigot.

Falcon took a bath, then a much-needed nap, waking up just as it was beginning to get dark outside. Going downstairs, he took a walk around the little town before winding up in the Lucky Strike Saloon.

Stepping through the batwing doors, Falcon moved to one side and placed his back against the wall. It was a habit he had developed over several years of being on the trail and encountering, and making, enemies as well as friends.

The symphony of the saloon was a familiar one: clinking glasses, loud talk, and a slightly-out-of-tune piano playing away from the back wall.

Once his eyes were accustomed to the low light in the saloon, he surveyed the crowd. It seemed to be a combination of cowboys and hard-rock miners. These were hardworking men, letting off a little steam after a day of labor. There was also the usual mix of gamblers, drifters, and bar girls in the room.

Smiling, one of the girls came over to greet Falcon.

"My, my," she said, looking up at him. "You're a big, good-looking man."

Falcon smiled. "What's your name?"

"Callie."

"Well, Callie, I wouldn't be a gentleman if I let a compliment like that go unrewarded. Can I buy you a drink?"

"I would like that," Callie said. "Thank you . . ." She paused, waiting for him to offer his name.

"Falcon."

"Falcon? That's an interesting name."

"My parents were interesting people. Barkeep," Falcon called. "I'll have a beer, and give the lady whatever she wants."

"Lady?" a man standing down at the other end of the bar said, scoffing. "Mister, I don't know whether you are blind, or just dumb. But that ain't no lady. That's a whore."

Falcon looked down toward the end of the bar. The belligerent man had dark hair and dark eyes and a scar on his cheek. He didn't look like either a miner or a cowboy, but Falcon had seen his kind before. They were drifters who supported themselves in any way that did not require work. Most of the time they were gamblers, cheats, and petty thieves.

"You know this asshole?" Falcon asked Callie. He said it loudly enough that several people heard it, including the belligerent man at the end of the bar. The others who did hear it laughed, including Callie.

"What? What did you call me?" the belligerent man asked in a blustering voice.

"I never met him before this afternoon," Callie replied. "He says his name is Pete. Pete Tucker."

"I asked you what you called me," Pete demanded.

"Oh, I'm sorry. Didn't I say it clearly enough?" Falcon replied. "I called you an asshole. Ass . . . hole," he said slowly and deliberately.

"Why, you son of a bitch!" Pete said, making a grab for his pistol.

Falcon threw his beer mug at Pete, hitting him in the forehead with it. Pete's first reaction was to put both hands to his head and when he did so, Falcon closed the distance between them in a rush. He hit Pete in the nose, and felt it break under his fist.

With a shout of pain, Pete dropped his hands to his nose. When he did, Falcon drove his fist into Pete's belly, causing him to double over as he gasped for breath. That enabled Falcon to grab him by his collar and belt. Picking him up, Falcon carried him to the front door, then tossed him out into the street, right into a pile of horse apples. Following him into the street, Falcon leaned down and took Pete's gun from his holster. He removed the cylinder, then stuck the gun, barrel down, into a horse turd.

When Falcon went back inside, he was greeted by applause and a smiling Callie, who was holding a fresh mug of beer for him.

"Mister," she said. "My job is to make men buy me drinks, so I've never bought a man a beer in my life. But after you came to the defense of my honor like that, buying you a beer is the least I can do."

"Well, thank you, Callie."

"I wish I could offer more, if you know what I mean," she said. She looked toward the clock. "But in ten minutes I have a . . . uh . . . engagement."

Falcon smiled at her. "Then I'll just enjoy your company for the next ten minutes until it is time for your . . . engagement," he said, setting the word apart the way she had.

In truth, Falcon didn't actually want to take her up on her offer, so it worked out better this way.

After Callie left with the man who had arranged for her services, a young, hard-rock miner, Falcon saw a poker game in progress. When one of the players got up, Falcon walked over to the table.

"Mind if I join the game?"

"No, we don't mind at all. Fresh blood is always welcome. Please, feel free to join in," one of the men said.

The game turned out to be a friendly, low-stakes game with enough good hands being passed around from player to player so that nobody was winning too much and nobody was losing too much.

The one who had invited Falcon to sit introduced himself as George Snyder.

"I run the express office," George said. "This is Paul Gibson, who runs the hardware store, and Mike Stovall, a rancher."

"I'm Falcon MacCallister," Falcon said.

Mike Stovall raised his eyebrows at hearing the name. "Falcon MacCallister?" he said. "Where have I heard that name before?"

"I get around," Falcon said offhandedly. He was never in a hurry to remind anyone of who he was for fear of dredging up some old enmity of which he might not be aware.

"Wait a minute, I remember you," Stovall said, snapping his fingers in recognition. "You're the fella who had a personal war with Naiche sometime back, aren't you?"

"That would be me," Falcon admitted. "You've got a good memory."

"Well, hell, mister, it's not hard to remember a fella that helped make this part of the country a lot safer," Mike said.

"Yeah, it's safer for the time being," Paul said. "The question now is, how much longer is it going to be safe?"

"Why do you say that?" Falcon asked.

"Keytano's as bad as Geronimo and Naiche. They should've taken care of him when they took care of the others."

"Keytano?"

"He's the chief now."

"Keytano has never given us any trouble," George said. "Damn, who dealt this hand?"

"You did," Paul said.

"Well, I'm obviously an idiot," George said, and the others laughed.

"What do you mean Keytano has never given us any trouble?" Mike asked. "What about those three prospectors they found a while ago? All three of 'em was dead and all three of 'em was scalped."

"Yes, well, they were found well into Indian land," George said. "They had no business being there. Besides, anyone could have killed them; we don't know that it was Keytano. It could have been someone else, angry because they were there. Dealer takes three cards."

Falcon held a pair of jacks and drew three kings to them. He won the pot, his first pot in the last three hands, and smiling at his good fortune, reached out to drag the money toward him.

"Mr. MacCallister, I liked the way you handled that fella a while ago," George said. "Most men would have drawn their gun, and we would've had another killing. But you didn't, though Lord knows, you had every justification to do so."

"Do you have many killings here?"

"Not so many as before. Sheriff Ferrell has done a very good job of cracking down on the lawlessness in this town."

"Yes, by making the town add two deputies to the payroll," Paul said.

"What are you saying, Paul? Would you would rather it go back to the way it was before?" George asked.

"No, I'm not saying that. I'm just saying that we're having to pay for it. The town is taxin' ever'thing now. Even the food you buy at the grocery store is bein' taxed to pay for the deputies."

"I don't care if it is costing us. I'm with George. I think it's worth it," Mike said.

George glanced over at the clock. "Speaking of the sheriff and his deputies, the wife and I are having them over for breakfast tomorrow. And if I want to stay in good with her, I reckon I'd better go home and see if she needs anything."

Paul laughed. "You just got a money shipment in, didn't you?"

"Yes."

"Why, you sly old dog you. That's a cheap way of hiring a few extra guards when you transfer it to the stagecoach tomorrow. Just feed them breakfast."

"Whatever is necessary," George said as he stood. "Gentlemen, this evening has been a pleasure. Mr. MacCallister, it was nice meeting you," he added, extending his hand.

"The same," Falcon replied, taking the hand George had offered.

It was just after first light the next morning when Pete Tucker sat on his horse at the edge of town. His nose still hurt, and it whistled every time he took a breath.

He reached up to press on the nostril to see if he could stop it from whistling, and the pain caused him to wince.

"I should've killed that son of a bitch," he said aloud.

About a mile out of town, he saw what he had been waiting for, the approach of Fargo Ford and four other riders. He waited patiently until they drew even with him.

There were no greetings. Instead Fargo asked, "Did the shipment of money come in?"

"Yes, it's down at the express office now," Pete answered.

Fargo squinted at him. "Son of a bitch, you look like shit. What the hell happened to you?"

It wasn't until then that the others noticed Pete's condition. His nose was misshapen and his eyes were black.

"My horse kicked me," Pete said.

Fargo laughed. "What kind of a damn fool would let his horse kick him?"

"It's not funny," Pete said, putting his hand to his nose and wincing in pain.

"No, I reckon not." Fargo pulled his gun out, then looked at the others. "Okay, ever'body check your guns. Make sure they're loaded."

Pete pulled his rifle from the saddle sleeve.

"You don't want to use a rifle here," Fargo said. "We're going to have to move quick. Use your pistol."

"I'd rather use my rifle," Pete said.

Fargo rode over closer, then reached down and pulled Pete's pistol. "I said use your . . ." He stopped in midsentence when he saw that the pistol was missing its cylinder. "What the hell happened to your pistol?" he asked.

"I don't know. The cylinder fell out somewhere."

"Mister, next time you agree to do a job with me, you make damn sure you got the right equipment," Fargo said. "Never mind. When we get there, you stay mounted and hold the horses."

"Whatever you say," Pete said in submission.

CHAPTER 3

Just a few minutes before Fargo Ford and the others gathered at the edge of town, Falcon MacCallister came downstairs to the dining room of the Railroad Hotel. Looking around the room, he chose a table in the corner, then sat with his back to the wall so he could observe everyone and everything. He was carrying his small grip with him, and he put it down by his chair.

A waiter hurried over to him, carrying a menu. "Good morning, sir," he said.

"Good morning," Falcon replied. He picked up the menu, which advertised the Railroad Hotel Dining Room as THE FINEST EATING ESTABLISHMENT IN CALABASAS, ARIZONA TERRITORY. What the menu did not point out was the fact that it was the only eating establishment in Calabasas. Though, to be honest, they did serve beans and tortillas at the Lucky Strike Saloon, because that had been Falcon's supper last night after the card game.

Falcon put the menu aside without opening it. "I'll have biscuits, a couple of fried eggs over easy, some fried potatoes, ham, and coffee," he said.

"Very good, sir," the waiter replied, picking up the menu and heading for the kitchen.

Shortly after buying the mine from Doc Holliday, Falcon had decided to come down and check on it. He was on his final leg now, but the last eighty miles would be by stagecoach to Oro Blanco, the location of his mine.

Oro Blanco.

The name meant "White Gold." He didn't know if the name was prophetic . . . or just hopeful.

The stage would be leaving for Oro Blanco at seven this morning, and according to the schedule, would arrive in Oro Blanco by suppertime.

The waiter brought Falcon his breakfast, including a generous supply of butter and jam for the half-dozen biscuits.

"Thanks," Falcon said, taking a bite of one of the biscuits as he surveyed his meal.

"I notice you are carrying a portmanteau. You takin' the train out today?" the waiter asked.

"No, the stage. It leaves at seven."

"Would you like to take a lunch with you? Only twenty-five cents."

"It was my understanding that the stage would be stopping in Pajarito at noon."

"Yes, but you never know what you'll get in Pajarito. I can fix a ham sandwich for you that'll be real tasty."

"Thanks anyway, but I'll take my chances at the stop in Pajarito," Falcon replied.

"Suit yourself," the waiter said, somewhat disappointed that he had not been able to make a sale. The sandwich arrangements were made strictly on his own, as he bought the makings from the restaurant and sold his products to passengers on both the train and the stagecoach.

"Waiter," someone called, and the waiter excused himself to answer the summons.

With the waiter out of the way, Falcon managed to get into some serious eating.

Falcon was just buttering his last biscuit as Fargo Ford was leading his five men by outside. They were unremarkable in appearance, except for the fact that the six were riding together. However, because it was so early in the morning, even that didn't arouse too much attention.

The six rode right down the middle of the street, keeping their horses at a slow walk.

"All right, we'll dismount here," Fargo said to the others, speaking authoritatively. "Pete, you stay mounted. You other fellas, give the reins to your horses to him. Hang on to 'em, Pete. If we have to get out of here in a hurry, I don't want to have to be chasin' down my mount."

"I know what to do, Fargo, you don't have to tell me," Pete said.

"Yeah, well, from the looks of your face, you ain't that smart around horses," Fargo said, and the others laughed.

The men dismounted, then started walking toward a building about fifty yards away, Pete following on horseback with the other horses. A large sign on the front of the building read WESTERN EXPRESS OFFICE.

"Are we sure the money is here?" one of the men asked Fargo.

"Pete said it is," Fargo answered. "So it damn sure better be, or he'll be answerin' to me."

"I still don't see why we're robbin' it here. Why don't we just wait until it gets put on the stagecoach?"

"And go up against the shotgun guard and whoever else might be on the stage? No, thanks. We hit them this morning; the expressman will still be at breakfast and half the town will still be asleep. Just keep your wits about you, we'll go in, get the money, and get out of here fast. By the time anyone figures out what happened, we'll be ten miles from here."

When they got within twenty yards of the building, the front door opened unexpectedly and four men came out.

"What the hell, Fargo? I thought you said nobody would be here. They're wearing badges! That's the law!"

"Pete?" Fargo hissed angrily. "What is this? What are these badge-packers doin' here?"

"I didn't know nothin' about this," Pete said. "You can't blame this on me!"

"What are we goin' to do, Fargo?"

"I don't know, I don't know. Let me think," Fargo said.

"I'm glad you and your deputies could come, Sheriff Ferrell," George Snyder was saying to his breakfast guests as he walked out to the porch with them.

"I'll tell you this, George," the sheriff replied as he patted his stomach. "For the life of me, I can't understand why you don't weigh three hundred pounds. I mean, what with a wife that can cook like that. I do believe that is about the best breakfast I've ever . . ."

"Who are you men, and what do you want?" one of the deputies shouted, interrupting the sheriff in mid-sentence. The deputy pointed to Fargo and the men who were approaching the express office in what the deputy perceived to be a suspicious manner.

"Sheriff?" George said. Like the deputy, George was concerned by the determined approach of the men.

Sheriff Ferrell looked up, as curious as the others. That was when he recognized the leader.

"Son of a bitch! It's Fargo Ford!" the sheriff shouted, going for his gun.

At this point neither Fargo, nor the men with him, had drawn their guns. But with the sheriff's confrontation, the guns came out at about the same time and, within seconds, the street was filled with the explosive sounds of gunfire and billowing clouds of white smoke. George Snyder, who wasn't armed, went down with the opening volley.

Falcon was taking a sip of coffee when he heard the sound of gunshots from out in the street. Getting up quickly, he ran out onto the front porch of the hotel and looked toward the sound of the guns. He saw someone standing in front of the hotel, looking toward the far end of the street. It was Paul Gibson, one of the men Falcon had played cards with last night.

"Mr. Gibson, what is it?" Falcon called from the front porch of the hotel. "What's going on?"

"It looks like someone is tryin' to rob the express office," Paul replied. "There's shootin' goin' on down there."

A bullet whizzed by, the angry buzz clearly audible to both men.

"Yeah, well, if I were you, I wouldn't be standing in the middle of the street like that," Falcon said.

"Damn, you're right!" Paul replied. He darted behind a watering trough and squatted down. The wisdom of Falcon's warning was demonstrated when a stray bullet kicked up dirt just behind where Paul had been standing but a second earlier. Another bullet whizzed by Falcon's ear and plunged into the post just beside him.

From here, Falcon could see three men, wearing badges, standing in front of the express office, exchanging fire with six men out in the street. He happened to remember that George Snyder, with whom he had played cards last night, planned to entertain the sheriff and his deputies for breakfast. And he remembered seeing the money shipment being taken off the train yesterday.

One of the six men out in the street was mounted, and he was holding the reins of five horses. The other five were in the street, backing slowly toward their horses, all the while shooting at the lawmen. Up on the porch of the express office, one man lay belly-down, and even from here, Falcon could see the downed man's blood pooling on the boards.

Pulling his pistol, Falcon started running toward the express office, staying up on the boardwalk. He fired once at the men in the street but hit no one. He hadn't really expected to hit anyone; it hadn't even been an aimed shot. He had fired at the outlaws only to let the lawmen know that he was not one of the outlaws, but was coming to join in with them.

"Fargo, the whole town is after us!" Pete shouted, pulling the rifle from his saddle holster. He jacked a shell into the chamber, then, seeing Falcon, recognized him as the man with whom he had had the run-in with yesterday.

"You!" Pete shouted. "You son of a bitch, I'm going to kill you!"

Pete let go of the horses and raised his rifle to his shoulder to aim at Falcon.

"Pete, what the hell are you doing? Hang on to them horses!" Fargo yelled when he saw what Pete had done.

Pete fired, and Falcon felt the bullet fry past his ear. Falcon fired back, an aimed shot this time. Pete tumbled from his saddle. When he did so, his horse galloped, causing the horses Pete had been holding to bolt off with him. The five remaining outlaws suddenly found themselves afoot in the middle of the street.

"Fargo! Fargo! Our horses is gone!" one of the other outlaws shouted.

"I can see that they are gone, damnit!" Fargo shouted back. "You think I'm blind?"

"Give it up, Fargo!" the sheriff called from the front porch of the express office. "Your horses is gone, one of your men is down, and none of the rest of you is goin' anywhere!"

"The hell you say!" Fargo shouted back, throwing a shot toward the front of the express office.

Falcon fired five quick shots then. He didn't hit anyone, but he didn't intend to. Instead, he put each bullet within an inch of the boots of each of the five men, showing them that he could kill them at will.

"Holy shit, Fargo, they've got us surrounded!" one of the men said.

"Give it up, Fargo!" the sheriff shouted again.

Fargo hesitated for just a second; then he put his hands up.

"Don't shoot, don't shoot!" Fargo shouted. "We give up!"

"Throw down your gun, Fargo. That goes for all of you," the sheriff added.

Looking toward Falcon, with a snarl on his lips, Fargo threw down his gun.

"Tell your men to do the same thing," the sheriff shouted. He made a motion with his own pistol. "Do it now!"

"Dagen, Ponci, Monroe, Casey, do like the man says," Fargo ordered. "Throw your guns down."

"I don't give up my gun for nobody," Dagen said with an angry growl.

"Have your own way, mister," Falcon said. "Throw down your gun and live, or hang on to it and die. Makes no difference to me." He aimed his pistol at Dagen and pulled the hammer back.

"Dagen, don't be a fool," Fargo said. "Look around you!"

Dagen and the other outlaws looked around as Fargo had instructed. By now several others, emboldened by Falcon's quick move to join the fray, had come from houses and buildings as well, and they were all holding rifles, pistols, or shotguns. The outlaws were surrounded and vastly outnumbered.

"Shit," Dagen said. He dropped his gun and, one by one, the others joined him, dropping their guns as well. Now, like Fargo Ford, they put their hands in the air.

"George!" a woman screamed, coming out of the express office. She knelt beside the man who was belly-down on the porch. "Oh, George!" she cried.

The woman turned him over; then, seeing that he was dead, she began crying uncontrollably.

"You boys are all goin' to hang for this," the sheriff said, coming toward them. "George Snyder was a good man, with a wife and two kids. Yes, sir, you're all goin' to hang, and I'm goin' to enjoy watchin' it. Wilcox, you and Baker take these men down the street and throw their asses in jail."

"Yes, sir, Sheriff, we'll be glad to," one of the deputies replied. "Come along, fellas," he said to the outlaws. "We've got a nice place all picked out and waitin' for you."

Seeing that everything was in hand, Falcon put his pistol back in his holster. The sheriff stepped down off the porch and started toward Falcon

"I don't know where you come from, mister, but I'm glad you showed up. I'm Sheriff Ferrell."

"Falcon MacCallister," Falcon said.

"MacCallister?" the sheriff replied suspiciously. He stroked his chin. "MacCallister? I'm pretty sure I've heard that name."

"I had some paper out on me a long time ago," Falcon said. "But it's been recalled."

Sheriff Ferrell shook his head. "No, I don't think it was anything like that. Never mind. Whatever it was, it'll come to me."

Falcon nodded toward the men who were being led away. "They were after the money shipment, I take it?" Falcon asked.

"Yes, it looks like it. George got in fifteen thousand dollars in cash yesterday," the sheriff replied. Again, he got a suspicious expression on his face. "By the way, Mr. MacCallister, you want to tell me how is it that you know about the money shipment? I thought it was supposed to be a secret."

"It was rather hard to keep it a secret from someone who came in on the train yesterday," Falcon said. "I saw you taking the pouch from the express car. Then, I played cards with George Snyder last night and some of the men around the table mentioned it."

"Yeah, I see what you mean. Too bad things like this get talked about," Sheriff Ferrell said. He pointed to the dead man and the weeping woman. By now a few others had come up to aid and comfort Mrs. Snyder. "If I had my way, nobody but the express company would have even known when money was being shipped."

"Is that his wife?" Falcon asked. He pointed to an attractive woman who was on her knees beside the body.

"Yes. Her name is Emma Snyder. You say you met George last night?"

"I did. He was down at the saloon, and I got into a friendly game of cards with him and some of the other fellas from town."

"Well, it's too bad you just met him. You never got to know what a good man he is, or was," Sheriff Ferrell said. He sighed. "I guess Fargo Ford thought that by hitting the express office early in the morning, nobody would be around. And ordinarily, he would've been right, but it just so happened that George had invited me 'n my deputies over for breakfast this mornin', so we just happened to be here when Fargo and his gang showed up. The Snyders live there in the back, you see."

"You called the leader of the outlaws Fargo?"

"Yes, Fargo Ford," Sheriff Ferrell said. "I'm sure you've heard of him."

Falcon shook his head. "'Fraid not."

"Oh. Well, let me tell you, he's a real bad one all right. He's been nothing but trouble ever since he come to this part of the country."

A short, balding man with a long beard came walking over from the stage depot, which was right next door.

"Sheriff, if all the excitement is over, I'd like to bring the team around now 'n get 'em hitched up," he said.

"Go ahead," Sheriff Ferrell replied. "There's no shootin' now."

As the short man returned to the depot, the sheriff resumed his conversation with Falcon.

"That was John Scanton. He's the stage depot manager,

about to hook up the team for the seven o'clock stage. Could I buy you a cup of coffee, Mr. MacCallister?"

"Thank you, no," Falcon replied. He nodded back toward the Railroad Hotel. "I just had breakfast. And as a matter of fact"—he pointed toward the stage, which sat, without a team, in front of the depot—"I'm planning on taking that very stage out of here."

"Oh, well, then, don't let me hold you up." Sheriff Ferrell said. Again, he stuck out his hand. "Thanks a lot for the help this morning. And if you're ever back in town, I'd like to buy you a drink. Hell, I'll buy you dinner."

Falcon chuckled. "I'll take you up on that, Sheriff," he said. "As a matter of fact, I should be back through here in a few days. I'm just heading over to Oro Blanco to check on a mine I recently bought."

"You just bought a mine over at Oro Blanco? Wait a minute, the Rey de Plata mine?"

"Yes, the Silver King. You know it?"

Sheriff Ferrell nodded. "I know it, all right. It belongs to Doc Holliday, or belonged, I guess I should say, seeing as you bought it."

Suddenly, and unexpectedly, Ferrell snapped his fingers. "Son of a bitch, I know who you are now. You were friends with Doc Holliday and the Earps, weren't you?"

"Yes."

"You also ran with Mickey Free and cleaned up some of the renegade Indians who were raising hell around here a while back."

"I did."

Sheriff Ferrell stuck out his hand. "Well, Mr. MacCallister, I am pleased to meet you. Especially now."

"Now?"

"Maybe you haven't heard about Keytano."

"Keytano? Yes, Keytano, I think I know that name. He's Naiche's brother, isn't he?"

"He's Naiche's cousin. He's also an Apache chief,

about the only one left around here now," Farrell said. "His band owns several thousand acres in between the Cababi and Quigotoa Mountains."

"Is he giving you trouble?"

"Well, I don't think it's Keytano himself. More'n likely it's just some renegades that's goin' out on their own. But whoever it is, they killed three prospectors not long ago. Of course, the prospectors was on Indian land, but the real thing has the Indians all up in arms is the fact that some settlers cut off their supply of water and their cattle are dying."

"That doesn't sound very smart, cutting off the water supply for a bunch of warlike Indians. I can't say that I would blame them," Falcon said. "Isn't there anything the government can do to get their water back?"

"The Indian agent has taken it to the territorial governor, asking him to demand that the settlers take down the dam and let the water flow again, but the settlers have gone to court claiming that the water is on their land, to use as they see fit."

"I see what you mean about trouble brewing," Falcon said.

"Yes, well, so far, except for some renegades, probably led by a hothead named Chetopa, Keytano has managed to keep most of his people out of trouble. But the whole thing is a tinderbox, and it wouldn't take much to set off another Indian war down here."

Falcon shook his head. "I've had enough Indian war," he said. "I wouldn't want to get involved in another one."

"Yeah, well, here's the thing," Sheriff Ferrell said. "That mine you bought from Doc Holliday? It's right on the edge of Keytano's land, so, like it or not, you're just likely to find yourself right in the middle of it."

"Mister?" someone called and, looking back, Falcon saw the waiter from the dining room of the Railroad

Hotel coming toward him. The waiter was carrying Falcon's canvas grip.

"Oh, damn, I nearly forgot that. Thanks," Falcon said, reaching for it.

"My pleasure," the waiter said. "I, uh, brought the check too."

Falcon chuckled.

"Oh, yes, I did run out of there in a hurry, didn't I? Here you go." He handed the waiter a dollar.

"Breakfast was only fifteen cents, mister, and I didn't bring no change with me."

"You keep the change," Falcon said.

A broad smile spread across the waiter's face. "Gee, mister, thanks!" he said. "Thanks a lot!"

By now, over at the depot, the team was connected to the coach and the passengers' luggage was being put into the boot in the back.

"Well, Sheriff, it looks like they are getting ready to leave, so I guess I'd better wander over there and get aboard," Falcon said.

"Good luck to you, Mr. MacCallister. And thanks again for your help," Sheriff Ferrell said.

"You're welcome," Falcon called back as he walked away.

As Falcon headed toward the stage, he crossed paths with a tall, dark-haired, bearded man who was going in the opposite direction. The bearded man was carrying a shotgun.

CHAPTER 4

"Sheriff," the man with the shotgun said, nodding his greeting as he reached the front of the express office.

"Hello, Kerry," the sheriff replied. "Could've used you and that Greener a bit earlier."

"Looks to me like you handled it pretty good," Kerry said. "You kept them outlaws from gettin' the money shipment, didn't you?"

"Yeah, we did that. But I reckon Mrs. Snyder's takin' scarce comfort about now."

Kerry looked toward Mrs. Snyder, who was still sitting beside her dead husband, weeping quietly.

"Yeah, I see what you mean. This don't hardly seem like the proper time an' all, but we got orders to get the money on to Oro Blanco. I hate to be botherin' her right now, but . . ."

"I'm sure Mrs. Snyder will understand," Sheriff Ferrell said, interrupting Kerry in mid-sentence. "Come on, we'll go see her."

Kerry stepped up onto the front porch and stood there for a moment, looking down at George Snyder. He'd known George for a couple of years now, ever since he took on the job as shotgun guard for the stage line. He liked George, who had a really good sense of humor and always had some funny story to tell.

Even now, there appeared to be almost a smile on his

face, as if he was laughing at something from the other side.

Kerry touched the brim of his hat in a salute. "Ma'am," he said. "I'm real sorry about your loss, and I'm sorry to bring up business now. But the driver sent me over to pick up a delivery."

Mrs. Snyder nodded, and wiped a tear from her eye. "Yes," she said. "I understand that it has to go, and George got it ready earlier this morning. If you'll come on inside, I'll get it for you."

"Thank you, ma'am," Kerry replied, following her inside.

Mrs. Snyder opened a safe, then took out a canvas bag and set it on the counter. The bag was sealed shut with a padlock, and Mrs. Snyder opened it. "There's fifteen thousand dollars here," she said. "Would you count it, then sign here, please?" she asked.

Sheriff Ferrell had come inside to watch.

"Yep, fifteen thousand, just like you said," Kerry said after he finished counting.

"Sheriff, would you sign here as a witness to the transfer, please?" Mrs. Snyder asked.

"Yes, of course."

"I'm real sorry about your husband," Kerry said again as the sheriff signed. "But I'm glad them yahoos is all in jail. I wouldn't want to run across them out on the road."

"Well, you aren't going to have to worry about them," the sheriff said. "The only place those people are going from here is hell."

As Kerry left the office, he met the undertaker. Significantly, the man Falcon had shot was still lying in the street, surrounded now by a handful of the morbidly curious. The undertaker and his assistant had gone first to see to George Snyder's body.

The undertaker, who was dressed in a black swallowtail coat and a tall black hat, touched the brim of his hat with a white-gloved hand.

"You have my sympathy in your bereavement, Mrs. Snyder," he said with professional somberness.

At the stage depot, there were four other people besides Falcon who were waiting to board the stage. One of the passengers was an attractive woman with copper hair. She was accompanied by her ten-year-old son. The little boy had fire-red hair and a face that was covered with freckles.

The only other male passenger was short, overweight, and had a round, puffy face. He looked to be in his early forties.

The last passenger was a very pretty young woman with black hair, deep brown eyes, and a smooth, golden complexion. Seeing her made Falcon catch his breath for a moment, because she reminded him so much of his own late wife, Marie Gentle Stream.

A second look confirmed that, like his wife, the young woman passenger was actually Indian. She was dressed as a white woman, though, wearing a calico dress of yellow with a pattern of tiny red flowers and green leaves.

The driver stuck his head into the waiting room.

"Folks, my name is Gentry. I'll be your driver today. We've got your luggage all stowed and the team hitched up. If you'll climb aboard, we'll get under way."

The five passengers went outside to the stage. Falcon glanced first toward the front of the express office, then out into the street. He was glad to see that both bodies had now been moved.

The short, fat man opened the door for the young mother, and graciously allowed her and her son to get into the coach first. When the young Indian woman started to board as well, however, the man stepped in front of her.

"Since when have they started letting Indians ride on the stage with white people?" he asked under his breath.

Falcon resisted the urge to reach up and jerk him

back down. Instead, he removed his hat and smiled at the young Indian woman.

"After you, miss," he said politely.

She smiled shyly back at him.

"Thank you," she said.

The seats inside the coach faced each other. They were quite wide, wide enough, in fact, to seat four across. The short fat man sat on the front seat, with the young mother and her son. Falcon and the Indian girl sat on the rear seat, facing forward.

Smiling broadly, the short fat man stuck his hand out toward Falcon.

"Arnold Johnson is my name and selling harness is my game," he said. "I'm what they call a drummer."

Falcon hesitated for a second, then took Johnson's hand. "MacCallister," he said. "Falcon MacCallister."

Falcon heard the Indian girl inhale sharply, and he sensed that she'd tightened up beside him.

"What brings you to our fair part of the country, Mr. MacCallister?" Johnson asked.

"Business," MacCallister said.

"Will you be staying long?"

"No."

Falcon's truncated answers finally convinced Johnson that he wasn't looking for conversation. Johnson leaned back in his seat, then took a collapsible fan from his pocket and began fanning himself. "Whew, I'll be glad when we get under way, so we get a little air. It's very hot in here."

"Oh, how clever," the young mother said, seeing the fan.

Proudly, the drummer turned the fan toward her so she could see.

THURMAN LEATHER GOODS it said on the fan.

"My company puts these out," he said. "I do a lot of traveling by stagecoach selling my goods, you see. So I learned a long time ago to always carry a fan with me."

"Are you folks all settled in down there?" the driver called from his seat up front and on top.

"We're ready," Johnson called back.

"Yeeeehah!" the driver shouted; then he whistled, and snapped the whip over the top of the team. The report of the whip was as loud as a gunshot, and the team started forward, putting the stage into motion with a jerk.

The stage rolled through town with little rooster tails of dust coming from all four wheels. As they passed through the town, Falcon looked through the window. It was small, but typical of the hundreds of Western towns he had visited over his lifetime, the only difference being that, instead of the false-fronted whipsawed lumber buildings he was more used to, these buildings were adobe, or mud-brick.

It was still early morning, so many of the businesses were not yet open. A man with an apron was sweeping the porch in front of the general store. A dog ran off the porch and followed the coach through town, barking at the spinning wheels.

When they passed the blacksmith shop, Falcon saw the smithy building his fire. The last building they passed was the livery barn, and a young boy of no more than four-teen was pitching hay into the feeding troughs. After that, they were out of town and rolling through the desert, which was pocked with hundreds of stately looking saguaro cactuses.

"Are you a Indian?" the little boy asked the young woman who was sitting beside Falcon.

"Timmy!" the mother said sharply.

"It's all right," the young Indian woman answered pleasantly. "Yes, I am an Indian."

"You don't look like one," Timmy said. "I mean, you're so pretty and all."

"Well, thank you," the Indian girl said with a lilting laugh. "Does that mean you've never seen a pretty Indian girl?"

"Oh!" Timmy said, putting his hand to his mouth. "I

didn't mean it like that. I mean, you don't look like a Indian because of your clothes."

The Indian woman smiled. "I know what you meant," she said. "I was just teasing you. I've been wearing these kind of clothes for the last two years while I was back East, enrolled in school."

"I'll bet that's why you speak English so good too," Timmy said.

"Well," the Indian woman said.

"Well what?"

"That's why I speak English so well." She laughed. "Excuse me for correcting you, but I learned to be a teacher while I was back East, so I'm just practicing."

"White man's clothes, white man's language," Johnson said sneeringly. "But it's like they say, you put a mule in horse harness . . . you still got a mule." He laughed at his comment.

"Sir, have I done something to offend you?" the Indian woman asked.

"You are Apache, aren't you?" Johnson asked.

"Yes, I am."

"You are Apache, and you ask if you have done something to offend me? I'm offended just by having to ride in the same coach with your kind."

"Well, hell, Mr. Johnson, if you don't want to ride in the coach with her, I can take care of that," Falcon said.

"I beg your pardon?"

"You say you don't like riding in the coach with an Indian?"

"I do not."

Falcon opened the door. "Then why don't you just get out?" he asked.

"What?"

Falcon reached across the stage, grabbed the drummer by his collar, jerked him off his seat, then pushed him through the open door.

"Hey!" the man shouted as he fell from the stage.

"Oh, my!" Timmy's mother said, putting her hand over her mouth.

Timmy laughed.

From outside, they could hear Johnson shouting. "Stop the stage, stop the stage!"

Either the driver or the shotgun guard heard him, because the driver started shouting at the team.

"Whoa! Whoa there!" he called.

The stage rolled to a stop.

A few seconds later, Johnson appeared alongside the coach, covered with dust and breathing heavily from the run, but otherwise none the worse for his ordeal.

"What the hell happened?" the driver asked. "How did you fall out of the coach?"

The drummer pointed toward Falcon with an angry expression on his face. Falcon looked back at him. Falcon's face was as devoid of expression as if the two were strangers in a casual encounter on the street.

"I . . . I," the drummer started, then he sighed. "I don't know what made me fall out. I must've leaned against the door, I guess."

"Well, hell, Johnson, you've ridden my stage enough times to know better than that. Be more careful from now on," the driver said. "We've got a lot of ground to cover today. I can't be stopping every mile or so just to be picking you up."

"I'll . . . be more careful," the drummer said. He looked pleadingly at Falcon, who, without a word or a change of expression, opened the door.

"Thanks," Johnson said as he climbed back inside.

The stage got under way again, but Johnson pulled his hat down over his head, leaned back, and pretended to go to sleep.

CHAPTER 5

Back in the Calabasas jail, Fargo Ford was lying on the bunk with his hands folded behind his head, staring at the bottom of the bunk above him.

"Easy pickin's, you told us," Dagen growled. "There wouldn't be nobody around at six in the mornin', you said. There won't be nobody there but just the express-man and his wife," you said.

"Yeah, well, how the hell was I to know that the sheriff and both deputies would be there havin' breakfast?" Fargo replied.

"You're supposed to know things like that," Dagen said. "That's why you're the leader."

"Anytime you want to be the leader, Dagen, why you just be my guest," Fargo invited.

"Yeah," Ponci said. "How 'bout you leadin' us, Dagen? You can lead us right up to the gallows!" He laughed out loud.

"Shut up, Ponci. That ain't funny," Dagen said. Almost unconsciously, he put his hand to his collar and pulled it away from his neck.

Ponci laughed again, but when Fargo heard the sheriff talking, he put his hand out as a signal to the others to be quiet.

"Shh," Fargo said.

"What is it?" Ponci asked.

"Be quiet, I want to listen."

"Listen to what?"

"To what the sheriff's got to say. Now shut up," Fargo ordered with a low hiss.

"Wilcox, keep an eye on things until Baker gets back," Sheriff Ferrell was saying from the front of the office. "I'm going down to the Western Union and send a wire off to Judge Norton up in Tucson."

"I'll keep an eye on things, Sheriff," Deputy Wilcox said.

The men in the cell heard the front door open and close.

"Good morning, Sheriff," someone said from just outside the jailhouse. "You and your boys sure did a fine job this mornin'. You done the whole town just real proud. Yes, sir, that was a fine job you and the deputies done."

"Thank you, Mr. Allen," Ferrell answered. He chuckled. "Hope you remember that come next election day."

"Oh, I'll 'member it all right. The whole town will remember it, if you ask me. So, how about it? Are we goin' to get to see us a hangin' soon?"

"Looks that way," Ferrell replied. "It sure looks that way. Course, that'll be up to Judge Norton, but if I was a bettin' man, I'd say we'll be building a gallows within a week or so."

"All right, that's good," Fargo said. He looked at the others.

"Good? What the hell are you talking about? All I heard the son of a bitch talking about was us hangin'," Dagen said. "I'd like to know what the hell is good about that."

"What's good about it is, he was outside when he was talkin'," Fargo replied.

"So he was outside. What's that got to do with anything?"

"Didn't you hear the sheriff when he told Wilcox to watch things until Baker gets back?" Fargo said.

"Yeah, I heard it."

"That means Wilcox is the only one here."

"Hell, Fargo, it wouldn't make no never mind if there wasn't no one here at all. Case you ain't noticed, we're locked up in this here cell. And they don't none of us have a key," Dagen said.

"One of us has a key," Fargo said.

"Who?"

"Wilcox."

"Wilcox has a key," Dagen said, scoffing. "That don't make a lick of sense. What the hell good does it do us if Wilcox has a key?"

"I got me an idea," Fargo said.

Up in the front of the sheriff's office, Wilcox used a folded-up cloth to keep from burning his hand as he picked up the blue coffeepot from the top of the stove. He poured himself a cup of coffee, and had just taken a swallow when he heard a loud commotion coming from the cells in the back. Everyone was shouting at the same time.

"Deputy! Deputy Wilcox! Get back here quick! Hurry!"

Wilcox put the coffee cup down, then started toward the back.

"What the hell is goin' on back here?" he called. "What's all the shoutin' about?"

As soon as he opened the door, he saw what had them all excited. One of the men had wrapped a blanket around his neck, then looped it over one of the overhead pipes. He was now hanging by the neck, twisting slowly in the cell.

"What the hell?" Wilcox asked. "Who is that? What is he doin' up there?"

"That's Casey and what he is doin' is, he's hangin' hisself," Fargo said.

"Son of a bitch, what'd he do that for? Couldn't he wait for us to do it?"

Wilcox stepped up close to the bars, his eyes on the hanging prisoner. But his curiosity got the better of him, and he got too close. He was paying too much attention to the hanging man to see what happened next.

Dagen reached out to grab him by his gun arm while, at the same time, Fargo got a handful of his hair. Fargo jerked the deputy's head hard against the iron bars, and though it didn't knock Wilcox out, it stunned him enough for Dagen and Monroe to twist him around until his back was against the bars.

Fargo took a leather shoestring and looped it around Wilcox's neck. He began tightening the string . . . drawing it so tight that it cut into the deputy's neck, causing blood to flow down on his shirt.

Fargo held it until Wilcox stopped struggling. Then he let him fall.

"Is he dead?" Casey asked.

"If he ain't dead, he's goin' to be sleepin' for about a thousand years," Fargo replied.

Ponci laughed. "Sleepin' for a thousand years. That's funny."

"Get me down from here," Casey said.

There were three belts hidden behind the blanket that connected Casey's neck to the overhead bars. Those three belts were buckled together, and attached to Casey's own belt so that his waist, and not his neck, had borne the weight of his body.

Dagen and Ponci lifted Casey up to release the pressure on the belt; then they pulled the blanket down and let him down.

"Does he have the keys on him?" Monroe asked.

"Yes," Fargo said. "They're hanging from his belt. Help me get him twisted around here."

The men moved Wilcox's body around until Fargo could reach the keys. It took but a moment to get them, then open the cell door.

"Let's get the hell out of here before Baker or the sheriff gets back," Dagen said.

"No, not yet," Fargo cautioned.

"What do you mean not yet? What are we hanging around here for?"

"We're goin' to wait until Baker gets back."

"What? Are you crazy?"

"No," Fargo said. "Think about it. If we leave now, the sheriff and Baker will form a posse and come after us."

"So? We need to put as much distance between us and this place as we can."

Fargo shook his head. "No, not yet."

Baker opened the door to the sheriff's office, then hung his hat on the peg. When he saw Wilcox sitting in the chair, leaning back against the wall with his hat pulled down over his eyes, he chuckled.

"Damn, Wilcox, you better be glad it was me caught you sleepin' and not Ferrell," Baker said. "Get your lazy ass up and make a few rounds."

When Wilcox made no move, Baker started toward the desk. "Didn't you hear me? Come on, get your ass out of that chair."

When Baker reached the desk, Fargo Ford suddenly jumped up from the other side of the desk.

"What the hell are you doin' up here?" Baker shouted in alarm. That was as far as he got before Fargo brought a hammer down on his head. So severe was the hammer blow that the head of the hammer sunk into Baker's head, allowing blood and brain matter to ooze out around the point of the blow. Baker fell, instantly dead, across his desk.

"Now we've got only one more person to take care of," Fargo said. "Sheriff Ferrell."

"Well you better get ready 'cause here he comes now," Ponci called from the window.

"Quick, get out of sight," Fargo said. He pointed to Baker. "Get him behind the desk."

The others moved Baker's body down behind the desk; then they hurried quickly into the back. Fargo went to the door, then stepped to the side so that as the door opened, he would be hidden. He raised his hammer and waited.

"I got the telegram off," Ferrell said. "We'll prob'ly get an answer sometime this after . . ." Something about Wilcox's still form alerted him, and he stopped in mid-sentence and started for his pistol.

He never reached his gun. Once again, Fargo made use of the hammer, hitting Ferrell so hard that the hammer made a popping sound as the sheriff went down.

"Now," Fargo said. "We can go down the alley to the livery, get ourselves some horses, and get on with our business without worryin' about the sheriff or anyone else."

"And just what business would that be, other than gettin' the hell out of here?" Casey asked.

"The same business we come into town for in the first place," Fargo replied. "Since we didn't get the money before they put it on the stage, we'll get it now."

"How the hell are we goin' to do that? The stage left three hours ago."

"Yeah, well, you can go faster on a horse than you can on a stage. Besides, come noon they'll be stoppin' at Pajarito for an hour or so to change teams and eat. We'll be caught up with 'em by then, and we can hit 'em just as they reach the top of Cerro Pass."

"Yeah," Dagen said. "Yeah, they won't be suspectin' anything. That's a damn good idea."

"So, Dagen, does that mean Fargo's our leader again?" Monroe asked jokingly. "Or do you still want to lead us onto the gallows?" He laughed.

"That ain't funny," Dagen said. "I told you, that ain't funny."

"Get your guns and let's get out of here," Fargo said, using the ring of keys to open the weapons locker. There, the men found their holsters and pistols, and quickly they put them back on.

"Damn, this feels good," Ponci said. "I don't mind tellin' you, I was feelin' plumb naked without my gun."

Casey laughed. "Ponci, don't be talkin' about you bein' naked. You want to give the rest of us nightmares?"

The others laughed.

"Hey, back when Ponci was a butcher, you think he got naked with them cows?" Dagen asked.

"Only with them pretty young calves," Monroe replied.

More laughter.

"You know too much about pretty young calves, if you ask me," Casey said.

More laughter.

"What are we hangin' around here for? Let's go!" Dagen said as he started toward the front door.

"Not that way," Fargo called out.

"Why the hell not?"

"You want the whole town to see us? Out the back door, then down the alley to the livery."

"Yeah," Dagen said. "Yeah, I see what you mean."

The five men left the back of the jail, then darted up the alley. Not one person saw them leave the jail.

Behind them lay the town's entire law-enforcement contingent . . . all dead.

Fargo was the first one to reach the vicinity of the livery. He stopped just behind the feed store, which was right next to the livery. Holding out his hand in a signal for the others to be quiet, he leaned around the edge of the building to check out the livery.

"Well, I'll be damn," he said.

"What is it?" Ponci asked.

"It looks like they got our horses in there," Fargo said. "That's good. If I'm goin' to be doin' a lot of ridin', I don't want to be breakin' in no new horse."

"What's our horses doin' here? I thought they run away."

"I thought they did too, but they must'a drifted back. Horses'll do that sometimes, you know," Fargo said. "Anyway, they got 'em all in there. The even got Pete's horse."

"How many folks they got watchin' 'em?"

"Looks like they's just one in there now, an' he's nothin' but a kid," Fargo said. "Ponci, go in there and take care of him."

Ponci nodded, but said nothing. The others watched as Ponci started toward the kid. The kid, seeing Ponci, started toward him.

"Yes, sir, mister," the kid said. "Something I can do for you?"

"Hey, kid, you see that sorrel over there?" Ponci asked, pointing toward the paddock.

"Sorrel? Where?" the kid asked.

"Come here, I'll point him out."

The kid came closer, then tried to look where Ponci was pointing.

Ponci was pointing with his left hand. As the kid tried to pick out the nonexistent sorrel, Ponci pulled his knife with his right hand. It took but one quick slice to cut the boy's jugular. The boy slapped his hands over his neck in surprise, then went down as the blood streamed through his fingers.

Ponci signaled the others.

"What about Pete's horse?" Dagen asked.

"Leave him."

"An extra horse might come in handy."

"Leave him," Fargo said. "One extra mount ain't goin' to do the five of us any good. And it'll just be a pain in the ass to keep up with him. Leave it."

"Whatever you say," Dagen said.

Fargo glared at Dagen. "Yes," he said more forcefully. "It is whatever I say. And if you don't like it, you can ride out of here on your own right now."

"No, no," Dagen said quickly. "I don't have no trouble with you bein' the leader of us, 'n I don't think there's no one else what has any trouble with it either."

"No one else has questioned it," Fargo said, gruffly. "You have."

"Yeah, well, you done good, gettin' us out of jail and all. I won't be questionin' it no more," Dagen said. "I promise."

All the time they were talking, the men were also putting saddles on their mounts.

"Everyone saddled?" Fargo asked, swinging onto his own horse.

"All done here," Dagen said. Ordinarily Dagen was the last to do anything, but right now he was straining to stay on Fargo's good side.

"Here too," Ponci said, and his response was echoed by all the others.

"Then get mounted. We've got a stage to catch."

CHAPTER 6

Timmy's mother's name was Jane Stockdale. At Oro Blanco, she would be connecting with another stage going on to Providence Wells, where her husband owned a ranch.

"What is your name?" Timmy asked the Indian girl.

The Indian girl smiled. "My name is Yaakos Gan."

"Yak . . . ?" Timmy couldn't repeat it.

"Ya-kos Gan," the Indian girl said, pronouncing the word phonetically. "Yaakos Gan. That means 'Cloud Dancer.'"

Timmy smiled. "Cloud Dancer. I like that. I can say that."

"For our first year at school, we lived with a white family, and the white family gave us all white man's names. I lived with the Walkers, so they gave me the name Nina Walker."

Timmy shook his head. "No, I like 'Cloud Dancer' better. It's prettier."

Cloud Dancer laughed. "I like it better too, because it is my name. But when we go away to school, we are given white man's names . . . white man's clothes"—she made a motion with her hand, taking in her yellow dress—"and we are told we can only speak the white man's tongue. If they caught us speaking in our native language, they punished us."

"But you can still speak Apache, can't you?"

"Yes, of course."

"Say something in Apache for me," Timmy asked.

Cloud Dancer pointed to Timmy's mother. "That is your mother. Mother is *shimaa.*"

"*Shimaa,*" Timmy repeated.

Cloud Dancer pointed to her head. "Head is *bitsitsin.* Hair is *bitsizil;* eyes, *bidaa;* ears, *bijaa;* hand, *bigan;* feet, *bikee.* It's easy. Just remember that each part of your body starts with the 'bi' sound, as in the word *bit.*"

Timmy repeated each word several times, until he was able to say them.

"Very good!" Cloud Dancer said, clapping her hands enthusiastically.

For the next few hours, Cloud Dancer taught Timmy her language while his mother looked on. Johnson stared out the window, his disapproval evident but not spoken.

Watching the interplay between Cloud Dancer and Timmy, Falcon MacCallister thought of his own wife, dead now for many years. Had she lived, it might be her sitting next to him now, and Timmy could be his own son, learning the language.

Marie Gentle Breeze, as she was called, had been captured by a band of Indians who tried to take her north with them as a slave. She fought them all the way, until they killed her. They crushed her head with a war ax, raped her many times, and threw her body in the river. Jamie MacCallister, Falcon's father, rode and walked for many miles on either side of the river, searching for Marie. He finally found her body wedged between a large rock and a tree, a few feet away from the west bank of the river.

Falcon stared across the coach at the drummer. Johnson's obvious Indian bias had triggered Falcon's memories of his own wife, and what happened to her. It was the memory of his wife's murder that had caused him to throw Johnson from the stage, and he had to fight against the urge to do it again.

Up on the driver's seat, Gentry and his shotgun guard were talking.

"As many times as Johnson has made this trip with us,

you'd think he'd have better sense than to fall out the door," Kerry said.

Gentry chuckled. "He didn't no more fall out that door than the man in the moon."

"What do you mean? He got off the stage somehow. You seen him come runnin' up alongside."

"Well, think about it, Kerry. Has he ever fallen out the door before?"

"No."

"No, and he didn't this time neither. Come on, you know him. You know how he can get on a person's nerves. If you ask me, that big fella MacCallister just threw Johnson's ass out."

Kerry laughed. "Damn me if I don't think you're probably right."

In order to get to Pajarito from Calabasas, the stage had to follow the road south for a while, then cut back west through Cerro Pass.

By horseback there was no need to follow the road, so Fargo Ford and his band started straight across the Sonora for Cerro Pass.

When they reached the Santa Cruz River, they stopped to fill their canteens, and to let the horses drink. Ponci stood at the edge of the river and started relieving himself.

"Ponci, what the hell are you doing pissing in the river like that? Can't you see we are filling our canteens, you stupid shit?" Monroe asked.

"I'm pissin' downriver," Ponci answered.

"Get away from the river or I'll kick the shit out of you," Monroe said menacingly.

"You want to try me?" Ponci replied, his hand hovering over his gun.

Suddenly a gunshot rang out, and a bullet hit the ground between the two men, then ricocheted off, the boom and whine bouncing back as echoes from the nearby mountains.

"What the hell is wrong with you two?" Fargo asked angrily. "Would you rather fight each other, or get your hands on that money?"

Ponci and Monroe stared at each other for a long moment.

"Look, if you two sons of bitches want to kill each other, be my guest. But do it after we get the money, okay? Hell, I hope you do kill each other, then . . . it'll be more money for the rest of us."

"We'll finish this later," Monroe said.

"I'll be here," Ponci said.

"Whichever one of you sons of bitches kills the other, you don't get his whole share. We'll split it up amongst us," Fargo said.

Ponci and Monroe stared at each other for a moment longer. It was obvious by the expressions on their faces that they had no intention of letting the argument get that far.

"Yeah, well, I didn't think so," Fargo said, reading their expressions. "Come on, get mounted," he ordered. "If we want to get our hands on that money, we've got to get to the pass before the stage."

The coach had been under way for about four hours when, from the driver's seat, came the blare of a trumpet.

"We must be coming into Pajarito," Falcon said. He pulled out his watch and looked at it. "And right on time, I see."

There was no railroad in Pajarito, and no telegraph line. Therefore, the arrival of the stagecoach, once each day from Calabasas and once each day from Oro Blanco, provided the only connection the town had with the outside world. Because of that, the arrival was a major event, and men and women stepped out of their homes, stores, and businesses to watch the stage roll in each day. Children would sometimes run down the street alongside the coach, often accompanied by their dogs. Today was no exception, and nearly every citizen in Pajarito stood outside their homes and businesses, watching the arrival.

Just before entering the town, the driver stirred the team into a trot so as to make a more impressive entrance. Then, as they approached the depot, Gentry called out to the horses and started hauling back on the reins. At the same time he applied the brakes and the coach slowed to just above a walk. It finally rattled to a stop just in front of the depot, where the stage sat there for a second or two as the dust cloud it had generated came rolling by them.

The driver climbed down then and, after patting some of the dust off himself, reached up to open the door. As he opened it, some of the dust rolled inside.

"All right, folks, this here place is the Pajarito stage depot. Since all of you is goin' on through, don't none of you be wanderin' off nowhere so's that you miss the stage. We'll be here for about an hour to change the team, take on fresh water, and let you folks grab somethin' to eat. Mrs. Foster fixes a good ham and 'taters, and if we're lucky, she'll have some kind of pie," Gentry said.

Johnson jumped down first and hurried toward the privies in back. Falcon was next, and he helped both Mrs. Stockdale and Cloud Dancer down.

The depot was one rather large room with a big table in the middle. A counter ran along one side of the room; a few bottles of whiskey sat on a shelf behind the counter.

On the other side of the room was a small store with a few items for sale, mostly handkerchiefs, soap, toothbrushes, things that travelers might need.

A door at the rear of the room opened onto the

kitchen, from which rolled the enticing aroma of roast beef, hot bread, and a touch of cinnamon.

A rather stout woman, wearing a dark blue dress and a white apron, stepped out of the kitchen. Her mousy-brown hair was done up in a bun behind her head, though one tendril hung down alongside a face that was covered with sweat. Picking up the hem of her apron, she rubbed her hands.

"Hello, Mrs. Foster," Johnson said, showing a feeling of proprietorship in that he had made this trip many times and knew her by name.

"Hello, Mr. Johnson," Mrs. Foster replied. She smiled at the others. "Well, you folks look like you could use a good meal," she said. She pointed toward a door on the back wall. "They's some washbasins out back. I reckon you'll be wantin' to wash off some of the dust. I know how dusty you folks get, ridin' in a stage, with all the dirt and dust blowin' in through the winders and all."

"Thank you, Mrs. Foster," Mrs. Stockdale said. "Come along, Timmy."

The other passengers followed Mrs. Stockdale outside, and all made use of the water, soap, and clean towels. Falcon had to admit that he felt considerably more refreshed when he went back inside.

"Oh, that was good," Mrs. Stockdale said.

"I'll have your meal out directly," Mrs. Foster offered.

"A meal does sound good, but something cool to drink sounds even better," Mrs. Stockdale said.

"I made some tea, my dear," Mrs. Foster said. "And I've kept it cool in the well house."

"That sounds good."

"The driver said you had pie," Timmy said.

"I do indeed, young man," Mrs. Foster said. "I just made a fresh apple pie this morning and you . . ." Mrs. Foster stopped in mid-sentence and stared at Cloud Dancer. "Well, for heaven's sake, I haven't seen you in a long time," she said. "You are Cloud Dancer, aren't you, my dear?"

"Yes, ma'am."

"I thought so. Why, you're a young woman now. Last time I saw you, you were just a girl. The school back East must have agreed with you."

"Yes, ma'am," Cloud Dancer said politely.

"Well, you folks go ahead and take your seats while I put some food on the table. I need to get you folks fed quick as I can, 'cause when it comes time for Mr. Gentry to leave, why, he just ups and do it, whether you're finished eatin' or not."

Cloud Dancer waited until the others were seated before she took her seat. Falcon waited with her.

"Mr. MacCallister, I want to thank you for coming to my defense in the stage," Cloud Dancer said quietly.

"You're welcome."

"But I am confused."

"Confused? Why are you confused?"

"You are Dlo Binanta."

"I beg your pardon?"

"My people say that you call yourself a bird. You are that man, aren't you?"

"Call myself a bird?" Falcon replied. Then he remembered. The last time he was down here, during his fight with Naiche, the Apache had referred to him as the man who calls himself a bird.

"Yes, I guess I am that man."

"Your given name is Falcon. I have been to the white man's school now, so I know what they mean when my people call you Dlo Binanta. That means the 'Leader of the Birds.'"

Falcon smiled. "Yes," he said. "My name is Falcon."

"That is why I am confused. If you hate Indians, why did you come to my defense?"

"Yaakos Gan, I don't hate Indians," he said. "I was

married to an Indian. Her name was Marie Gentle Breeze."

"Where is your wife now?"

"She is dead," Falcon said. "Killed by renegade Indians."

"So that is why you killed so many of my people? To avenge the death of your wife?"

"I'll admit that played a role in it," Falcon said. "But only a role. The main reason I killed so many Apache was because they were renegades on a killing spree. And killing them was the only way to stop them."

"Folks, the food is on the table," Mrs. Foster called to them. "Aren't you going to sit down?"

"After you," Falcon said, holding out his arm in invitation.

"Thank you."

Cloud Dancer sat at the table, directly across from Timmy and his mother. Falcon sat beside her and seeing her there, the drummer made a point of moving down to the farthest end of the table.

"Mr. Johnson, why are you sitting down there all alone?" Mrs. Foster asked.

"I prefer to sit here, thank you," Johnson replied in clipped words.

"Well, suit yourself."

Outside, Gentry was overseeing the changing of the team. Mr. Foster, the depot manager, was leaning back against the fence with him as they watched the hostlers go about their business.

"Hear anything new about Keytano and his bunch?" Gentry asked.

"No, nary a thing," Foster answered. "As far as I know, there ain't nothin' happened since them three prospectors come up dead 'n scalped here couple weeks or so back.

"Yeah, well, I don't think they're likely to come down onto the road and attack a stagecoach," Gentry said. "Still, I don't mind tellin' you, from here on to Oro Blanco, the hair will be standin' up on the back of my neck."

"The hair on the back of your neck, huh? Tell you what, Gentry. If it was me 'stead of you makin' this trip, why, it sure wouldn't be the hair on the back of my neck that I'd be a-worryin' about," Foster said, laughing and running his hand across the top of his head.

Gentry took his hat off, and ran his hand through his own hair. "Yeah," he said. "Yeah, I reckon I see what you mean."

"Go on in and get yourself somethin' to eat," Foster said. "Don't worry none about the team. I'll see to it that all the connections is done right."

"Thanks," Gentry replied. "I'll just do that. What do you say, Kerry?" he called to his shotgun guard. "Let's me'n you go get us somethin' to eat. I smelled apple pie and I aim to make sure I get me a piece."

Nodding, Kerry picked up the canvas bag and followed Gentry toward the front of the depot.

When Gentry and Kerry came inside, Kerry was carrying his shotgun in one hand and the canvas bag in the other.

"Oh," Timmy said. "Does that mean we have to go? Mama, I haven't had my pie yet."

"We haven't either, young fella," Gentry said. "And we don't plan to leave until we do, so you don't have to worry about that."

Timmy smiled. "Good," he said.

Gentry and Kerry drew up a couple of chairs; then Kerry put the bag down in front of him.

"Eat up, folks," Gentry said. "We'll be pullin' out of here in . . ." He looked over at the clock that stood against the wall. "Thirty-two minutes."

CHAPTER 7

No more than five miles away from where the stage-coach passengers were taking their meal, Fargo Ford and the four men with him waited at the top of Cerro Pass. Fargo walked over to the rock overhang and looked down into the valley, some 3500 feet below.

"You think we got here afore the stage?" Ponci asked.

"Yeah," Fargo said.

"How do you know?"

"You see any tracks on the road?"

"No."

"Then we beat the stage."

"So what do we do now?"

"Now? We wait," Fargo said. He walked back over to the shade of a rocky ledge, sat down, and pulled his hat over his eyes. "Wake me when you see it," he said.

"Fargo?" Dagen said.

When the outlaw leader didn't open his eyes, Dagen called him again. "Fargo?"

"Yeah?"

"It's a-comin'."

Fargo got up, stretched, then walked back over to his earlier vantage point. Far below, just coming off the valley floor and starting up the winding mountain road, was the stage. From this distance it was so tiny that it looked like a toy stage and team he had once seen in a store window.

"I told you we'd beat it here," Fargo said. "Now all we have to do is wait for it to get to the turnout. The driver will have to stop there to give the horses a rest and check his brakes before he goes down the other side."

"If you ask me, we should'a just took the stage down there," Dagen said. "'Stead of practically killin' the horses bringin' 'em up here. If we have to ride fast, the horses ain't got nothin' left in 'em."

"Do you see anyone up here that's goin' to come after us?" Fargo asked.

"No."

"Then don't be worryin' none about havin' to ride somewhere fast."

They waited behind some rocks for about half an hour. Then Ponci got up. "I gotta walk around a bit," he said. "I'm gettin' kinks just sittin' there."

"Walk around, but stay back away from the road. Wouldn't want them to see anyone up here and get spooked," Fargo warned.

"You know what I need right now?" Ponci said as he stretched his arms out.

"What's that?" Casey asked.

"I need me a cold piece of pie and a hot piece of ass."

Casey laughed. "Well, you might get yourself a cold piece of pie somewhere," he said. "But you ain't goin' to be gettin' you no hot piece of ass. Leastwise, not soon."

"What do you mean, not soon?" Dagen asked, laughing. "What woman would have anything to do with Ponci?"

"I've got me a woman," Ponci said. "She's a good woman too."

"Hell, the only kind of woman who would have anything to do with you would be a whore," Casey said. "And anyone can get theirselves a whore if they have money."

"Yeah, well, they's whores and they's whores," Ponci said. "And back when I was butcherin', I had me a special whore." He looked at Fargo. "She was a real special whore, wouldn't you say so, Fargo?"

"Enough talk about whorin'," Fargo said, holding up his hand. "Quiet, here comes the stage."

The five men pulled their guns and waited behind the rocks for the stage to reach the turnout. They could hear the driver shouting to his team, the whip snapping, the harness clanging and creaking, and the stage squeaking as it worked its way laboriously up the hill.

It arrived a few minutes later, the horses snorting tiredly, straining into the harness.

"Whoa, hold it up there, team," the driver shouted, pulling on the reins. The stage rumbled to a stop. "Folks," he called down. "We gotta let these here animals blow for a bit before we start down the other side, so we goin' to be here for the better part of an hour. But they's a real purty view from up here, and they's a private place over there behind them rocks for you ladies if you're a'needin' it. So why'n't you take a break and stretch your legs a mite?"

The outlaws, watching from behind a nearby rock outcropping, saw five passengers get out of the stage: two men, two women, and a young boy.

"Hey, Fargo," Dagen said, pointing. "Is that tall son of a bitch there who I think he is?"

"Yeah," Fargo answered. "That's the one who killed Pete back in Calabasas."

The driver was not wearing a side arm, and was near the lead horses, adjusting a loose harness. The shotgun guard leaned his gun against the front wheel and took several steps away from it to stretch.

"Damn, they are making it almost too easy for us," Fargo said. He raised his pistol. "The rest of you, take out the shotgun guard."

"What about the son of a bitch who killed Pete? He's wearin' a gun, and we know he can shoot."

"He's mine," Fargo said, aiming. "Ready? Now!"

All five men fired at about the same time. Fargo had the satisfaction of seeing a spray of blood come from the top of the head of the tall man standing by the back wheel of the stage.

Kerry and Falcon went down.

Hearing the gunshots, and seeing his guard and one of the passengers go down, Gentry ran back from the front of the team, heading for the shotgun that Kerry had leaned against the front wheel.

"Hold it, driver!" Fargo called, stepping out into the open. "You pick up that scattergun and it'll be the last thing you ever do."

Gentry, realizing that he would never make it to the gun in time, stopped. As he looked toward the robbers, his face registered surprise when he recognized them. These were the same men who had attempted to rob the express office back in Calabasas.

"What are you doing here? I thought you fellers was in jail back in Calabasas."

"They realized they made a mistake, and they let us out," Fargo said.

"Yeah, they let us out," Dagen repeated, and he and the others laughed.

"I doubt that. Not after you kilt Mr. Snyder like you done."

"How we got out don't matter. What I want you to do is climb up there and throw down that money pouch," Fargo said with a wave of his gun.

"We ain't carryin' any money," Gentry said.

"What do you mean you ain't carryin' any money? What do you think all that ruckus was about back in

Calabasas this mornin'? You think we was just shootin' to hear the sound of our guns? We was tryin' to steal the money shipment."

"That's right, and you kilt the expressman, so they didn't send the money. They won't be able to send it till they get another expressman."

"He's lyin', Fargo," Dagen said. "Look at the son of a bitch sweat."

Fargo pointed his gun at the drummer and pulled back the hammer. "Tell me the truth, or I kill another one of your passengers."

"I told you, we ain't carryin'. . . ."

"For God's sake man, give him the money!" the drummer shouted, his voice breaking in terror. Then, to the outlaws, he said, "He's got the money. I seen the shotgun guard bring a pouch from the express office. It's up there under the seat right now."

"You chicken-shit son of a bitch," Gentry said to Johnson.

Fargo nodded, then eased the hammer back down. "Now don't be too hard on him, driver. He's what I call bein' a good citizen. I thank you for your help, friend." He looked back at the driver. "Get up there and throw that money down."

Gentry hesitated, and Fargo pointed his gun at him.

"Driver, you don't want me to kill you and leave these folks stranded out here, do you? 'Cause you know damn well this little pipsqueak ain't goin' to be able to drive this coach."

Glaring at the drummer, Gentry climbed up onto the box and reached under the seat. Again, he hesitated for a moment, then looked at Fargo. A sixth sense, sometimes developed by creatures on the run, told Fargo that the driver was thinking of reaching for a gun.

"Driver," Fargo said coolly. "If you come out from

under that seat with anything other than a canvas pouch, you will be dead one second later."

The driver picked up the pouch and held his hands in the air.

"That's better," Fargo said. "Now, throw the pouch down here."

The driver did as instructed.

"Hey, Fargo," Ponci said. "I think we ought to take one of these here women with us."

"Why?"

"Well, just seems to me like it might be a good idea," Ponci said.

Dagen laughed. "Looks like ole Ponci's wantin' to do a little sportin'."

"Yeah, but he might be right," Fargo said, stroking his cheek as he looked at the two women. "Having us a hostage along to keep as insurance might not be a bad idea."

Protectively, Jane Stockdale pulled Timmy closer to her.

"You better not take my mama!" Timmy said, not out of fear, but defiance.

Fargo chuckled. "He's a feisty little shit, ain't he? Get the hell out of the way, boy," he said, shoving Timmy down. "Come here, you! You're goin' with us." Fargo grabbed Jane.

"No!" Cloud Dancer said quickly, stepping toward the men. "Let her go! Take me instead."

Fargo looked at Cloud Dancer for a moment. "You serious? You're volunteerin' to go in her place?"

"Yes."

Fargo shoved Jane back roughly. "All right," he said, pointing at Cloud Dancer. "As far as I'm concerned, one of you's as good as the other. Come on."

"Son of a bitch! Look at her, Fargo, that's a Indian woman!" Casey said.

"So she is," Fargo said.

"Well, what kind of a hostage is a Indian goin' to make? I mean, there ain't goin' to be anybody who gives a shit what happens to her," Casey said.

"We'll take her," Fargo insisted. "Let's go."

"Where at is the girl goin' to ride? We didn't bring a spare horse," Monroe asked.

"She can ride with me," Ponci said. He rubbed himself pointedly. "Oh, yeah. She can sit right in front of me." He walked over to Cloud Dancer and grabbed her by the arm. "Come on, girlie. You are goin' to like ridin' with ole Ponci."

"Dagen, get the horses," Fargo said.

As Dagen went to get the horses, Fargo climbed up to the front of the stage and reached down under the seat. He pulled out a Winchester rifle, then turned and smiled down at the driver.

"This here what you were goin' after while ago?" he asked.

With the Winchester in hand, he jumped back down, then picked up the shotgun that was leaning against the front wheel. By that time, Dagen had returned with the horses.

"You boys get mounted now," Fargo said. "Let's get out of here."

"Get up there, girlie," Ponci said, patting the saddle. "Course, you bein' Indian 'n all, you prob'ly ain't never rode in no saddle before."

"Wait a minute, Ponci. Better let me hold the reins once she's mounted, else she might try'n run off," Casey said.

"Yeah, you're right," Ponci said. He handed the reins over to Casey, then looked back at Cloud Dancer, who, having made no effort to mount, was still standing there.

"I told you to get mounted, girlie," he said, growling at her.

"I can't ride straddle with this dress," Cloud Dancer said.

"Well, hell, if that's all it is, I can take care of that,"

Ponci said, giggling. Pulling his knife, he cut a slice down through the front of her dress and petticoat, then did the same thing to the rear.

"Now you can ride," he said. "Get up there."

Cloud Dancer put her foot in the stirrup, then swung easily, gracefully, onto the back of the horse. The slit in her dress allowed it to fall to either side of the horse.

"Scoot up to the front," Ponci said, reaching up to grab the saddle horn. He swung into the saddle behind her. "Oh, yeah," he said when he was in the saddle. "This'll do fine. Yes, sir, this'll do just real fine."

"Let's go," Fargo said when all were mounted.

As the riders started away, Cloud Dancer glanced back toward Jane. Jane saw the look of fear in the young Indian woman's eyes, and she felt guilty that she had allowed Cloud Dancer to take her place. But she also knew that she had a son to look out for and, involuntarily, she put her arm around Timmy and pulled him to her.

After just a few feet, the horses broke into a gallop and started down the other side of the pass. Within moments, they were out of sight.

"That there is about the bravest thing I've ever seen," Gentry said.

"Yes, it was," Jane said in a quiet, plaintive voice.

Realizing that she might be feeling guilty, Gentry looked at her.

"Miz Stockdale, don't you go be holdin' on to no guilt feelin's or nothin'," Gentry said. "She done what was right, and you done what was right."

"I know," Jane said. "But that doesn't make it any easier."

Gentry glared at Johnson. "And you, you lily-livered son of a bitch. You had to go 'n tell them about the pouch, didn't you?"

"I had no choice, I had to tell them. They would have killed me if I hadn't told them," Johnson said. He pointed at Gentry. "And you. You're supposed to look after your passengers, but you would have let them do it, wouldn't you?"

"We'll never know now, will we?" Gentry said. "'Tell you what, if you're all that easy to bluff, why, I'd sure love to get you in a poker game."

"You weren't bluffing. You were serious. You would've let him shoot me," Johnson insisted, pouting his displeasure.

"Yeah, well, maybe I would have and maybe I wouldn't. But there ain't no sense in arguin' over it now. Help me get these two bodies up on top of the coach so we can get 'em into town."

"Why don't we just leave them here, and send someone back for them?" Johnson suggested.

"Send who back?" Gentry asked. "I would be the one who came back for them. We're not going to leave them out here. Now are you going to help me, or do I have to do it myself?"

"How are we going to get these two bodies all the way on top?"

"I'll climb up onto the seat and you get them up this far. I'll put 'em on top."

"Are we going back to Pajarito?" Jane asked.

Timmy walked back to have a closer look at Falcon MacCallister, who was lying facedown by the rear wheel of the stage.

"Timmy, get back here," Jane said.

"No, we're closer to Oro Blanco now. I figure we may as well go on through," the driver said, answering Jane's earlier question.

"Hey," Timmy said. "Mama, come look! Mr. MacCallister ain't dead!"

"Isn't," his mother corrected automatically.

"He isn't dead," Timmy said.

Falcon groaned once, then got up on his hands and knees. He stayed that way for a moment, then stood the rest of the way up. Doing so made him dizzy, however, and he fell back toward the coach, and Jane, who had come over at Timmy's bidding, had to reach out to steady him or he would have fallen down.

"Whoa, take it easy," she said solicitously.

"Thanks," he said, taking her hand for stability.

"Are you all right?"

"Yeah, I guess so. What happened?" Falcon asked, confused by what he was seeing and hearing.

"You've been shot."

"Shot?"

Falcon put his hand to his head and felt a ridge running from front to back, just above his right ear. When he pulled his hand back, he saw blood on the tips of his fingers.

He looked at the blood for a second; then he saw the shotgun guard lying belly-down in the dirt.

"I see that I wasn't the only one," he said. "Road agents?"

Gentry nodded his head. "We was robbed," he said. "When we stopped to rest the horses, they was hidin' behind them rocks over there, and they opened up on us. They kilt Kerry right off the bat, and we thought they kilt you. They shot you in the head."

Falcon chuckled. "Yeah, well, that's where they made their mistake. Folks always did say I was hardheaded." He looked around. "Where's Yaakos Gan?"

"Who?" Gentry asked.

"That's the Indian girl's real name," Timmy said. "Yaakos Gan."

"Oh. They took her with them," Gentry said.

"They took her? Why?"

"They were going to take me," Jane said. "But that

dear, sweet girl volunteered to go in my place. So they took her."

"That still doesn't explain why they took her," Mac-Callister said.

"Fargo Ford said somethin' about usin' her as a hostage," Gentry suggested.

"Fargo Ford? Wait a minute, isn't he the one that tried to rob the express office back in Calabasas?"

"That's him, all right."

"How did he get out here? I thought he and his men were in jail."

"Yeah, I thought so too, and I asked him about it. He said the sheriff let 'em go, but I don't believe that for a moment. I believe they escaped."

"I believe you are right."

"We need to get going if we are going to make Oro Blanco by dark. Come on, Johnson, give me a hand with Kerry."

Gentry climbed up onto the driver's seat, then held his hands down while the drummer tried, unsuccessfully, to pick up Kerry.

"Here," Falcon said, pushing Johnson aside. "I'll do it."

"Mr. MacCallister, be careful. You've got a bad head injury," Jane said.

"Yes, well, it's my head, not my hands," Falcon said. He picked up Kerry and handed him up to Gentry, who was able to pull him the rest of the way up, then position him on top of the coach.

"Get on board, folks," Gentry said. "The sooner we get going, the better."

CHAPTER 8

Ponci held the Indian girl on the front of his saddle, pulling her back hard against him. As he did so, he felt himself growing aroused, and he reached a hand up to squeeze her breast.

"Please don't," Cloud Dancer said.

"Please don't," Ponci mimicked. He grabbed her breast again, and this time she slapped it away.

"Please don't," she said again.

"Ponci, leave her the hell alone," Fargo said. "We ain't got time for any of your foolishness."

Slowly, so slowly that Cloud Dancer didn't realize that he was doing it, Ponci stuck his hand in the slit of her dress. Going in under the dress, he reached up and put his hand on her inner thigh.

"Now, don't tell me you don't like that, girlie," Ponci said.

Cloud Dancer said nothing, nor did she try and slap his hand away.

"Uh-huh, I thought you might like that. All you Indian women is nothin' but whores anway," he said.

Cloud Dancer reached down and gently rubbed Ponci's arm. She leaned back into him.

"Damn!" Ponci said. "You little whore, you really are a'likin' this, ain't you?"

Suddenly, Cloud Dancer reached back and grabbed

Ponci's knife. Pulling it, she stabbed him in the leg, just below the knee.

"Oww!" Ponci shouted. "You bitch!" Ponci pushed her off his horse.

"What the hell is going on back there?" Fargo asked, twisting around in his saddle.

Cloud Dancer was very quick and athletic, so, instead of landing on her back, she landed on her feet with his knife still in her hands. She made another swipe at him, making a big slice in the calf of his leg.

"Ahhhh!" Ponci shouted with pain. Pulling his pistol, he shot her. His bullet hit her in the forehead, and she fell back, dead before she even hit the ground.

"Son of a bitch!" Fargo shouted. "You shot her!"

"Hell, yes, I shot her! This Indian whore damn near cut my leg off," Ponci replied, his voice strained with pain. "If you want to know why I done it, that's why I done it."

Fargo rode back to Ponci and looked down at the Indian girl. She was lying on her back alongside the road, a black hole in her forehead, blood and brain matter on the ground at the back of her head.

"Shit, Ponci, you killed her," Fargo said angrily. "Damn it, what'd you do that for?"

"Why did I do it? I did it because she cut me. She cut me bad."

Fargo looked toward Ponci and saw blood streaming down his leg.

"Yeah, I'd say she did cut you," he said. "If you didn't keep that knife honed like a razor all the time, maybe it wouldn't of been so bad."

"No sense in having a knife if you don't keep it sharp," Ponci said.

"Yeah, well, maybe that's true when you're butcherin' cows and pigs, but you ain't butcherin' anymore," Fargo said.

"Damn, it hurts," Ponci said, his voice raw and edgy with pain.

Fargo looked back toward Cloud Dancer and sighed. "She was supposed to be our hostage," he said. "You can't have a hostage if she's dead."

"Yeah, and besides that, now we can't have no fun with her," Dagen said. "I hope you're happy, Ponci. You dumb son of a bitch, you've done screwed it up for everyone now."

"Fargo, we better get a bandage on ole Ponci there or he's goin' to bleed to death," Monroe said, pointing to Ponci's leg. The bottom of his trousers was soaked red with blood.

"You want to patch 'im up, you do it," Fargo said with a scowl. "If you ask me, the son of a bitch got just what he deserved. I wouldn't be surprised if he wasn't feelin' her up or something."

"What are we goin' to patch him up with?" Monroe asked.

Dagen laughed. "Pull the dress off the Indian woman," he said.

"What?"

"Why not? We need a bandage, don't we? And we ain't goin' to have no fun with her, so we might's well see what she looks like nekkid."

"Dagen, you are one crazy son of a bitch," Monroe said.

"You don't have to look none if you don't want to," Dagen said, starting for Cloud Dancer's body.

"I didn't say I wasn't goin' to look," Monroe said. "I just said you was one crazy son of a bitch for thinkin' about it, that's all."

Dagen tore the dress off, then handed it to Monroe. "Tear strips out of this," he said.

Ponci weaved back and forth in the saddle a couple of times, then fell, raising a little puff of dust as he hit the ground.

"Son of a bitch, he fell off," Dagen said.

"Is he dead?" Fargo asked.

Dagen leaned over for a closer look. "No, I think he's just passed out."

"Now what?" Monroe asked.

"Son of a bitch," Fargo said disgustedly. He sighed. "Shit," he swore. "All right, get the son of a bitch bandaged up and get him back into the saddle. And be quick about it. We got to keep movin'."

Dagen pulled Cloud Dancer's petticoat, camisole, and underdrawers off while Monroe wrapped strips around Ponci's wounds. Ponci came to while Monroe was working on him. He groaned.

"Ponci, you son of a bitch," Dagen said as he stared at the Indian girl's nude body. "Lookit them nice little titties. Damn me if she ain't better-lookin' than any whore I've ever seen."

"Get Ponci back on his horse and let's get out of here, you dumb bastards," Fargo said.

The stagecoach was under way again. Timmy and Johnson were sitting in the front seat; Falcon was in the backseat. Jane Stockdale was sitting beside Falcon.

"Let me get a closer look at your wound," she said.

Obligingly, Falcon lifted his hat and lowered his head so she could examine it more closely. After a moment of study, she lifted the hem of her skirt, then tore a strip off her petticoat.

"I know this isn't very ladylike," she said. "But what has to be done has to be done."

She took a dipper of water from the water barrel, then poured it over the piece of petticoat. Then, using the wet cloth, she gently cleaned the wound on Falcon's head.

"It doesn't look as bad now as I thought it did at first," she said as she worked. "The crease wasn't very deep, and there's not much blood. Nevertheless, I think you should hold this against your wound for a while, just to keep out some of the dust that's coming in through the stage windows."

"Thanks," Falcon said, holding the compress to his head. "You did that well."

"I was raised on a ranch, Mr. MacCallister," Jane said. "Nursing becomes a necessary skill."

Holding the cloth to his wound as she suggested, Falcon leaned back in his seat and closed his eyes.

"Are you feeling all right?"

"Yes," Falcon replied. "I'm a little nauseous, but other than that, I'm fine."

"Nausea is normal for head wounds," Jane explained. "I don't think you'll have much trouble with it."

"Whoa! Whoa, there!" they heard the driver call from atop the coach. The stage came to a stop.

"Now what?" Johnson asked irritably. "Will this accursed stage trip ever be completed?"

"I wonder why we are stopping," Jane said.

Falcon put the compress down and drew his pistol. "I don't know," he said. He cocked his pistol. "But I don't intend to be caught by surprise this time."

"Mr. MacCallister, you might want to see this," the driver called down. "I think the rest of you should stay in the coach."

With his cocked pistol in hand, Falcon stepped down from the coach, then moved up to the front.

"What is it?" he asked.

Falcon was standing at the right front of the coach. The driver pointed over to the left side of the road. "It's over there," he said.

Looking in the direction the driver pointed, Falcon saw some yellow cloth on the ground.

"Don't that look like the dress that Indian girl was wearin'?" Gentry asked.

"Yes," Falcon said.

"Yeah, that's what I thought when I seen it. So the question is, what do you reckon it's doin' there on the ground?"

With his gun still at the ready, Falcon walked over for a closer look at the dress. That was when he saw the other items of clothing.

And then he saw Cloud Dancer.

The young Indian woman was lying on her back, totally naked. The bullet hole in her forehead was round and black.

Shaking his head slowly, Falcon put his gun back in his holster and returned to the stage. He reached out and grabbed the front of the wheel, then looked up at the driver.

"She's over there," he said quietly.

"Is she . . ."

Falcon began nodding before the driver could finish his question. "Yes, she's dead."

"Damn."

"She's also naked."

"What's that you say? She's nekkid?"

Falcon nodded again.

"Why, them sorry sons of bitches," the driver swore angrily. "It ain't bad enough they took the girl, and it ain't bad enough that they kilt her. They had to do this to her. So, what do we do now?"

"We can't leave her out here," Falcon said.

"No, I don't reckon we can."

Falcon stepped back to the coach window.

"What is it?" Johnson asked, still irritated by the unscheduled stop. "What is so important that we can't continue our journey?"

Falcon ignored Johnson's question. Instead, he looked directly at Jane.

"Mrs. Stockdale, I wonder if you would step out here for a moment?" he said.

"Yes, of course," Jane Stockdale said, stepping down.

She looked at Falcon and the driver with a questioning expression on her face.

"What is it? What's going on?" Johnson asked, even more irritated now because he got no reply to his earlier question. He stepped out of the coach just behind Jane.

"Mrs. Stockdale, I'm going to ask you to do something," Falcon said. "Something that's not going to be easy or pleasant, and if you don't want to do it I'll understand, and I'll take care of it myself. But I think what needs to be done should be done by a woman."

"I'll do it," Jane said without hesitation.

"You haven't heard what I want you to do."

"It doesn't matter. If you want me to do it, then I know it must be something important. I'll do it," she said.

Falcon pointed toward the side of the road.

"You'll find the young Indian woman over there, in that ditch," he said.

"Is she . . ."

"She's dead."

Jane put her hand to her mouth. "Oh, my! The poor thing."

"She's also naked," Falcon added.

"She's naked?" Johnson asked, looking toward the side of the road. "You don't say." He took a couple of steps toward the direction indicated by Falcon.

"Hold it right there, Johnson," Falcon said.

"I was just going to . . ."

"You are just going to do nothing," Falcon said. Then, turning back to Jane, he said, "You can understand that I don't want to take her body into town like this. I could dress her, but I think it would be more respectful if a woman put her clothes back on her."

"Yes, I think you are right," Jane said. "I'll do it."

"Thanks."

Jane walked across the road, stopped, then gasped visibly as she looked down into the ditch. Gathering her resolve, she pulled her shoulders back, leaned over to pick up the dress from the road, then climbed down into the ravine. For the next few minutes, Jane couldn't be seen, shielded as she was by the berm along the edge of the ravine.

"You think we ought to let Mrs. Stockdale be down there all by herself?" Johnson asked. "Shouldn't one of us be there with her?"

"Why?" Falcon asked.

"Why? Well, just to, uh, look out for her."

"You are volunteering, are you?"

"Well, I would do it."

"I'm sure you would," Falcon said.

"Do you . . . do you think those men had their way with her?" Johnson asked. "With the young Indian girl, I mean."

"Had their way with her?" Falcon asked.

"Yes, you know. What I mean is, do you think maybe they raped her?"

There seemed to be a little more than idle curiosity in Johnson's question. Falcon thought he saw a little red glint way in the bottom of the drummer's beady little eyes, and he turned away in disgust, for fear he would backhand the son of a bitch.

After a few minutes, Jane returned to the stage. She put her hand on the side of the coach and stood there for a moment with her eyes closed. Falcon saw tears sliding down her cheeks.

Falcon took a scoop of water from the barrel and handed it to her. "Are you all right?" he asked.

Jane nodded as she received the dipper. She drank the water, then wiped her mouth with the back of her hand. "That poor girl," she said. "She was so sweet and innocent, so nice to Timmy."

Falcon took the dipper back from her and returned it to the water barrel.

"Thank you for doing this," he said. "I know it was hard on you."

"Mr. MacCallister, I know you was wounded, but do you feel up to helping me get her back here?" Gentry asked.

"I'll help," Johnson said.

"No, you won't," Falcon said sharply, pointing at Johnson. "If you so much as touch her, I'll kick you from here to Sunday."

"Now, what was that all about?" Johnson asked as Falcon and the driver started toward the dead girl.

"Mr. Johnson, have you always been this insensitive? Or did you have to study to attain this level?" Jane asked.

When the five men rode into Oro Blanco, nobody paid any attention to them at first. Then a few noticed a bright yellow piece of calico wrapped around one of the riders' legs. A couple of them laughed at the incongruous sight, but then another noticed that the calico was stained with blood.

The riders stopped in front of the saloon.

"Fargo, I need a doctor," Ponci said. "This leg is hurtin' somethin' fierce."

"Ahh, you'll feel better once you've tossed a few drinks of whiskey down your gullet," Fargo said. "Come on, boys, let's go in and celebrate." Fargo swung down from his horse and tied it off at the hitching rail.

"Fargo, don't you think we ought to go on a little farther before we stop?" Dagen asked. "That stagecoach ain't that far behind us."

"What the hell for?" Fargo asked. "It'll be four more hours before the stage gets here, if it comes here at all. Like as not, he turned around and went back to Pajarito."

"I'd just feel better if we would divide the money up now and go our way," Dagen said. He rubbed his hands together. "I got me some big plans for my share."

"We'll divide up the money when I say we'll divide up the money," Fargo replied. "Now, I say we're goin' to have us somethin' to drink and somethin' to eat. We ain't eaten this live-long day and I'm hungry."

"Yeah," Monroe said. "I'm for that. Let's get somethin' to eat and drink."

By now everyone had dismounted but Ponci.

"What the hell, Ponci? You plannin' on just sittin' there on your horse the live-long day? Or are you comin' in with the rest of us?" Fargo asked.

"I can't get down from my horse," Ponci replied weakly.

"Well, if that ain't the shits. All right, a couple of you help him down."

Casey and Monroe helped Ponci down. When the five men went into the saloon, Ponci managed to walk under his own power, but with a severe limp.

The saloon was only about one-third full, and most of the men who were present were standing at the bar. Fargo led his group to a table toward the back of the room.

"Barkeep, whiskey," Fargo called.

"If you gentlemen will step up to the bar, I'll be glad to serve you," the barkeeper replied.

"Nah, we want to be served here."

"I'm sorry, but I'm the only one working right now and I can't leave the bar."

Fargo held up a twenty-dollar bill. "Will this get you over here?" he asked.

The bartender smiled broadly. "Yes, sir," he said. "I do believe that will."

The bartender walked over to the table to take their order.

"Whiskey all around," Fargo said. "You got 'ny food in this place?"

The bartender looked over at the clock. "Consuelo is our cook, but she don't come in until five o'clock," he said.

"Go get her. Tell her to come now."

"I . . . I can't leave the saloon now."

"You!" Fargo said, pointing to someone who was standing at the bar. "Do you know this woman Consuelo?"

"Yeah, I know her."

"I'll give you five dollars to go get her."

"Give me the five dollars."

"How do I know you won't take the money and not come back?"

"What if I bring her and you don't pay me?"

"Give me your hat," Fargo said.

"What?"

"I'll give you five dollars, you give me your hat. When you bring Consuelo back, I'll give you your hat back."

The young man smiled, then took off his hat. "You got yourself a deal," he said.

A few minutes later, the man returned with Consuelo. When she saw Ponci's leg, she gasped, then crossed herself.

"Este hombre muere."

"What did she say?" Ponci asked.

"She wants to know what we want to eat," Fargo said with a dismissive wave of his hand.

"That ain't what she said," Dagen said. He looked at Ponci. "She said you're dying."

"What?" Ponci asked, his eyes wide with fear. "I ain't dyin', am I? Fargo, am I dyin'?"

"No, you ain't dyin'."

"But she said. . . ."

"Who the hell are you goin' to listen to?" Fargo asked gruffly. "Your ole pard? Or some Mexican bitch who don't know her ass from a hole in the ground." Then, to Consuelo, he said, "Get back in the kitchen and cook some grub for me'n my pards. Lots of it."

"Look, mister, I don't know who you are," the bartender said. "And I don't care if you are throwing money around here. You don't talk to my employees that way."

Fargo whipped his pistol out and pointed it at the bartender. He pulled the hammer back.

"My name is Fargo Ford," he said. "And I'll talk to anyone in any way that I please."

"F-Fargo Ford?" the bartender stammered. The name alone was enough to cause him to start shaking in fear.

Fargo Ford smiled. "I see that you have heard of me."

"Yes, sir, I've heard of you."

"Good, good. When someone knows who I am, it always makes things go a little easier. Now you tell your cook to get her ass into the kitchen and cook us up some grub like I said. And it better be good grub too. Me'n my friends ain't et for a day or two."

"Consuelo. Cocina para ellos. No haz éste enojado."

"Dagen, what did he say to her?"

Dagen chuckled. "He told the bitch to go cook for us and not to make you angry."

Fargo Ford held his glass out toward the bartender. "I like you. You learn fast."

"Hey, Fargo," Monroe said.

"What?"

"I think ole Ponci has done passed out on us."

Ponci was sitting in his chair, his head lolled back, his mouth open and his eyes shut.

"Maybe we better get him to a doctor," Monroe suggested.

"Yeah," Fargo said. "We'll do that, soon as we eat."

It took less than fifteen minutes for the food to be delivered, and for the next thirty minutes, four of the five men sat around the table eating, talking loud, and laughing boisterously. The fifth man sat in the chair, neither eating nor participating in the activity.

The rest of the saloon grew quiet as the patrons, aware that this was Fargo Ford and his gang, were very careful not to do anything to incur Ford's wrath.

"Hey, Fargo," Casey said after a while.

"What?"

Casey nodded toward Ponci. "Maybe we'd better get him to a doctor now."

"Yeah, all right," Fargo finally agreed. He turned toward the bar. "Hey, bartender. You got a doctor in this town?"

"Yes, sir, Mr. Ford, we sure do," the bartender answered. "That would be Doc Andrews. He's just down the street, you can't miss him. His office is above the hardware store."

A small white sign with black letters hung from the corner of the hardware store. A hand with an extended index finger pointed up the stairs that climbed the outside of the building. The sign read SETH ANDREWS, M.D.

"I can't climb up them stairs," Ponci said.

"Help him up," Fargo said, bounding up the steps before them. He pushed the door open and walked inside. The office was rather small, with a desk, an examining table, and an assembled human skeleton hanging from a wooden arm that protruded from the wall.

Hearing Fargo come in, Dr. Andrews stepped in from the back. He was just beyond middle-aged, with hair still a little more black than gray. He was wearing a gray suit and a gray silk vest.

"Can I help you?" he asked.

"I've got a friend that they're bringin' up the stairs now," Fargo said. "He's been hurt, and I'd like for you to look at him."

At that moment the door opened and Ponci was carried in, supported on the right and left by Dagen and Casey. Ponci's face was white, and he was in obvious pain. Dr. Andrews saw the piece of blood-soaked calico around his leg.

"Get him up here on the table," he said. "And get his boots and pants off."

"Damn," Casey said as he began removing Ponci's boots. "I sure never thought I'd be tryin' to take off a man's clothes."

The others laughed.

With the pants off, the two wounds on Ponci's legs were very obvious: one a puncture wound, just below the knee, and the other a deep gash across the calf muscle, running from the front of the leg to the back of the leg.

In addition to the crusted blood around each of the wounds, there were patches of blue-green skin, along with a network of lines of color running away from them.

"How did you get these wounds?" the doctor asked, examining Ponci's leg.

"He fell off his horse into some cactus," Fargo said.

Dr. Andrews shook his head. "These aren't cactus wounds," he said. "These wounds came from a knife."

"If you know what they are, why the hell did you ask? It ain't none of your business how he got 'em," Fargo said. "All we want from you is for you to fix him up."

"It isn't going to be that easy," the doctor said. "What we have here is tissue necrosis, brought on by arterial ischemia."

"What? What the hell are you talking about? Talk English, Doc," Fargo said.

"I'm talking about a serious wound. Your friend has the beginnings of gangrene."

"Gangrene? Damn, you mean you're goin' to have to chop off his leg?" Dagen asked.

"Son of a bitch! No way!" Ponci said angrily. Sitting up, he put his hand down protectively over his leg. "Huh-uh," he said, shaking his head vigorously. "You ain't goin' to take off my leg!"

"I didn't say anything about taking off your leg."

"You said I had gangrene."

"I said you have the beginnings of gangrene. It hasn't gone far enough to consider amputation. I can still save it."

"That's good," Ponci said, his expression of relief evident. He lay back down on the examining table. "That's good."

"So, what you're sayin' is, you can give him something to fix it up, then we can go on, right?" Fargo asked.

"Oh, no, I didn't say that. This is going to require a very aggressive treatment."

"Aggressive treatment? Like what?"

"I'll have to get some meat from the butcher, then leave it outside until I can cultivate some fly maggots," Dr. Andrews said.

"Fly maggots? What the hell do you want them nasty things for?"

"To treat his leg," Andrews said. "You see, the fly maggots eat away the dead flesh. And they eat only dead flesh. That will keep the infection from infesting any more of the leg."

"How's he goin' to keep them maggots on his leg while he's ridin'?" Fargo asked.

Dr. Andrews chuckled and shook his head. "He's not going to be doing any riding," he said. "He's going to have to stay right here in bed."

"For how long?"

"Well, it'll take a day or two to cultivate the maggots. Then, they'll need to work for at least four or five days in order to get all the dead flesh out of there and stop the spread. Your friend is going to be laid up for the better part of a week at least. And to be sure that all the infection is gone, I'd recommend that it be even longer."

"Well, Ponci, I reckon this is where we part company," Fargo said. "Me'n the others has got to keep going."

"Wait a minute, you plannin' on just leavin' me here?"

"Yeah, that is my plan."

"You son of a bitch! You damn sure better not leave me here," Ponci said.

"You heard the doctor, Ponci. He said it was goin' to take a while to get you well."

"I ain't stayin' here," Ponci said again. He looked at the doctor. "Ain't you got somethin' that'll make it stop hurting?"

"Well, yes, I can give you some laudanum," Dr. Andrews said. He shook his head. "But all that'll do is stop the pain. It won't make your leg any better."

"Just give me somethin' for the pain," Ponci said. "I'll let the leg heal itself."

"Don't you understand? The leg won't heal itself," Andrews said. "If it isn't treated, it will only get worse. Then it will be too late for any kind of treatment. Then the leg really will have to be amputated."

"They ain't nobody goin' to take off my leg!" Ponci said again.

"Then you will die," Dr. Andrews said flatly.

"What do you say, Ponci?" asked Fargo. "You want to stay here and be treated, or go on with us?"

"What about my share?"

"We divide it when we get to where we're goin'."

"I want my share now."

"No," Fargo said resolutely. "Either come with us and get your share when we all divide . . . or stay here with nothin'. It's up to you."

"Well, now, you are givin' me a hell of a choice to make, ain't you?" Ponci said angrily. "Either stay here and get cheated out of my share, or come with you and die. Is that what you're sayin'?"

"Yeah, that's pretty much what I'm sayin'," Fargo agreed.

"Ponci, you brung this on yourself," Dagen said. "Fargo told you to quit messin' aroun' with that little ole girl. Well, you didn't and she cut you. So, whatever happens, you got no one to blame but your ownself."

Ponci glared at Dr. Andrews for a moment. "Give me some laudanum."

"I told you, the laudanum won't stop the infection," Andrews said.

"I said give me the damn laudanum!" Ponci shouted.

Dr. Andrews sighed, then went to his medicine cabinet and started to pour some laudanum into a small bottle.

"Give me all of it," Ponci said, grabbing the entire bottle.

"That will be twenty dollars," the doctor said.

"Here, Doc, don't think we ain't grateful," Fargo said, handing the doctor a handful of bills.

Dr. Andrews looked at them, and his eyes grew wide with surprise. "This is one hundred dollars," he said.

"Like I said, I don't want you to think we ain't grateful. Ponci, if you are going with us, get your pants back on," Fargo ordered.

Andrews counted eighty dollars out, then handed it back to Fargo.

"I'm keeping twenty dollars for the laudanum. I can't accept the rest of the money."

"Why the hell not?" Fargo asked.

Andrews looked pointedly at Ponci.

"Because your friend is going to die," he said.

Staring defiantly at the doctor, Ponci turned the bottle up and took a couple of swallows.

"And if you don't watch the way you use that stuff, you'll be dead before you get out of town," Andrews said.

Ponci pulled on his trousers, wincing with pain as he did so.

"Look, we ain't goin' to hang back none for you neither," Fargo said to Ponci. "If you come with us, you are going to have to keep up."

"I'll keep up," Ponci said. "Don't you worry none about me. I'll keep up."

CHAPTER 9

It was dark by the time the stagecoach rolled into Oro Blanco. The depot manager stepped out onto the front porch, carrying a lantern with him.

"I was beginnin' to get a little worried about you folks," the depot manager said. "You ain't never been this late before."

"Sorry, Clark, but we was held up," Gentry said.

"What held you up? Was there another rock slide across the road?"

"No, I mean held up, as in a holdup. We was robbed by a bunch of road agents."

"The hell you say." Clark held the lantern a little higher and looked more closely. "Where's Kerry?"

"They kilt 'im, Clark," Gentry said. "He's lying up here on top of the stage."

"Oh, hell. I hate to hear that. Kerry was a good man. A little strange sometime, but he was a good, God-fearin' man."

The door to the stage opened then, and Johnson was the first one to step out. He held his finger up.

"Mr. Clark, don't you think for one moment that the stagecoach company is not going to hear from me," he said. "When a person buys a ticket for passage on the stagecoach, he should have every right to think that the stagecoach will get him safely to his destination."

"Was you hurt any in the holdup, Johnson?" Gentry asked.

"No, I wasn't."

"Well, then, this is your destination and you got here safe, so what are you bitchin' about?" Gentry asked curtly.

"I got here safe, yes, but it was no thanks to you," Johnson replied. "You would have let them kill me if I hadn't told them where the money was."

"Wait a minute," Clark said. He stared at Johnson. "You told the robbers where the money was?"

"I had to. I didn't have no choice," Johnson said. "They would've killed me otherwise." He pointed to Gentry. "And he was just going to let them do it."

"Get out of my sight, you little pissant," Gentry said. "And you best find yourself some other way to travel from now on, 'cause I ain't ever carryin' you on my stage again."

"What? How dare you talk to me like that?" Johnson said. He looked at Clark. "You are in charge. Are you going to let him talk to me like that?"

Gentry stepped down onto the front wheel, then jumped down right in front of Johnson.

"Did you hear what I said?" Gentry asked.

"No!" Johnson shouted in fear, jumping back from him and holding his hands out in front of him. "Mr. Clark, you saw him threaten me."

Gentry just glared at him, then stepped behind the stage to the boot . . . opened it, and pulled out Johnson's bag and samples kit. He tossed them onto the ground in front of Johnson.

"Get, I said!"

"Mr. Clark?" Johnson said again.

"If I was you, Mr. Johnson, I'd be gettin' about now," Clark said.

With a whimper of fear, Johnson picked up his luggage, then hurried on down the street, disappearing in the dark.

In the meantime Jane, Timmy, and Falcon climbed out of the stage.

"Ma'am," Clark said, touching the brim of his hat. "I hope you weren't hurt."

"I wasn't hurt," Jane said. "But the poor little Indian girl who was traveling with us was killed."

"Indian girl?" Clark asked.

"Yes," Gentry said. "She's up on top of the coach with Kerry."

"Was her name Cloud Dancer?"

"Yes, it was. How did you know?" Gentry asked.

"We got word she was comin' back home," Clark said. "This ain't good. No, sir, this ain't good at all."

"Did you know her?" Jane asked.

"Oh, yes, ma'am, I know'd her all right," Clark replied. "What's more, I know her papa, Keytano."

Jane gasped and put her hand to her mouth. "She was the daughter of the chief Keytano?"

"Yes, ma'am."

"She never said a word about that."

"She wouldn't," Falcon said, speaking for the first time. "That's not her way."

"You knew her, did you?" Clark asked.

Falcon shook his head. "No. I met her for the first time on the stage. But I know her kind."

Clark squinted his eyes as he looked at Falcon. "Have we met before, mister?" he asked.

"I don't know," Falcon said. "I live in Colorado, but this isn't my first time here."

"What's your name?"

"MacCallister. Falcon MacCallister."

"I knew it!" Clark said, snapping his fingers. "You and Mickey Free cleaned out Naiche and his bunch here a few years ago. That was you, wasn't it?"

Falcon nodded. "Yes, it was me."

Clark stuck out his hand. "Well, mister, I'd like to shake your hand."

Falcon shook his hand.

"Wow!" Timmy said. "I didn't you was a hero!"

"Hardly a hero," Falcon said.

"Hah, that ain't what all the dime novels say," Clark said. "My boy collects them. He must have half a dozen about you."

Falcon chuckled. "I can't be held accountable for what someone writes in one of those dime novels. And from what I've been able to determine, there's very little truth in them."

"Well, what they wrote about you and the Indians here 'bouts was true," Clark said. "There ain't none of us around here that don't know that story.* What brings you to Oro Blanco?"

"I bought the Rey de Plata mine."

"The Rey de Plata. That the mine that belonged to Doc Holliday?"

"Yes. I bought it from him."

"Oh," Clark said. "Oh, that's not good."

"Not good? You mean the mine is worthless?"

"No, I don't mean that. Fact is, ever'body thinks that mine is a rich producer. But . . . it's right at the very edge of the Apache land, and it's too dangerous to work."

"You're having Indian trouble again?"

"Some trouble, yes. We had some prospectors killed a couple weeks ago, not more'n a mile from your mine as a matter of fact. And now, what with the chief's daughter bein' murdered 'n all, well, it can't do nothing but get worse."

Falcon felt a little spasm of pain from the wound on top of his head, and he winced slightly. Noboby but Jane noticed it.

Cry of Eagles

"Mr. Clark, do you have a doctor in Oro Blanco?" Jane asked.

"Yes, ma'am, we have one. That would be Dr. Andrews," Clark replied. "You needin' a doctor, ma'am?"

"No, but I think a doctor should look at Mr. MacCallister."

"Mr. MacCallister?" Clark replied. He looked at Falcon. "Are you hurt?"

"No."

"He was shot in the head," Jane said. She reached up to remove Falcon's hat, showing the blood streak through his wheat-blond hair.

"Holy . . ." Clark started to say, then, realizing there was a woman present, checked his language. "I reckon you was at that. Well, sir, the doc's office is right down the street on top of the hardware store. You can't miss it. He lives in some rooms behind his office."

"If you folks will pardon me, I think I'll find the nearest saloon and have a drink," Falcon said. He put his hat back on, then nodded toward Jane. "Ma'am," he said.

Falcon walked away from the coach then, and like Johnson a few moments earlier, disappeared into the darkness.

"He really should have it looked at," Jane said.

"Like as not, the doc is in the saloon anyway," Gentry said. "He generally takes his supper in there and visits for a while this time of night. I'll have him look at Mr. MacCallister."

"Thank you," Jane said. She looked at Clark. "I wonder if you would arrange to have the smaller of my three suitcases sent to the hotel. And if you would, keep the other two here for me. I'll be taking the morning stage on to Providence Wells."

"Yes, ma'am, I'll take care of it for you," Clark said. He sighed, and looked up at the coach. "I'd better get Gene

Nunlee down here as well. He's got two bodies to take care of."

Falcon was eating a supper of beans and tortillas when a couple of men stepped up to his table. Looking up from his meal, he recognized Gentry.

"Mr. Gentry," he said. "What can I do for you?"

"This here is Doc Andrews," Gentry said. "You can let him look at your wound."

Falcon waved him off. "I told you, there's no need."

"Sorry, you can't get rid of me that easy. I promised Mrs. Stockdale I'd have the doctor take a look at you," Gentry said. "And she ain't a woman that can be easy put off."

Falcon chuckled. "I think you're right about that. But there's nothing to my wound."

"Then you won't mind me taking a look at it," Doc Andrews said.

Falcon sighed, then took off his hat and leaned his head forward. "All right, go ahead, take a look at it if you must."

"Gentry, get that lantern over here and hold it close so I can see."

"All right," Gentry said, going over to take a burning lantern down from a shelf. He brought it back over and held it above Falcon's scalp while Andrews examined it.

"You are a lucky man," the doctor said. "If that bullet had been half an inch farther to the left, you'd be dead."

"Yeah, I know," Falcon said. "But so far my luck has held out."

"Looks like you cleaned it out pretty well. That was smart of you."

"I can thank Mrs. Stockdale for that," Falcon said.

"Thing is, if it festers it could still kill you, so you better let me treat it," Dr. Andrews said. He opened his bag and took out a bottle. "This is going to sting a little," he said as he poured alcohol onto the wound.

"Ouch! Damn right it stings," Falcon said.

"Shame on you," Dr. Andrews said. "Think of all those kids who are reading about you in dime novels now. What would they think if they saw you wincing like this?"

"They'd think it hurts," Falcon said.

"Yes, well, at least you came out on top of the deal. I saw the other man."

"You saw the other man? What do you mean, what are you talking about?"

Dr. Andrews turned to Gentry. "Didn't you tell me it was Fargo Ford that robbed the stage?"

"Yes."

"Well, I treated one of the men who robbed you. They called him Ponci. He's in real bad shape."

"You say one of them is hurt?" Gentry said. He shook his head. "Don't know how that could be. Didn't none of us get a shot off."

"It wasn't a gunshot wound," Dr. Andrews said as he finished treating Falcon's wound. He put his equipment away and closed his bag. "They came through town about mid-afternoon," he said. "There were five of them, including Fargo Ford."

"And one of them was hurt?"

"More than just hurt. He's going to die if he doesn't get treatment."

"I thought you treated him."

Dr. Andrews shook his head. "No. I tried to, but he wouldn't let me."

"How was he hurt?"

"Well, to quote Fargo Ford, he brung it on by himself by messing with some girl, and she cut him in the leg."

"I'll be damn," Gentry said. "It had to be the Indian girl."

"It's a leg wound, yet you say he will die if he doesn't get treatment?" Falcon asked.

"He has the onset of gangrene," Dr. Andrews said. "It's going to require a very aggressive treatment to stop the spread, but Ponci isn't going to allow it. In fact, it may already be too late. The idiot is trying to treat it with laudanum."

At that moment a tall thin man with white hair and a white handlebar mustache came into the saloon. He was wearing a white collarless shirt and a black leather vest. A star was pinned to the vest. He stepped up to the bar.

"Dooley, is Gentry in here?" the sheriff asked.

"I'm back here, Sheriff," Gentry called to him, having heard the question.

"Mr. Gentry, I understand you were robbed today," the sheriff said, coming toward the table where Gentry, Dr. Andrews, and Falcon were.

"That's right, Sheriff," Gentry said. "We was robbed, Kerry was killed, an Indian girl was killed, and Mr. Mac-Callister here was shot."

"Yes," the sheriff said. He stuck his hand out. "Mr. MacCallister, Sheriff Corbin. I've heard a lot about you."

"Sheriff," Falcon replied, taking the proffered hand. "I understand from the doc here that these men came through your town this afternoon."

"They did indeed," Corbin said. "But of course, none of us knew then that they had robbed the stagecoach."

"Yes, well, they were also escaped prisoners," Falcon said. "They killed a man back in Calabasas and Sheriff Ferrell put them in jail. I know damn well he didn't just let them out."

"No, I know Sheriff Ferrell and I don't reckon he would do something like that. The problem is, we don't have the telegraph here, so we're almost always the last ones to know anything. Truth to tell, I looked through my files and couldn't even find any paper to serve on them."

Falcon stared at the sheriff for a moment and saw him wince, then look down. He knew then that the sheriff was lying; he was sure there was paper. On the other hand the sheriff was one man, and Fargo Ford alone was more than most lawmen could handle. Fargo Ford with his gang would be impossible.

Falcon smiled to let the sheriff know that he understood. Then he held up his hand. "Nobody is blaming you, Sheriff."

"Yes, well, right now, we've got us a bigger problem than those robbers," Sheriff Corbin said. "Fact is, it is one hell of a problem."

"Yaakos Gan," Falcon said.

"I beg your pardon?"

"Yaakos Gan," Falcon said again. "That's Cloud Dancer's Indian name."

"Oh, yes," the sheriff said. "Well, if you know that much about her, you may also know that she is the daughter of Keytano. And here lately, Keytano's band has been giving us a bit of trouble. The funny thing is, Keytano is the one who has been holding the others . . . the young troublemakers . . . back. But now . . ."

Sheriff Corbin sighed, and shrugged his shoulders. "Now, I don't know what is going to happen."

"The only thing you can do is deliver her body and explain what happened," Falcon said.

"Yeah, well, that's what should be done. But what is going to be done is, we are just going to take her out to the edge of Apache land and leave her there."

"No," Falcon said. "You can't do it that way. That would start a war for sure."

"Maybe. But I figure whoever takes her out there is going to die. I damn sure ain't goin' to do it, and I can't ask anyone else to do it."

Falcon chuckled and shook his head. "Well, hell, Sheriff, in a roundabout way, didn't you just ask *me?*"

Sheriff Corbin smiled and nodded his head. "I reckon maybe I did. All right, so I'm not very subtle. The point is, Mr. MacCallister, you, being who you are, are probably the only white man alive who could deliver that poor girl to her parents and come out of there alive."

"What makes you think I would come out alive? Especially after what I did to them a few years ago."

"Dlo Binanta," Sheriff Corbin said. "You do know that's what they call you, don't you?"

Falcon nodded. "Yes, I know that."

"Apaches don't give names to just anyone. They only give names to those they respect."

"But they regard me as their enemy," Falcon said.

"This is true, but an Apache holds a worthy enemy in as high regard as a trusted friend."

"And you think that translates into me being able to get into the village, deliver the girl, and get out with my scalp intact?"

Sheriff Corbin nodded. "I think you can do it," he said.

MacCallister smiled. "You aren't just saying that to talk me into doing this, are you?"

Corbin laughed. "Well, maybe I am. What do you say, Mr. MacCallister? Will you do it? Or do I dump the girl at the edge of their land?"

"That's blackmail, Sheriff."

Corbin put up both his hands. "I know it. I'm guilty of it, and I admit it."

"All right," MacCallister said. "I'll do it. I don't like having a cinch jerked into me like this. But I don't intend to let that young woman's body just lie out there and rot until her people find her."

"Thank you," Corbin said. He put his hand in his pocket, then brought out a star. "Oh, and I'm making you a deputy."

Falcon waved his hand and shook his head.

"I don't want to be a deputy," he said.

"You ought to reconsider that, Mr. MacCallister,"

Sheriff Corbin said. "With this star, you can do anything you need to do."

"Sheriff, I'll do anything I need to do, with or without the star, and with or without permission."

Corbin nodded. "Yes," he said. "Well, I rather thought you were like that. I was just going to give you the cover of a star, that's all."

"By the way, Sheriff, if I happen to run across Fargo Ford and his men, and in that encounter if I happen to kill them, would you arrest me?"

Sheriff Corbin laughed. "Only Falcon MacCallister would suggest that he could single-handedly run across Fargo Ford and his gang and kill them. Arrest you? Hell, no, Mr. MacCallister. If you kill those sons of bitches, I'll give you the keys to the town," the sheriff said.

"Thanks, but no thanks. I don't need the star, or the keys to the city. I'll do what needs to be done. And for that, I will need a couple of horses. Know where I can buy them?"

"You don't worry about that, Mr. MacCallister. I'll get you two of the best damn horses you've ever seen, and they won't cost you a penny."

Falcon recalled his horse Diablo, and he shook his head.

"I don't think you can get me the best horse I've ever seen," he said. "But do what you can."

CHAPTER 10

Falcon rode one horse while leading another. The horse he was leading was dragging a travois, and on the travois was Cloud Dancer's body, sewn into a canvas shroud. Falcon rode out in the open, making certain that he was in plain sight. He was doing that to send a clear message to the Indians: that his coming represented no danger to them.

He had gotten directions to the village from the sheriff, and was heading straight for it. He wondered how long it would be before someone spotted him, and he knew the moment it happened. He knew, not because he saw them, but because he felt them.

He rode on for another half hour, feeling the hair standing up on the back of his neck. The Indians trailing him were good, they knew how to use the lay of the land to keep themselves hidden, and if they had been trailing ninety-nine out of a hundred men, their presence would be unknown.

Finally, either because the Indians sensed that Falcon was aware of them, or because they no longer felt it necessary to keep their presence a secret, they grew bolder. Falcon saw them then, six or seven Indians on horseback, riding parallel but managing, always, to keep a ridge or an outcropping of rocks or a small hill between them, no longer to stay out of sight, but just to be able to control the situation.

The sheriff in Oro Blanco told Falcon that the village was on the banks of a small stream, a tributary from the Santa Cruz River, so when he reached the tributary, or what was left of it, he followed it until he saw the village itself. It was easy to see the source of some of the trouble between the Indians and the whites, because the stream banks showed that it was once a rather substantial flow of water several feet wide. Now it was a trickle, so narrow in places that a man could stand with a foot planted on either side of the water flow.

The village consisted of several wickiups, not scattered loosely alongside the bank of the stream, but carefully aligned with every structure in the same relative place it was at their last location, and would be at their next location. In this way, individual members of the village had an address, as certain as the address of residents in any town or city.

The wickiups were circular and dome-shaped, with conical tops. These dwellings, which Falcon knew were erected by the women, consisted of a framework of poles and limbs tied together, over which was placed a thatch of bear grass, brush, yucca leaves, and rushes. For those who had it, a canvas was stretched over the windward side, and the structure was open at the top to allow smoke to escape from a fire built in a pit near the center of the house. The doorway was a low opening on one side, over which a blanket was hung.

In addition to the houses, there were also several "coolers," which consisted of posts in the ground that were covered by a roof of brush, thus providing shade from the hot sun. The squaws did their work under these covers. Falcon knew from his previous exposure to the Apache that they also suspended clay water pots from the edge of the coolers and, as the water evaporated, it had the effect of cooling the surrounding air.

As Falcon entered the village, the warriors who had

been riding parallel suddenly galloped by him with whoops and shouts as they raced ahead of him.

Those who were in the village drifted forward to meet him, for a single white man, riding in as boldly as Falcon had just done, was a strange enough experience to create interest. The men and boys came from the outskirts of the village, where they had been tending to the animals; the women and girls came from the coolers; and the old men awoke from their naps and stepped out of their wickiups to see what was causing the excitement.

One of the old men recognized Falcon, for he had seen him in the days of the Geronimo and Naiche wars.

"Dlo Binanta," he said, and the word spread so that, as Falcon rode deeper into the village, he heard his name spoken many times.

"Dlo Binanta."

"Dlo Binanta."

"Dlo Binanta."

Men, women, and children repeated his name and drew close to him. When he reached the inner circle, he saw an impressive-looking Indian standing in front of him. The Indian, who was being deferred to by the others, held his arms folded across his chest. His dark eyes were questioning.

"Are you Dlo Binanta?" the Indian asked.

Falcon started to reply with his own name, but he recalled what Sheriff Corbin told him about Indians only giving names to those they respect.

"I am Dlo Binanta," Falcon replied.

A ripple of exclamations passed through the gathering of Indians; some sounded angry, some sounded awestruck. Some were even frightened, and Falcon saw many of the children step behind their mothers in fear. He felt bad about that. He didn't want his name used to frighten children.

"I am Keytano," Keytano said.

Falcon nodded. "I have heard of the great Keytano."

"What have you heard?"

"I have heard that the great chief Keytano is a brave and wise man," Falcon said.

Keytano nodded. "This is true."

Falcon fought the urge to smile at Keytano's response, but under the circumstances, a smile would not be good at all.

"Why is he here?" Chetopa shouted.

"Yes. This man is the killer of our people!"

"Ask this man why he has come to our village now!" another shouted.

"We should kill him!" Chetopa said.

The shouting was in Apache, so Falcon didn't understand it, though he could tell by the tone of the voices that it was challenging and unfriendly.

Keytano held up his hand to those who were gathered around him. He glared at Chetopa. "We will not kill this brave man," he said. Then, he turned to one of the others. "I will ask the questions of this man," he said authoritatively. Keytano turned his gaze back to Falcon, staring at him intently.

"You are the killer of many of our warriors."

"Yes," Falcon said. "I fought fiercely against brave men, and killed many of your warriors."

"You made many women and children cry because you killed their husbands and fathers," Keytano challenged.

"This is true," Falcon answered without equivocating.

"Because of you, many wickiups were made empty."

Falcon wondered for a moment as to how best to respond to Keytano. He couldn't deny it, because everything Keytano said was true. He thought about saying he was sorry, but that wouldn't be true. Everyone he killed needed killing. Besides, saying he was sorry might be misconstrued as a sign of weakness.

"We were at war," Falcon said. "The Apache are brave

and fierce warriors. I would not be showing my respect if I did not fight against my enemies with all my strength."

Keytano took in Falcon's response, not only this one, but his earlier responses. Then he nodded. "Yes," he said. "This is true. A good enemy is a valued and sacred thing."

"We will not harm this man. He has shown courage by riding into our village to speak with us. And he knows the Apache way of speaking truthfully to a respected enemy," Keytano said to the others in Apache.

It had the desired effect, for many of the warriors nodded and made positive-sounding grunts.

"Why have you come to our village?" Keytano asked.

This was the moment Falcon had been waiting for. It was also the moment he was dreading. But this was why he was here, and he couldn't turn around now.

"Keytano, I come with very bad news for you."

"Bad news?"

"Yes."

"What is this bad news?"

"It is about Yaakos Gan."

"Yaakos Gan? My daughter? What news do you have of my daughter?"

Falcon started to speak, but decided instead to just point to the canvas shroud that lay on the travois. "You will find the bad news there," he said.

Keytano looked questioningly at Falcon. Then he said something to one of the warriors, pointing to the shroud. The warrior cut the shroud and spread it open, then jumped back in alarm.

"Uhnn!" the warrior gasped.

Noting the expression on the warrior's face, Keytano hurried back to look at what was in the shroud. As soon as he saw it, his confusion gave way to shock . . . then to grief.

"Aiyee!" he called, spinning away from Cloud Dancer's body. He started hitting his fist to his forehead. An Indian woman, seeing his strange reaction, ran from the crowd and looked down at Cloud Dancer. Without having to be told, Falcon knew this must be Cloud Dancer's mother, and she began weeping out loud. Within moments, everyone was gathering around to look at Cloud Dancer's body and react to it.

For the next several moments there was a general outbreak of lamentations and weeping. During that time the Indians forgot all about Falcon, and he just stood there, allowing them to vent their grief.

"We will kill him!" two warriors shouted, and they started toward Falcon with their battle axes raised. Falcon drew both his pistols, cocked them, and pointed them at the two warriors.

"Wait!" Keytano shouted.

At Keytano's shout, the two warriors stopped, and for a long moment they faced Falcon with their axes raised while Falcon faced them back, both his pistols aimed and cocked.

"Dlo Binanta, did you kill my daughter?" Keytano asked.

"If I had killed her, I would not have brought her to you," Falcon said. "I would have run with fear from the rightful anger of Keytano, the great warrior and chief of the mighty Apache."

"I think this is true. I think you did not kill her." Again, Keytano spoke in his own language, and the two Apache lowered their war clubs.

Seeing his two would-be attackers backing off, Falcon put his guns away.

Cloud Dancer's mother was sitting on the ground now, her head on Cloud Dancer's chest. She was still weeping, though the loud wails had given way to a quiet sobbing.

"Why did you bring her to me?"

"I met Yaakos Gan on the stagecoach as she was returning from school in the East," Falcon said. "She was a woman of much courage and much honor. When she was killed, I knew she would want to come back to her own people."

Keytano pointed to Falcon. "You are a man of courage and honor. I thank you for bringing her here to me and to her mother who now weeps over her."

Keytano said something in Apache to the weeping woman and she looked up at Falcon. Falcon nodded in sympathy, but said nothing.

"Do not leave," Keytano said. "After we have seen to my daughter, we will talk."

"I will stay to pay my respects to Yaakos Gan; then we will talk," Falcon said.

Keytano spoke again to his people and Falcon stepped back, then watched as the village began making preparations for Cloud Dancer's funeral.

The first thing they did was take her out of the shroud and wrap her face in a piece of cloth. Next, they completely stripped her, apparently showing no concern for the fact that she was now naked. That situation changed quickly, however, when they clothed her in a dress that was more in keeping with her Indian tradition. After that, they folded her arms across her chest, though this was difficult, as rigor mortis had already set in. Her hair was parted and brushed smooth with a hairbrush. Her wrists were covered with bracelets and beads, and around her neck, her mother placed a squash-blossom necklace of silver and turquoise. Finally, they laid her on a litterlike bed of reeds, and a medicine man circled around her, scattering ashes and pollen to the four cardinal directions. Following the scattering of ashes and pollen, everyone in the village grew very quiet.

Nobody told Falcon that this was a part of the ceremony, but it was his way to watch and learn, so he found a place to sit and wait, watching as the Indians maintained their silence.

Then, after about an hour of silence, a gourd of *tiswin* was passed around and several took a drink. When the gourd was brought to Falcon, he drank as well. He had tasted *tiswin* before and knew that it was an alcoholic beverage made of fermented corn and fruit. In strength, it was equal to a rather weak beer, but it didn't taste as good as beer. Like many things in the Apache culture, though, *tiswin* was more important for its ritual application than for its ability to bring on intoxication.

After all had a drink of *tiswin,* the wailing for the dead woman began in earnest, with every man, woman, and child in the village howling like a coyote. After a few minutes of this, the chief medicine man stepped into the center of the circle and held up his hands to call for quiet.

When the howling ceased, the medicine man prayed, and spoke words of condolence.

"Hio esken eskingo boyonsidda?" the medicine man asked. Then he glanced toward Falcon.

"So that Dlo Binanta will know the sorrow he has brought to our people, I will speak in English.

"Where is this woman now? We don't know. Where will she be day after tomorrow? We don't know. Where will she be ten years from now? We don't know. It is not for us to say where she will be. It is for Usen, he who resides in the mountains, to receive into O'zho . . . heaven . . . the spirit of this woman."

Two warriors lifted the reed bed upon which the body of Cloud Dancer lay. They started toward the nearby hills, with the entire village following. Falcon followed as well.

Once they reached the hills, they set her down, then looked about for a bit until someone shouted and pointed. Falcon saw that he was pointing toward a crevice between two layers of rock. The others hurried to him, and after some consultation, which at times grew into heated discussion, the village elders, and especially Keytano, decided that this crevice would do.

"This is where our sister will lie as she waits for Usen," the medicine man said.

They rolled Cloud Dancer's body off the litter—rather unceremoniously, Falcon thought. For a moment she lay at the lip of the crevice, but several of the villagers pushed and shoved her body until it was well down into the crevice. After that, they covered it with dirt and rocks until the crevice was so completely closed that to the casual passerby there was little evidence that it even existed.

After Cloud Dancer was interred, ashes and pollen were sprinkled in a circle around what was now her grave. They began at the southwest corner and laid the ashes and pollen down in a rather intricate pattern the meaning of which was lost on Falcon.

Seeing Falcon's respectful interest, Keytano pointed to the elaborate design.

"This is the story of the life of Yaakos Gan," Keytano said, pointing to one end of the design. "She was born at the time of the great burning of grass." He continued through the pattern, showing other milestones in her life. "Here the elk ran, and here the father of her mother died." He continued until he reached the part where she went East to go to the white man's school. That was the end of the design because, as Keytano explained, they did not know what events occurred while she was away.

After the burial all returned to the village.

"Come," Keytano said. "You are now my guest."

Falcon knew that he was more than simply a guest. If he tried to leave now, he would be taking his life into his own hands. He nodded at Keytano.

"I will be pleased to stay with you and honor your daughter with my mourning."

Fifty miles south of where Falcon was at this very moment was the small town of Sassabi Flat. Sassabi Flat was less than two miles from the Mexican border. The town, which had its beginnings in the days when Arizona was a part of Mexico, was considerably more Mexican than American.

Like many of its counterparts south of the border, Sassabi Flat consisted of two-dozen or more adobe buildings, perfectly laid out around a center square. One end of the square was anchored by a church, the other end by a livery stable.

As Fargo Ford led his band of riders into the town, Father Rodriguez and a young altar boy were at the well in front of the church, drawing up a bucket of water. They looked up as the men rode by.

"Father," the boy said. "Did you see those men as they rode by?"

"*Sí,*" Father Rodriguez said. "I saw them."

"What sort of men are they?"

"*Creo que ellos son malos. Ellos tienen sobre ellos el olor de azufre,*" Father Rodriguez said.

"Yes," the boy said. "I too think they are evil and have about them the scent of sulfur."

Father Rodriguez crossed himself as he watched the men ride toward the center of town, and seeing his priest make the sign of the cross, the altar boy did the same.

There was no saloon as such, but there was a cantina, and Fargo Ford led his band directly there.

All dismounted except for Ponci.

"Hey, Fargo, Ponci is still mounted," Casey said as the others started toward the cantina.

"You goin' to stay out here?" Fargo asked.

"What?" Ponci had been hitting the laudanum pretty hard, and he was having a hard time focusing on what was going on around him.

"Are you going to stay out here, or come inside and have a few drinks . . . maybe get something to eat?" Fargo asked.

"Oh," Ponci said. He took another drink of the

laudanum. "I think I'll come in," he said. He made an effort to dismount, but couldn't.

"Help his sorry ass down," Fargo said with a dismissive wave of his hand. As Monroe and Casey went to Ponci's aid, Fargo stepped up onto the low wooden porch. Dagen followed him as he pushed through the dangling strings of beads that hung across the door of the cantina.

Because it was so bright outside and darker inside, the cantina managed to give the illusion of being cooler. But that was an illusion only. It was out of the direct sunlight, but it was also without any flow of air, so it wasn't any cooler, and might even have been a little warmer than outside.

Once the two men stepped through the door, they moved to one side for a second, keeping their backs to the wall as they looked around the room. This was always the most critical time because if there was anyone here who intended to harm them, that person would have the early advantage until their eyes adjusted to the darkened interior.

"Do you see anyone?" Fargo asked.

Fargo's question didn't have to be any more specific. Dagen knew that he was asking if there was anyone in here who posed a threat to them.

"No, it looks clear," Dagen answered.

"There's a table back there," Fargo said, pointing to the far corner of the room.

The two men started toward the table Fargo had pointed out.

"Fargo, he's going to die," Dagen said. "You know that, don't you?"

Fargo was quiet for a long moment before he answered. "Yeah, I know it," he finally said.

"Well, what are we keeping him with us for?"

"What do you mean, what are we keeping him with us for?"

"I mean, look at him, Fargo. Right now he's more

dead than alive. If you ask me, all he's doin' is just slow-in' us down."

"Hell, Dagen, if you want to shoot the son of a bitch, go out there and shoot him," Fargo said. "I ain't goin' to do nothin' to stop you."

Dagen shook his head. "It ain't my place to shoot him. You're the leader. It's your place."

"Now, what kind of leader would I look like if I went around killin' my own men?" Fargo asked.

By now they had reached the table and, deferring to Fargo, Dagen let him be the first to choose where he wanted to sit. After Fargo was settled, Dagen sat down. Then he looked around the room again, this time making a more careful observation.

There were about a dozen people in the cantina—ten men, counting the bartender, and two women. Not one of the people in the place looked American.

"Damn," Fargo said. "Are you sure we're still in America?"

"Yes," Dagen said. "That is, I think so."

"You think so? Look around. Do you see one Ameri-can in here?"

Dagen called over to the bar. "*Señor, es esta Norteamérica o México?*"

"Territorio de Arizona, Estados Unidos," the bar-tender answered.

"Yeah, we're still in America."

"Ask the son of a bitch if anyone in here speaks English."

"I speak English, Señor," the bartender replied. "We all speak English." With a wave of his arm, he took in everyone in the room. "We are Americans."

"Americans, huh? Well, you sure as hell can't prove it by me," Fargo said.

Casey and Monroe came in then, half-dragging, half-supporting Ponci between them. Ponci's arms were across their shoulders, and he was hopping on one leg, dragging his useless leg behind him.

"What happened to your friend?" the bartender asked.

"His horse fell on him," Fargo said. "Bring us some whiskey and something to eat."

"No whiskey. Tequila."

"Tequila is fine," Fargo said as he watched Casey and Monroe pull out a chair and very carefully help Ponci sit down. Then they sat as well.

A moment later the bartender brought a bottle and five glasses.

"You can take one of the glasses back," Fargo said. "Ole Ponci here isn't going to be drinkin' none. Are you, Ponci?"

"What?" Ponci asked.

"See what I mean?" Fargo said. "Hell, he's been suckin' down so much of that laudanum that right now he don't know if it is daylight or dark outside."

The other men around the table laughed as, nodding, the bartender took the extra glass back.

One of the women laughed out loud, her voice rather shrill over the subdued conversation, mostly in Spanish, of the other patrons.

Fargo took a drink, then looked over at the two women. The women, obviously bar girls and probably whores, appeared to be in their mid-to-late thirties. They were attractive in a garish sort of way. Both were wearing blouses that showed a lot of cleavage, and skirts split to show long, shapely legs. They had dark hair, black eyes, and olive complexions highlighted by bright red lipstick.

"What do you boys say that we get us a couple of women?" Fargo asked the others.

"Good idea, but they seem to be busy now," Casey said.

"I'll take care of that." Fargo got up from the table and started toward the bar.

"You and you," he said, pointing to the two women.

"You see my friends over there at that table? We'd be much obliged if you'd come join us for a few drinks."

The two women looked at him just for a second, then returned their attention to the men they were with.

"You," Fargo said to the woman nearest him. "I asked you nice to join me'n my friends over at the table.

"The señorita is with me, Señor," the man who was standing with her said.

"Yeah? Well, she is going to be with us now," Fargo replied.

The Mexican's hand moved toward his pistol. "No, Señor, I think she will stay with me," he said, his eyes glaring menacingly.

Fargo found it amusing that the Mexican had threatened him by making a move toward his pistol. As he stared at the Mexican, a big smile spread across his face.

"Well now, mister, are you goin' to pull that hog leg, or just hold your hand over it tryin' to scare me?" Fargo asked.

The Mexican had not expected this kind of reaction to his threat, and the expressions on his face went the gamut, from menacing, to surprise, and then, as he realized that he had started down a path from which there was no return . . . to fear.

Fargo read the range of emotions, and decided to push the man further.

"Go for it, Mex. That is, if you've got any cojones. Otherwise, crawl on out of here like a coward."

The fear on the Mexican's face now turned to anger and determination. He let out a yell of rage, and made a ragged attempt to draw his gun.

Fargo had his own gun out in the blink of an eye. The Mexican was surprised at how fast Fargo had drawn. It was almost as if the gun had just magically appeared in Fargo's hand. Seeing that he was badly beaten, he interrupted his own draw, pausing, just as his gun cleared leather.

The Mexican held his hand out and tried to smile.

Fargo smiled, as if greatly enjoying this moment. Then, while still smiling, he pulled the trigger.

The heavy .44-caliber bullet hit the Mexican just under his left eye, and blood and brain matter flew out of the exit wound in the back of his head, leaving a smear on the mirror behind the bar. The Mexican fell, dead before he hit the floor.

The drama had unfolded so quickly, and so unexpectedly, that everyone else in the cantina looked on in shock.

The woman who had been with the Mexican screamed, then looked down at him. She looked back at Fargo with a shocked look on her face.

"Usted mató Pablo!" she said in a quiet, choked voice.

"Hey, Dagen, what did this here whore just say?" Fargo asked, waving his gun. A little stream of smoke was still coming from the end of the barrel, and it drifted up to join the cloud of acrid-smelling smoke that was gathering over the barroom.

"She said you killed him," Dagen replied.

"Ha!" Fargo said. "Yeah, I reckon I did kill the son of a bitch at that." He looked at the woman. "This is all your fault, you know," he said.

"Why is it my fault, Señor?" the woman asked, surprised by Fargo's accusation.

"If you had done what I asked you to do, Pablo here would still be alive. But because you didn't leave him and come join us for a little friendly get-together, he is dead." He looked over at the other woman, who was standing halfway down the bar. She too was with someone, but the person she was standing with backed away from her very quickly when he saw Fargo looking toward him.

"You," Fargo said to the other woman, "I want you too. I'm invitin' both of you, real friendlylike, to come join my friends and me."

Without further hesitation, the two women hurried over to the table to join Fargo Ford's men. In the meantime, Fargo walked over to the bar and stared down at the body of the man he had just killed.

"Bartender," he called. "Come here."

"*Sí?*" the bartender answered. Like the others in the room, the bartender was still in a state of shock over what he had just witnessed. And now, added to that shock was fear. He hung back.

"I said come here," Fargo repeated, more authoritatively this time.

Hesitantly, and visibly shaking, the bartender closed the distance while keeping the bar between them.

"The whore said this man's name was Pablo?" Fargo asked.

"*Sí*, Pablo Bustamante."

"Tell me, did Pablo Bustamante have a wife? Did he have any kids?"

"No, Señor, he was not married. He lived with his mother on the edge of town."

Fargo pulled one hundred dollars from his pocket and handed it to the bartender. "Give this money to his mother. Tell her I'm sorry that her son was so foolish as to draw on me."

The bartender made no effort to take the money from Fargo.

"Do you want Pablo's poor mama to do without this money?" he asked.

The bartender hesitated a second, then reached for the money.

"*Gracias.*"

Fargo pulled it back slightly. "Now, what are you going to tell her?"

"I will tell her that you are sorry her son was so foolish as to draw on you."

"That's a good man," Fargo said. He looked at the

others in the room. "And as for the rest of you. If there is anyone in here who does not think this was a fair fight, then step up and let me hear from you. We may as well settle this now," he called out loudly.

There were several men in the cantina staring at him, and they had been staring at him from the moment his confrontation with Pablo began. But now, at his challenge, they all looked away. It was as if they had suddenly found their drinks much more interesting.

"I didn't think anyone would disagree with me. Bartender, how about getting some food over to the table now? And be quick about it, I don't want to wait for it all day."

"*Sí, muy rápido, Señor,*" the bartender replied nervously.

When Fargo returned to the table to rejoin the others, the two women were already there, though the expressions on their faces showed that they were frightened.

"Can you imagine that dumb shit pulling his gun on me just to keep a whore to himself?" Fargo asked. "What the hell was he thinkin'?"

Monroe chuckled. "Well, there's one thing for sure, Fargo. Ole Pablo won't be pullin' his gun on you no more. I'd say he's learned his lesson."

"Learned his lesson," Casey repeated, laughing out loud. The others, except for Ponci, joined him in the laughter.

"How do you know he's learned his lesson?" Dagen asked. "He might be down in hell right now trying to bluff the devil."

"He don't have to bluff the devil; hell is full of whores," Monroe said, and everyone laughed again.

"*Incluso las putas en el infierno no tendrían nada que ver con este hombre,*" one of the women said in biting tones. This was the woman who had been standing next to Pablo when Fargo shot him.

Dagen laughed.

"What the hell did she say?" Fargo demanded.

"She said even the whores in hell would want nothing to do with you."

Fargo glared at the woman, and she shook with fear at what he might do. Then, suddenly and unexpectedly, Fargo laughed out loud.

"You got guts, I'll give you that," he said. "But we ain't in hell right now, so I'm more worried about the whores up here." Fargo put his hand on her cheek and she shrank back from him. "Don't be scared. You can't have no fun if you are scared. Are you scared of me?"

"*Sí, Señor,*" the woman said.

"What is your name?"

"Carmelita."

Fargo looked at the other one.

"Rosita."

"Well, Carmelita, Rosita, will this make you less scared?" Fargo asked. He handed each of them a twenty-dollar bill.

"Señor! So much money? Why?" Carmelita asked.

"Don't you want it?"

"*Sí,* but what must we do?" Carmelita asked.

"You got a room here?"

"*Sí.*"

Fargo smiled broadly. "Well, when we get to your room, I'm sure we can figure out something to do. I figure between the two of you, you can make me'n my friends just real happy."

"This one too?" Rosita asked, looking at Ponci. The expression on Ponci's face was devoid of any interest, or even awareness of what was going on around him. "I do not think he looks like a man who wants a woman."

"I think you are right," Fargo said as he stared at Ponci. Even though they were now talking about him by name, Ponci continued to stare straight ahead, obviously not following the conversation. "Nah, don't worry about him. You don't have to mess with him," Fargo said.

"Jesus, Fargo, look at ole Ponci," Casey said. "The son of a bitch looks like hell."

"What is wrong with your friend?" Carmelita asked. "Why does he look so?"

"Oh, never mind him. He is dying," Fargo said flatly.

"Madre de Dios," Carmelita said, and she and Rosita crossed themselves.

The food was brought to the table then, and all conversation halted as the men dug into the beans and tortillas.

Ponci did not eat; nor did he give any indication that he even knew there was food on the table.

CHAPTER 11

The fire in the middle of the village, fed by mesquite wood, burned brightly. Escaping sparks rode the rising column of heat high into the night sky, mixing their golden glow with the soft blue wink of the stars.

The mourning period was over, and true to Keytano's referring to Falcon as a "guest," he was invited into Keytano's wickiup and treated well by Keytano's wife, who provided him with food and drink. Even so, he still had the distinct impression that he would not be able to leave the village without Keytano's approval.

Falcon didn't know how much longer he would be required to stay, but he decided that he would remain a while longer just to see what was going to happen. If things took a turn for the worse, he would leave, with or without Keytano's permission.

"Come," Keytano said right after Falcon finished eating the rather large and surprisingly good meal he had been served. "The council meets now."

Falcon nodded, then stood up and followed Keytano from the wickiup.

The warriors were sitting in concentric circles around the fire, with the oldest, and those who had established themselves as leaders, in the first circle. As the circles grew more distant from the fire, their occupants were younger and held positions of less importance in the social structure of the village. The women were in the outermost circles.

Beyond the last circle the children, who were too young even to sit in the last circle, played in the night, watched over by a few of the older women of the village.

Falcon, by Keytano's personal invitation, was sitting beside him in the inner circle. There were a few sentences passed back and forth between Keytano and Chetopa, but as they were spoken in Apache, Falcon had no idea what they were saying. Then Keytano held up his hand to call for quiet.

"Because Dlo Binanta is among us, we will speak only in English," he said. He turned to Falcon. "Dlo Binanta, tell us what you know of my daughter."

"I will tell of Yaakos Gan," Falcon said.

Using Cloud Dancer's Indian name had the impact Falcon had hoped for, because several of the Indians repeated her name, then nodded in approval.

"I am pleased that you knew my daughter by her name," Keytano said.

"I am pleased to have met and known your daughter," Falcon said. "As I told you, I met her on the stagecoach and we knew each other only a short time. But the desert flower that lives for but one night differs not in heart from the mighty saguaro that lives for five hundred years. So too is the time I spent with your daughter, for I learned in that short time that she was a very smart, and very brave, young woman. You and the entire village should be very proud of her, and you are rightly grieved . . . as am I . . . that such an evil thing was done to her."

"Who did this evil?" Keytano asked.

"The leader of the evil ones is a man named Fargo Ford."

"Why did you not stop the evil?" Chetopa asked.

"When the stagecoach stopped, I was shot," Falcon

said. He took off his hat to show the scalp wound, a visible scab line through his hair.

Several got up and came forward to bend over and personally inspect the wound, and it was a moment or two before the conversation resumed.

"The bullet knocked me out," Falcon continued when everyone had regained their seat. "When I came to, I saw that our shotgun guard had been killed, and Yaakos Gan had been taken from the stage by the evil men."

"Taken by them?" Keytano asked.

"Yes."

"I do not understand. If they took her, why did they kill her?"

"I believe she fought them," Falcon said. "And she fought very bravely. I know this because when the men stopped in Pajarito, one of them had knife wounds in his leg. Some way Yaakos Gan managed to get a knife and she stabbed him."

"Better she should have stabbed him in the heart," Chetopa said.

Falcon shook his head. "No, it is better this way," he said. "A doctor in Pajarito saw the wounded white man. The white man has gangrene."

"What is gangrene?" Keytano asked.

"It is when you begin to die here first," Falcon said, putting his hand on his leg. "And it moves up so that your body dies a little at a time until your heart dies as well."

Several in the village nodded, for all had seen cases of gangrene, which they referred to as the "creeping death."

"Yes, it is good that he has the creeping death," Keytano agreed. "He will die slow and in much pain." He nodded. "I am glad that my daughter killed the man who killed her."

"We must go to war to avenge Yaakos Gan," Chetopa said.

"No," Keytano replied.

"Yes!" Chetopa said.

"No," Keytano said again.

Angrily, Chetopa stood, then walked back and forth within the inner circle.

"Why do you say no? Are we women, to do nothing?" Chetopa challenged. "Or are we warriors?"

Some of the others shouted out then, some in support of Chetopa, some in support of Keytano.

Keytano held up his hand to call for quiet. Then, when silence was restored, he looked at Falcon.

"Dlo Binanta, I would ask that you wait in the wickiup," he said. "We must speak of this, and the things we say are for our ears only."

Falcon could have told him that, if they spoke in Apache, he wouldn't understand what they were saying, but he knew that Keytano knew that and had his own reasons for asking Keytano to leave.

Nodding, Falcon stood up, brushed the dirt from the seat of his pants, then stepped into the wickiup indicated by Keytano. Almost immediately thereafter, one of the Apache women came in behind him, offering him a piece of fry bread.

"Thank you," Falcon said, accepting the proffered food.

The woman withdrew then, and Falcon ate the bread, pleasantly surprised to learn that the inside of the bread was filled with honey. He enjoyed the treat as he listened to the discourse from outside. They were speaking in Apache so he had no idea what they were talking about, but it sounded quite heated.

"I do not believe this white man," Chetopa was saying to the others in the council. "I think we should kill him. Give me the word, and I will kill him."

"Why should we kill the one who brought my daughter back to me?"

"I believe he killed her. I believe he lies when he says there were others who killed her."

"If he killed her, why would he bring her back?"

"Like all white men, he is a man of deceit. Remember, this is Dlo Binanta. He has killed many of our people. I believe we should kill him. Then we should take up the path of war and kill the others who come to our land."

"Dlo Binanta killed your brother, so you are angry," Keytano said. "But your brother was making war against the white man, and those who kill in war are honorable. I believe Dlo Binanta to be such a man. He is an enemy of great honor."

"He is a white devil!" Chetopa shouted loudly. "And I say kill him now!" He held his war ax above his head and gave a blood-curdling yell that caused fright among some of the children.

Chetoka and Keytano were beginning to get very angry with each other. Then Lapari, a medicine man who was known for his wisdom, held up his hands to call for both to be quiet.

"I have the answer," he said.

"What is the answer?" Keytano asked.

"We will ask Dlo Binanta to find the white men who did this to Yaakos Gan. He will find them and kill them, then return to us with word that he has done so."

"How will we know he has killed them?" Chetopa said. "He is a man of deceit. He might say that he has killed them when he has not."

"We will make him prove that he has killed them," Lapari said. "We will ask him to bring their scalps so that we might see them."

"A white man will not scalp another white man," Chetopa said.

"I will ask if he will do this," Keytano said. "I believe if I ask this of him, he will do it."

"What makes you believe he will do it? Remember, he is an enemy of the Apache."

"Yes, he is an enemy of the Apache, but he is an enemy of much honor. If he says he will kill these evil men and bring their scalps to us, I believe he will do it."

"Call him from the wickiup and ask him," Chetopa challenged. "He will say no."

Keytano shook his head. "I will not ask him before others. I will ask him alone."

Chetopa shook his head. "No, that is not good. If he says he will not do so, I think you will not tell us."

Keytano glared at Chetopa. Chetopa was younger and stronger, but he had just questioned the veracity of his chief, and in doing so, was stepping into very dangerous ground, for Keytano had many who would fight for him.

"Do you say that I lie?" Keytano asked challengingly.

"No," Chetopa replied, dissembling. "I call back the words I spoke. I do not believe the great chief Keytano would lie."

Keytano glared at him for a moment longer. Then he looked at Lapari, the medicine man.

"Lapari, you may come with me and watch and listen as I question Dlo Binanta. Then, you can bear witness that what I will tell the council is true."

"You do not need Lapari," Chetopa said quickly. "I will believe the word of Keytano."

"I will take him so that all may believe," Keytano said resolutely.

The conversation outside the wickiup had grown quiet, and Falcon was beginning to wonder if he should be concerned about his fate. They had not taken his guns from him when he arrived and that was a good sign. He didn't believe they would let him keep his guns unless they planned to release him.

Still, the argument in the council had grown very heated, and he knew, instinctively, that he was not only the subject of the conversation, but the cause of the heat.

He loosened his guns. Whatever happened, he was not going to go down peacefully.

The flap opened and Keytano and an even older Indian came in. Falcon stood, not only to show the Indians respect, but also to be ready for any contingency.

"We have talked much about you in our council," Keytano said.

"Yes, I have heard the talk," Falcon replied. "I know there is much anger."

Keytano looked surprised. "You speak our language?"

"No," Falcon said. "One does not always need to understand the words to know what is being said. I can tell by the sound that there is anger."

"This is true."

"And the anger is with me," Falcon said. It wasn't a question, it was a declaration.

"Yes."

"Keytano, do the people believe that I killed Yaakos Gan?"

"No," Keytano answered. "Chetopa has said this, but I do not think that even he believes you killed my daughter."

"That is good."

"But Chetopa and many want to kill you anyway," Keytano said in a matter-of-fact tone. "And they want to take up the path of war against the whites."

"This would be wrong," Falcon said. "I will not let anyone kill me easily. And if they try, I will kill many before I die."

"Yes," Keytano said. "I know this is true, because I know you are a brave warrior."

"Why do you wish to take up the path of war?"

Keytano pointed in the direction of the stream. "You have seen our water," he said. "Once, the water was wide, and so deep, that one had to find places to cross. Then, the white men build a . . ." He made a motion with his hands.

"Dam," Falcon said, supplying the word.

"Yes, a dam. The white men build the dam to steal the water, and now we have but a small amount. Our horses and our cattle die of thirst. And sometimes, if we go long without rain, there is no water in the stream at all, and even our people die of thirst."

"Keytano, I must tell you that if you take up the path of war, this time the white man will not stop. His soldiers will kill all of you, not just the warriors, but the women and children as well. Your numbers are small now. When the war is finished, there will be no Apache left."

"Yes," Keytano said again. "I know that this is also true."

"So, what is going to happen?" Falcon asked. "Are you going on the path of war?"

"I think there is a way to not have war, if you will help."

"I'll do what I can," Falcon replied. "What do you want?"

"We want you to find the men who killed Yaakos Gan and kill them," Keytano said.

Falcon smiled, and nodded. "That I will do with pleasure," he said.

The medicine man said something and Keytano nodded.

"There is something else," Keytano said.

"Something else?"

"Yes," Keytano said. "When you kill these men, we want you to take their scalps and bring them to us so that we may see that you have done as you said."

Falcon took a deep breath, then let it out in a long sigh. He shook his head.

"Keytano, I will find them and kill them, but I will not scalp them."

"You must, for it is the only way the council will know

that you have done as you promised. And only if the council knows that the evil ones are dead, will I be able to keep the village from following Chetopa on the path of war."

"I'm sorry," Falcon said, "but scalping isn't something I do."

"Did you not take the scalp and gouge out the eyes of many of our young warriors during your war with Naiche?" Keytano asked.

Falcon was caught and he knew it. He had done that very thing, in part out of anger, and in part to send a message to the Indians: that he was someone to fear.

Sighing, Falcon nodded.

"Yes," he said. "You speak the truth. I did scalp your people."

"You took the scalps of our people, but you will not take the scalps of these evil men? Are these evil ones not as evil as the Apache you killed?"

"Keytano, the Apache I killed were not evil," Falcon said. "They were just warriors fighting me."

"Is Fargo Ford evil?"

"Yes."

"Then, why will you scalp my people who are not evil, but you will not scalp the white men who are evil?"

Suddenly, and inexplicably, Falcon laughed.

"Why do you laugh?" Keytano asked.

"Keytano, you should be a lawyer," Falcon said. "I believe you could get a light sentence for ole Satan himself. All right, you win. I will chase Fargo Ford and his group down, and I will kill them. And I will bring you their scalps to prove that I have."

Keytano smiled. "That is good," he said. "Come, we will tell the council, then you will be free to go."

Falcon chuckled again. "Free to go, huh? Yes, I figured it was sort of like that . . . that I would not be able to leave until you gave me permission."

Falcon followed Keytano back to the council fire. Most of the Indians were still there, though by now as many were standing as were sitting. Chetopa was with a group of five or six rather fierce-looking young men. The expression on his face was one of anger and hate and, regardless of what Keytano promised, or what Falcon did, Falcon knew that he was going to have to deal with Chetopa. If not now, someday.

"Hear these words," Keytano said, addressing his assembled people in English. "I have spoken with Dlo Binanta, and he has said that he will find the evil ones and he will kill them."

"And he will bring the scalps back as proof?" Chetopa asked.

"Yes, he has said that he will do this," Keytano replied.

"Let the council hear him say this in his own words," Chetopa demanded.

"Is the word of your chief not good enough for you?" Falcon asked Chetopa.

"It is not the word of Keytano that I question," Chetopa said. "It is the word of Dlo Binanta, killer of Apache. I will not believe you unless I hear the words you speak."

"Keytano has told you of the words that I spoke," Falcon said. "You do not wish to believe me and I think you would not do so no matter what I said."

"We will not speak of this again!" Keytano said, angrily. "I have told you what Dlo Binanta said. Do you say that I am lying?"

"I do not say that you are lying," Chetopa said, backing down.

Yes, sir, Mr. Chetopa, Falcon thought. The day is going to come when I am going to have to kill you. Or you me.

Keytano said something in his own language, then, looking at Falcon, pointed to the outer edge of the circle.

"You are free to leave," he said. "Go now, find the evil

ones. Kill them as you have said, then bring their scalps back so that we may all see."

Standing just outside the edge of the circle, Falcon saw a young Indian boy holding the two horses he had come in with. His horse was already saddled.

Falcon walked to his horse and swung into the saddle. Then the boy handed him the reins of the second horse. Falcon shook his head, then looked at Keytano.

"Keep this horse," he said. "This is a gift to you, to express my grief over the death of your daughter."

Keytano said nothing but nodded.

Falcon rode out of the village, fighting the urge to break into a gallop, depending upon Keytano's honor to keep Chetopa from shooting him in the back. It didn't take too long before he disappeared into the night.

CHAPTER 12

A fly landed on Fargo Ford's face. Without waking, he brushed it off, but the second time it landed, it woke him up. He lay there for just a second to get his bearings; then he realized where he was.

Last night he had brought Carmelita to his room. He had kept the whore all to himself, telling the others to share Rosita. Turning his head, he saw her in bed beside him. The bedsheet came up only to her waist and she was naked above it. In the bright light of the morning sun, she didn't look nearly as attractive to him as she had last night. The dissipation of her profession was beginning to show, and she looked older now than he had thought she was last night. There was a terrible scar on one of her breasts, ending with a split nipple.

"Damn, woman, someone cut you pretty good," he said under his breath. He got out of bed, then walked over to the window and looked outside. The window opened onto the back of the cantina, so he raised it, then relieved himself over the windowsill, shooting a golden stream out to glisten in the morning sun.

"There is a chamber pot under the bed," Carmelita said from behind him.

"This'll do fine," Fargo said, shaking himself off. He walked over to the chair and started pulling on his trousers. "How'd you get your titty all cut up like that?" he asked.

As if just now realizing that she was naked from the waist up, Carmelita jerked the sheet up to cover herself.

"A very bad hombre," she said.

"Woman, you ain't never seen an hombre as bad as I am," he said.

"You . . . you are going to hurt me, Señor?" Carmelita asked in quick fear.

"No, I ain't goin' to hurt you," he said. He looked at her as he buttoned his shirt. "But if I had seen how ugly you was last night, I sure wouldn't of give you as much money as I did."

"I'm sorry I do not please you, Señor."

Fargo laughed. "Oh, hell, I didn't say you didn't please me. You was good enough in bed last night. And like they say, in the dark all cats are gray."

Fargo pulled on his boots, strapped on his gun, and picked up his saddlebags.

"Well, I guess I'll be gettin' my pards and movin' on. We got a ways to . . ." He paused in mid-sentence, then hefted the saddlebags again. His eyes narrowed, and quickly he opened the flap and looked inside. "Where's my money?" he asked.

"*Qué?*"

"You heard me! My money, you ignorant bitch! Where's my money?" Fargo pulled his pistol, cocked it, and shoved the barrel of it into her nostril, pushing so hard that her nose began to bleed. "You stole my money!"

"*Señor. No entiendo!* What are you talking about? I know nothing about your money!"

Fargo pulled the pistol back, then ripped the sheet off the bed. Seeing nothing, he pushed her onto the floor, then pushed the mattress off, so he could look under the bed.

The money wasn't there.

"Where is the money?" Fargo demanded again, this time hitting her across the face with the flat of his pistol.

Now, both her nostrils were bleeding, and he left a cut on her lip.

"Por favor ayúdeme. El gringo trata de matarme!" Carmelita screamed.

"Where is my money?" Fargo asked again, shouting at the top of his voice.

Suddenly the door to the room opened and, turning toward it, Fargo saw the bartender rushing in, holding a shotgun. Fargo shot first. The .44-caliber bullet punched through the bartender's chest, then broke through his back, leaving a quarter-sized hole. The bartender fell back into the hall, firing his shotgun as he fell back. The charge from the shotgun tore a hole in the ceiling.

By now the others, except for Ponci, were out in the hallway, guns in hand. All were in their underwear.

Casey walked over to look down at the bartender. The bartender was on his back, lying in a pool of blood. His eyes were open, but unseeing.

"Fargo, what the hell happened?" Casey asked. "What'd you shoot him for?"

Fargo turned toward Carmelita. "This bitch stole our money," he said. He nodded toward the bartender. "He must'a been in on it, 'cause he come runnin' in with that scattergun."

"The whore didn't steal the money," Monroe said. "Don't you remember?"

Fargo looked at Monroe. "Don't I remember what? What do you mean, the whore didn't steal the money?"

"You put all the money in Ponci's saddlebags last night. You said bein' as how he was the only one who wouldn't be with a woman, it would be safer there."

"That's right, Fargo, that's what you done," Dagen said.

Fargo looked at them for a moment. Then he chuckled. "I'll be damn," he said. "You're right. That is what I done." He looked over at Carmelita, who was using the edge of the sheet to wipe the blood away from her face. She was weeping quietly, joined now by Rosita, who sat on the bed beside her, trying to comfort her.

"Look, I'm sorry about all this," Fargo said to her. "I forgot I gave all the money to Ponci. I thought you stole it."

"Usted bastardo. Usted es el hijo del Diablo," the woman spat.

"Yeah, yeah, well, I guess you got a right to be mad," Fargo said. He looked at the others. "Where is Ponci?"

"Well, since we was all goin' to be busy, he got a room by hisself," Dagen said. He pointed to a closed door. "He's in that room there."

Fargo walked over to the room Dagen indicated and tried to open the door. It was locked.

"Ponci," Fargo called, knocking on the door. "Ponci, you still alive this morning?"

When he didn't get an answer, he tried the door again. "Ponci?" He looked at the others and chuckled. "Well, what do you know? Ole Ponci must've died during the night." He kicked the door open, then walked inside. "What the hell?" he asked.

"What is it?"

"Come look for yourself."

The bed in the room was not only empty, it showed no signs of ever having been slept in.

"Son of a bitch," Casey said. "Where's Ponci? You think he wandered off somewhere and died?"

"No," Fargo said. "I think the son of a bitch has skedaddled! The son of a bitch has run off and he took our money!"

"How the hell could he do that?" Dagen asked. "The bastard could hardly sit up on his own, let alone take our money and run."

"Fargo, you ain't behind this, are you?" Monroe asked.

Fargo looked shocked at the accusation. "What? Are you saying I took the money?"

"I'm just saying we're wondering about it," Monroe said.

"Yeah," Casey added, and Monroe breathed a sign of relief that he wasn't issuing the challenge alone. Though Dagen didn't say anything, he stepped over to stand beside the others.

Fargo could handle any one of them by himself. That was why he was the leader. But even he couldn't handle all three if they turned against him.

"Look, fellas," he said, less belligerent now than he had been. "I don't know how Ponci pulled this off. Maybe he wasn't near as bad as he let on to be. Or maybe he was just soused down with that laudanum and figured to take his chance. But I didn't have nothin' to do with this."

There was a long beat of silence before Dagen answered.

"I believe you," he said.

"Yeah, me too," Monroe added.

"So, what do we do now?" Casey asked.

"Now? We run the son of a bitch down, kill him, and take the money. I mean, faking it or not, he's more dead than alive. How damn hard can it be to find him?"

When Falcon rode into Oro Blanco that morning, his reception was exactly as it had been when he rode into the Indian camp. Because everyone had known of his mission, nearly everyone in the town came out of houses and stores to stand on the boardwalk and watch him. A few children even ran alongside, keeping pace as he headed for the sheriff's office.

By the time he reached the sheriff's office, Sheriff Corbin was standing out front to greet him. Falcon dismounted, and tied his horse off at the hitching rail. The townspeople who had followed him as he rode into town now gathered in the street around the sheriff's office to find out what had happened.

"Well, I'll be damned," Sheriff Corbin said, pushing his hat back on his head with a bemused smile. "Here you are, back again, and all in one piece, I see."

"Still alive," Falcon said. "Although I'm sure there are more than a few people here and there who might be disappointed by that fact."

"Did you . . ." Corbin started to say, but Falcon answered before he could complete the sentence.

"I personally delivered the Indian girl to her parents," he said. "If that is what you were about to ask," he added.

"Yes, it was."

"Did the Indians give you any trouble?" one of the men in the gathering crowd asked.

"Did you see ole Keytano hisself?" another asked.

"How did Keytano act when you brung his daughter back to him?" still another shouted.

"I had no trouble," Falcon replied. "Yes, I did see Keytano, and he was like any other parent would be at having their daughter's body delivered to them. He was grieved, and he was upset."

"Would you like some coffee, Mr. MacCallister?" the sheriff said. "I've got some fresh made just inside. Come on in and have a cup."

Falcon welcomed the sheriff's offer of coffee for what it was, an invitation for them to talk more privately.

"I don't mind if I do," Falcon answered, stepping up onto the boardwalk.

"How they goin' to act now? They holdin' the girl's killin' against all whites?" someone shouted from the crowd.

"Is there goin' to be an Indian war?" another man called.

The sheriff stepped in front of the crowd and held up his hands as if pushing them back. "Now listen, you people, go on now," the sheriff said. "Haven't you got something else to do? Shoo, get away."

"Sheriff, now by damn we got us a right to know if there's goin' to be an Indian war or not," one of the men said challengingly. "And you ain't got no right to keep us in the dark."

"I have no intention of keeping you in the dark, but there ain't no way Mr. MacCallister can get told what all has to be told with all of you standin' around here shoutin' at him. If there is somethin' you need to know, I'll tell you first thing," Sheriff Corbin said. "But for now, there ain't none of you goin' to find out anythin' unless I find it out first. Get on back to your business, all of you."

"This ain't right, Sheriff."

"I tell you what, Chandler," the sheriff said, growing impatient now. "You can come inside if you want to, and spend the next twenty-four hours in the cell."

"On what charge?" the man named Chandler challenged angrily.

"On the charge of you're too damn ugly to be standin' out in public," the sheriff replied, and it had the desired effect of causing everyone, including Chandler, to laugh.

"All right, all right," Chandler said. "But don't you forget to let us know what you find out." Chandler walked away then, and his action led the others away as well.

"Come on inside," the sheriff said, "and I'll pour you that coffee."

Falcon followed the sheriff inside, then sat down in a chair, removed his hat, and ran his hand through his hair.

"Thanks for getting me away from the mob," he said.

"How is it?" the sheriff asked as he poured a cup of coffee.

"Beg your pardon?"

"The wound you have in your head. I see you're runnin' your hand across it. Is the wound botherin' you any?"

"No, not really," Falcon said. "It's just a force of habit, I guess." He put his hat back on.

The sheriff handed Falcon the cup of coffee. "So, are we? Going to have us an Indian war, I mean."

"Not if I can help it," Falcon replied. The coffee was hot, and he extended his lips and slurped it in order to cool it.

"Not if you can help it? Good Lord, man, you mean the issue is in doubt?"

"Yeah, you might say that."

"How? Why?"

"I had to promise Keytano and the council that I would track down the men who killed his daughter."

The sheriff looked relieved. "Well, that is understandable. And by the way, we have even more reasons to track them down now."

"How is that?"

"It turns out that when they escaped from jail back in Calabasas, they killed the sheriff, both his deputies, and the kid who worked at the livery stable," the sheriff said. "We just got word of it today."

"So, counting the expressman back in Calabasas, the sheriff, his two deputies, the kid at the corral, the shotgun guard, and Cloud Dancer . . . that makes seven people they've killed just in the last few days," Falcon said. He sighed. "They have really been on a tear."

"Seven that we know of," Sheriff Corbin said. "There's no telling what they have done since they left here."

"If somebody gets in their way, they won't hesitate to kill them, that's for sure," Falcon said.

Sheriff Corbin walked over to his desk, opened the drawer, and pulled out a star.

"What's that for?" Falcon asked.

"You may recollect that I offered this to you before, when you took the girl back to the Indian village. I reckon you were right to turn it down then. But I'm offerin' it to you again." He crossed over to where Falcon was sitting and held the star out toward him. "I wish you'd take it."

Falcon held up his hand. "Sorry, Sheriff, but I'm goin' to have to turn it down again."

"Why? It might come in handy for you, havin' the law on your side."

Falcon shook his head. "What I have to do, the law would want no part of," he said. "And I wouldn't want to put the burden of my action on the law."

Sheriff Corbin stared at Falcon. "What are you talking about? Huntin' down those folks . . . even huntin' them down and killin' them would be doin' the work of the law."

Falcon pointed to the star. "Sheriff, if I'm wearing that badge, I would be honor bound to try and bring them in alive for trial," he said.

"Well, yes, I suppose you would, if you could. But the truth is, these are desperate and dangerous men, so I doubt that anyone would fault you if you don't bring them in alive."

Falcon shook his head. "Still, if I was wearing the star, I would be honor bound to try to bring them in. But I'm going to be truthful with you, Sheriff. I don't have any intention of bringing them back alive. I plan to track them down, then kill them. And I mean every last one of them."

"There are five of them. There is one of you," Sheriff Corbin said.

"By now there's probably only four of them," Falcon said. "And even if Ponci is still alive, I expect he is pretty much out of it."

Sheriff Corbin stood there for a moment, rolling the star over in his hand. Then he nodded and put the star back in the drawer.

"Yeah, I guess you're right," he said. "You don't need a star for that. I suppose that was part of your deal with the Indians?"

"Yes."

"Well, if it prevents war . . . then I say kill the bastards. They're worthless murderers anyway. Better them dead than some of the good citizens of Pima County, and that's what would happen if the Indians go on the warpath."

"I thought you might see it that way."

"The only problem is, if you don't let me deputize you, I can't send a posse. Pin on this badge and I guarantee that half the able-bodied men in town would go with you."

"I don't want a posse."

"With odds of five to one . . . or even if it is only four to one, a posse might come in handy," the sheriff suggested.

"I told you what I was going to have to do, Sheriff," Falcon said. He shook his head. "I see no need in getting good citizens mixed up in this."

"Listen, Mr. MacCallister, I don't think you have to be worryin' about getting any of our good citizens mixed up in this," Sheriff Corbin said. "Don't you believe for one moment that I wouldn't be able to find people in this town who would be willing to turn a blind eye if these outlaws didn't make it back alive."

Falcon paused for a second before he spoke again. "Yes, well, that's not all there is to the promise," he said quietly.

Sheriff Corbin picked up the coffeepot to pour himself a cup. "What do you mean that isn't all there is to the promise? You're going to track them down and you're going to kill them. Seems to me like that's about all there is. What else would ole Keytano be wantin' you to do?"

"I'm going to scalp them," Falcon said flatly.

Sheriff Corbin put the pot back down in surprise, and he turned to look at Falcon.

"What did you say?"

"I said I was going to scalp them."

"You are planning to scalp white men? God in heaven, man, why would you do such a thing?" the sheriff blurted.

"I told you. It is part of the promise I made to Keytano."

"Well, to hell with Keytano," Sheriff Corbin said. "Killin' them murderin' bastards is one thing, but killin' 'em and then scalpin' 'em . . . that's something else again. That ain't somethin' white men do to one another. It ain't civilized."

"No, it isn't civilized," Falcon agreed. "But if you think about it, after I kill them, they'll be dead. So it won't make any difference to Fargo Ford and his bunch whether I scalp them or not. And it might prevent an Indian war."

"Might? You mean there is a chance that, even if you kill these bastards, and then . . ." Sheriff Corbin paused for a moment, as if struggling to say the word. "And then . . . scalp them . . . we still might have a war?"

"Yes."

"How so?"

"Turns out Keytano isn't the only one we have to worry about," Falcon said. "He's got a young buck in his band named Chetopa."

"Chetopa, yes, it would be him," Sheriff Corbin said.

"You know him?"

Sheriff Corbin nodded. "I've never had any real run-ins with him . . . but he's come off the reservation a few times to harass some freight wagons, frighten the passengers in the stagecoaches. As far as I know, that's all he's ever done. Unless he's the one who killed those three prospectors."

Falcon nodded. "I'm sure he is the one. Chetopa has a wild hair up his ass, and I don't think anything is going to calm him down."

"So what you are telling me is that, even if you track down and kill Fargo Ford and his gang, the Indians, or at least Chetopa, might still go on the warpath?"

"Yes."

"Well if that's the case, why are you willing to do this?"

"Because if I don't do this, it won't only be Chetopa on the warpath, it will be Keytano too. And I have a feeling that if Keytano ever went bad, it would be Geronimo all over again."

"I guess you've got a point there," Sheriff Corbin said.

"Besides," Falcon added, "Fargo Ford and those sons of bitches with him need killing."

"You've got a point there too," Sheriff Corbin said again.

CHAPTER 13

Ponci Elliot's leg hurt him. There was no denying the pain that had by now infested his whole leg. But he wasn't nearly as crippled or as out of it as he had been pretending to be. Although it was painful to do so, he could still walk, and ride, and stay alert.

Ponci had exaggerated his condition around the others for one reason. He had done it to put them, and especially Fargo Ford, off guard. He hadn't even been hitting the laudanum as hard as everyone thought, but was saving it for later, when he would need it.

This entire ruse was all a part of his plan to steal the money during the first opening he had. His only problem was finding the right chance. Then, last night, the opportunity was handed to him on a silver platter. He was very pleasantly surprised when the others went upstairs with their whores and Fargo figured that, somehow, the money would be safer with him. It was all he could do to keep his face expressionless over the gift that was dropped in his lap.

"What do you think about that, horse?" Ponci asked his mount. "They were going to leave me in Oro Blanco without the money. Did you know that? Well, let's see how they like it now." He chuckled. "Damn me, if I wouldn't enjoy bein' a fly on the wall when ole Fargo discovered his money's all gone, though."

Ponci had ridden out of town right after midnight, and rode hard through the long, dark hours, putting as much distance between himself and Sassabi Flat as he could. Now, as the sun rose over the Quigotoa Mountains, he slowed his horse to a more leisurely pace. After all, there was no sense in killing his animal, and he doubted that Fargo was even awake yet.

Back in Sassabi Flat, Fargo Ford was awake. So were Dagen, Casey, and Monroe. They were not only awake, they were already aware that Ponci had taken the money. The four of them hurried down to the livery to claim their horses. That was when they saw that Ponci's horse was gone.

"Son of a bitch!" Fargo swore loudly. "I didn't think the bastard could even get mounted without help. Son of a bitch!" he said again in his anger.

"Hey!" Monroe shouted to the stableman. "You! Come here!"

The stableman was an older man with white hair and a white beard.

"*Sí, Señor?*" the man asked when he answered the summons.

"The roan," Monroe said, pointing to the stable. "Where did the roan go?"

"I do not know, Señor. I did not see him leave."

"What do you mean, you didn't see him leave, you ignorant bastard? It's your job to see people leave when they take a horse," Fargo said angrily. "Otherwise, why do we pay you to watch after our horses."

"I do not know, Señor," he said again.

"Ahh! You don't know shit!" Fargo said, shoving the old man roughly. Then to the others: "Let's get saddled and get after him."

"Get after him? Get after him how? We don't even know which way he went," Dagen said.

Fargo smiled. "Yeah," he said. "We know which way he went."

"We do?"

"He went north," Fargo said resolutely.

"How do you know that?"

"I know that he did 'cause he's got hisself a whore up in Mesquite," Fargo said. He chuckled. "Oh, yeah, he figures he can get up there, lay low with his whore while he's gettin' his leg fixed, and we won't know nothing about it."

"Yeah, he's talked about that whore from time to time, but who knows if she is real?" Casey asked. "I mean, when you think about it, I can't picture Ponci with no woman, be she whore or not."

"Most of the time that is true," Fargo agreed, "but I know that this one is real."

"How do you know this one is real? How do you know he ain't makin' this one up like he does all the others?" Casey asked.

"I know this here one is real 'cause she's my sister," Fargo said.

"Your sister?" Casey said in shock.

"Yeah, you got anything to say about that?" Fargo challenged.

"No," Casey said quickly. "No, I don't reckon that I do."

"Come on," he said. "Get your asses in the saddle and let's go."

Within minutes after saddling and mounting, Fargo Ford and the others were riding north out of Sassabi Flat. By now it was incredibly hot and even the breeze, what little there was of it, emphasized the terrible heat. When the wind did blow, which was seldom, it did little by way of amelioration. Quite the opposite, in fact, for it was like a breath of air from a blast furnace, rattling the tinder-dry grass and shifting the sand about in abrasive clouds.

The four men were riding in single file, even though there was plenty of room for them to ride abreast. Fargo was at the head of the file, pushing them hard to catch up with Ponci.

"I'm going to kill him," he said. Then, shouting into the desert: "Do you hear me, Ponci, you son of a bitch? I'm going to kill you!"

The echo rolled back from the Quigotoa Mountains.

"Kill you . . . kill you . . . kill you!"

Keytano's wife awakened him. He sat up in the blankets and reached for the wooden shingle she offered him. On it was his breakfast of boiled beef and bread.

"He is gone," he wife said.

"Who is gone?" Keytano asked as he bit into the meat.

"Chetopa. He is gone, and he has taken five warriors with him."

Keytano sighed, then put down his meal. "This is not good," he said.

"Will he make war?" she asked.

"He cannot make war, he can only make trouble," Keytano said.

"But he can make much trouble," Keytano's wife suggested.

"Yes," Keytano agreed. "He can make much trouble."

Keytano sat there for a long moment, just staring ahead. His wife picked up the food he had put down and held it out to him.

"Eat, my husband," she said. "You cannot be strong here, and here"—she put her hand to her heart, then to her head—"if you do not eat."

"Yes," Keytano agreed. "I must eat. Then I must consider what to do."

Arnold Johnson drove the rented team and buckboard toward Arivica. He had two accounts in Arivica, which he normally serviced by stagecoach, but after his run-in with Gentry, he would not be using the stagecoach again. They could just get their revenue somewhere else. They would not get one more cent from Arnold Johnson, or from Thurman Leather Goods.

His samples were in the back of the buckboard, plus he was even carrying the fulfillment of one order. When he traveled by stage, all he could carry was his samples. He could never fulfill an order because there was rarely room for the extra baggage on the stage.

The more he thought about it, the more he believed that he should have been traveling this way all the time anyway. It was certainly more comfortable than being inside a hot, airless coach box. And if he had to share another coach with someone like Falcon MacCallister . . . well, he just didn't know what he would do.

He didn't know which was worse, having to share the coach with MacCallister, or with the Indian woman. There should be a law prohibiting Indians from traveling with white people, just as there was a law prohibiting the Colored from traveling with white people.

Indians and Coloreds should know their place, and their place was definitely below a white man.

"Below a white man," he said aloud, and he laughed. "Yeah, I would like to have one of them below me right now."

He rubbed himself as he thought of Cynthia. Cynthia was a black woman who had set herself up with her own crib back in Calabasas. Johnson was one of her best customers.

And, up in Harshaw, he was a frequent visitor to an Indian woman named Sasha.

The Indian girl who had been riding in the coach with him was prettier than either one of them. He thought of her lying naked in the ditch, and he wished he had gone up with MacCallister to see her. He wondered if the men who took her did have their way with her.

What would it be like, he wondered, to be an outlaw, to be completely free of all convention? Why, anytime you wanted a woman, you would just take her. And you wouldn't have to pay her either. He imagined himself as one of the more storied outlaws of the West.

"Johnson the Terrible," he said out loud.

No, that didn't sound good.

"Kid Johnson."

He shook his head. That didn't sound right either. Maybe his first name.

"Arnold the Outlaw."

"Arnold the Evil One."

"Evil."

"Evil Arnold! Yes!" he said aloud.

For the next several minutes, as Arnold drove the buckboard, he fantasized himself as Evil Arnold, robbing banks, holding up stagecoaches, and raping women. He felt himself getting an erection.

While one of his warriors held the reins to his horse, Chetopa slithered on his belly up to the crest of the ridge. Looking down onto the road that ran through the valley floor below, he saw a single buckboard, occupied by only the driver. There appeared to be some things in the back of the wagon, though from his distance, he had no idea what they were.

He went back to the others and looked at the war party he had gathered. There were five of them, ranging in age from sixteen to thirty. Each warrior was in paint, having chosen his own particular design.

Chetopa's war paint consisted of yellow around one eye, black around the other, and three red slashes on each cheek.

It had not been hard to gather his band. Some he had known since they were boys growing up together. Others had come to the village during the breakup of the Chiricahua. All had a thirst for adventure, and most had their own reasons to hate the white man.

Early that morning he had walked though the village calling for all who were brave of heart to join him. These five joined him, while the others, especially the older men, merely stared at them from the openings of their wickiups.

"Will we attack this white man?" one of the Indians asked.

"Yes," Chetopa answered.

"Eeeyaah!" the others shouted, and Chetopa motioned for them to be quiet.

"We will wait until he passes," he said. "Then we will strike from behind."

So deep was Johnson into his fantasies that he didn't even see the Indians as they came over the ridge and started after him. In fact, his very first indication of danger was when one rode up right beside him on the left and another on the right.

For a second, Johnson was shocked by their sudden and unexpected appearance. Then he became frightened, and he slapped the reins against the back of his team, urging them to run.

The team broke into a gallop, and the buckboard flew down the road, leaving behind it a billowing rooster tail of dust. The Indians easily kept pace with him, and as he looked left and right, he saw that they were laughing, actually enjoying his panic.

He was not armed, and had no way to fight back. As soon as the Indians realized he wasn't armed, they rode ahead of him, still one to either side, and reached down to grab the harness of his team. The Indians slowed the team, finally bringing them to a halt.

For a second the buckboard just sat there, surrounded by the swirl of dust the wheels had stirred up, as the whole war party gathered around.

"What do you want?" Johnson asked. He pointed to the harness and tack he was carrying. "Do you want my samples? You can have them! Take them."

"You should not have come here," Chetopa said.

"What do you mean I shouldn't have come here? This is a public road. I'm on my way to Arivica."

Chetopa spoke in Apache to the others, and Johnson saw them all raise their rifles and point at them.

"What? No!" he shouted.

The report of six rifle shots rolled back from the nearby mountains, and Johnson's body jerked under the impact of the bullets. He slumped forward, prevented from falling only by the footrest of the buckboard.

Chetopa dismounted, drew his knife, and advanced toward the body. Grabbing the dead white man by his hair, he made the scalping cut; then he jerked the scalp off and held it up while it was still bleeding.

"Eeeyahh!" he shouted, and the others, denied the scalp, took out their anger and left their mark by further disfiguring of the body. They hacked and cut at the dead man while, overhead, buzzards circled, waiting patiently for their unexpected feast.

By now the pain Ponci was feeling was so severe that it was almost unbearable. Every step his horse made transferred a shooting pain up his leg and into the rest of his body. He had half a bottle of laudanum left . . . but he didn't want to use it. Not yet anyway.

Up ahead, he saw what he had been looking for, and he guided his horse toward an unusual rock formation:

an obelisk, with two round stones at the bottom. To Ponci, it looked like a pecker and a pair of balls. It looked like that to the Indians as well, which is why they called it Dzil Ndeen, or "Mountain Man."

What made the rock formation particularly significant now was the fact that Ponci knew it shielded a cave from view. And right now, Ponci needed the cave as a means of getting out of the sun, staying out of sight, and providing a place to recuperate after he did what had to be done.

Ponci rode his horse toward the rock formation. When he passed a patch of vegetation, he stopped and let his horse graze.

"Eat what you can," he said. "It's going to be slim pickin's for a while."

Once in the cave, Ponci climbed down from his horse, removed the horse's saddle, then secured him. After that he started a small fire, then took his knife out and cut his pants leg off, just above his right knee. He took off his boot, and slid the cut sleeve of the pants leg down and off.

"Oh, damn," he said quietly as he examined his leg. From the knee down, the leg was blue. The wound was puffy, with abscesses and dead flesh all around it. "This son of a bitch is bad."

Ponci built a small fire, then put the knife blade in the fire.

"How damn hard can it be?" he asked aloud. "Hell, when I was butcherin', I would sometimes cut off a dozen legs a day."

Ponci fortified himself with a few swigs of laudanum, making sure to hold some back for later. Then he took the knife from the fire and looked at his leg, just below the knee.

"Of course, them legs was on cows or pigs. This here will be the first time I ever cut my own leg off."

Almost hysterically, he giggled. Then, holding his breath, he started to cut.

CHAPTER 14

There was a comforting familiarity to the interior of a general store. It was redolent with the scent of coffee beans, ground flour, smoked meat, and various spices. The shelves behind the clerk's counter were colorful displays of can labels—yellows, reds, blues—advertising beans, peaches, peas, and tomatoes. A calendar on the back wall had the smiling picture of a young girl holding a bar of soap.

BUY PEARL'S SOAP, the legend said.

A long string of peppers hung from a nail, adding their own aroma to the other smells.

Falcon was here, buying the supplies he would need to sustain him during the time he would be on the trail of Fargo Ford and the others. As he called for each item, the store clerk, a tall, thin man with snow-white hair and a beard, would find it, then bring it back to the front, adding the item to an increasing pile. As he added each item, he would take a pencil from behind his ear, sharpen it between his teeth, then add the item and the price to his running total.

"Will there be anything else for you, Mr. MacCallister?" the store clerk asked, putting his pencil back behind his ear. He wiped his hands on an apron that might have been white at one time.

"Let's see," Falcon said, looking over the pile. "Bacon, flour, beans, coffee, salt, matches, tobacco." He paused and looked up at the clerk. "Do you have any horehound candy?"

"Horehound is it? Yes, sir, I believe I do. How many sticks do you want?"

"Around twenty, if you have that many," Falcon said.

The store clerk chuckled. "I wonder if the people across the country who read in the dime novels about the exploits of the great Falcon MacCallister know about this sweet tooth of yours?"

"Shh," Falcon said, laying his finger across his lips. "We'll keep it our secret, won't we?"

"Turn out, turn out!" someone was yelling from outside the store. "Everyone, turn out!"

"What in the world is going on out there?" the store clerk asked.

"I don't know. I'll take a look," Falcon said. He walked to the front window and looked out onto the street. In response to the man's shout for everyone to turn out, the street was beginning to fill with the citizens of Oro Blanco.

"Do you see anything?" the clerk asked.

"No, just a bunch of people milling about," Falcon said back over his shoulder. "Maybe I'll go out there to have a look. What do I owe you?"

"Just a minute, let me sum it all up," the clerk answered. Once again he took the pencil from behind his ear, sharpened it with his teeth, then began writing on the little piece of paper. "Put down the five and carry the two," he said, talking to himself as he figured.

At that moment the door opened and Sheriff Corbin stepped inside. The clerk looked up as he did so.

"I'll be right with you, Sheriff," the clerk said. "I'm just finishin' up here." He held up the paper and examined it. "Mr. MacCallister, it looks like the whole thing is goin' to come to six dollars and forty cents."

"Six dollars and forty cents for that little dab of

supplies," Falcon said. He shook his head. "It's getting real expensive just to live."

"Put it on my bill, Mr. Dobbins," Sheriff Corbin said to the clerk. "As he is doing a job for the city, I just got authorization from the city council. Give him anything he wants."

"Very good, Sheriff, if you say so," Mr. Dobbins replied.

"Sheriff, what's all the commotion out there?" Falcon asked.

"Do you know that harness drummer Johnson? Arnold Johnson, I think his name is. He's from Calabasas."

"Yes, I know him. We came into town on the same stage. Not a pleasant man."

"Yeah, well, right now he is also not a living man," Sheriff Corbin said.

"What happened?"

"Yesterday, Mr. Johnson rented a team and a buck-board from the livery. His plan was to go up to Arivica and call on some of his clients up there. Evidently, he ran into trouble on the way up. This morning the rented team came back into town pulling the buckboard."

"Without Johnson?" Falcon asked.

"No, Johnson come with 'em, all right. He's in the buckboard," Sheriff Corbin said. "Dead." He paused for a moment, then added, "He don't look pretty. The thing is, I don't know if it was done by Indians, or by someone who wanted to make us think it was Indians."

"By someone, you mean, like Fargo Ford?"

"Yes."

"Let me take a look," Falcon said.

"Come on, I'll show him to you. He's still in the buck-board, and that's over at the livery. I told the undertaker to keep him there until you got a look at him. I figured you'd be able to tell a bit more about what happened than the rest of us."

When Falcon followed the sheriff out into the street, he saw that a rather substantial crowd of people had gathered in the street at the front of the livery. It wasn't just curious men, though. Women and children were in the crowd as well, all of them buzzing about the excitement.

"Look's like the whole town has turned out," Falcon said.

"Not much happens in Oro Blanco," the sheriff said. "So when something does happen, it creates a lot of interest. We're comin' through, so make way," he called as they approached the crowd. "You folks make way, let us through here."

The crowd separated enough to let Sheriff Corbin and Falcon pass. When they approached the buckboard, they saw that a tarpaulin had been put over the body.

"Pull the tarp back," Falcon said. "I want to have a look."

"It ain't pretty," the liveryman said as he reached for the piece of canvas that covered the body lying in the back of the buckboard.

"Hold on a minute, Jimmy," the sheriff said, holding out his hand to stop the liveryman from turning the tarp back. Corbin turned to address the crowd. "Now, some of you already know this fella has been butchered up pretty good," he said. "So if there's anyone among you that's got a queasy stomach and don't want to see this, I'd advise you to turn your heads now," he said. "I'm sorry to do this, but we've got to take a look."

A few of the women did turn away, forcing their children to turn away as well, but most did not. And some of the more morbidly curious actually moved nearer to the buckboard for a closer look.

The liveryman put his hands back on the tarp and looked up at the sheriff. Corbin nodded, and the liveryman pulled the tarp back.

There were several gasps from the crowd.

"Oh, my God!" one of the women who had not turned away said.

"Would you look at that?" a man said.

Johnson was lying on his back. His eye sockets were bloody holes. His stomach had been cut open and his entrails were hanging out. His right hand was missing. He had also been scalped, and Falcon examined the method by which the scalp was taken. The knife cut had started in the forehead, then made a complete circle around to the back of the neck. Following the cut, the hair was jerked off the top of the head, bringing the scalp with it.

This was, Falcon knew, the way the Indians scalped their victims.

Falcon looked into Johnson's inside jacket pocket and pulled out a billfold. When he opened the billfold he found forty dollars in cash. He held the money up for the sheriff to see.

"Damn, whoever did it didn't rob him, did they?" Corbin said.

Falcon shook his head. "All right, you can re-cover him now," Falcon said.

The liveryman pulled the tarp back over Johnson's body and Falcon walked away without saying a word, leaving the crowd behind him. He heard the sheriff moving quickly to catch up with him.

"It wasn't Ford, was it?" Corbin asked. "Otherwise, he would'a took the money. Damn, I should'a checked that first thing myself."

"It was Indians," Falcon said simply.

"So, does this mean that Keytano has gone on the warpath?"

"Not necessarily. If I had to guess, I would say this is Chetopa's doing. Chetopa and whoever he has managed to get to ride with him. I don't believe it's Keytano. And

I'm sure that Chetopa only managed to get a handful to ride with him."

"Nevertheless, I'd better ride up to Fort Lowell and let the Army know about this," Sheriff Corbin said.

"I'll go with you," Falcon offered.

"I thought you were going after Fargo Ford and his bunch."

"I am," Falcon said. "But for the moment it's clear that Chetopa represents the most danger to the people that live around here. So I think the first thing I'd better do is go after Chetopa."

It was after dark when Fargo Ford and the others rode into the tiny town of Mesquite. Although it was dark, the town was still sweltering, slowly giving off the heat it had absorbed during the day.

It lay before them, bathed silver under the full moon. The buildings of the little town were, for the most part, low-lying structures of adobe. However, here and there, and prominent by the contrast, could be seen houses made of unpainted ripsawed lumber. Straw appeared to be the building material of choice for the roofs, though on a few of the more substantial buildings the roofs were of tile.

Little squares of light projected through a few of the windows, forming dim yellow splashes in front of the buildings. As the four men rode up the street, they passed in and out of these splashes of light so that sometimes they were visible, and sometimes they were not.

The yap of a barking dog came from behind one of the houses. The sound of a crying baby came from one of the other houses. Guitar music and the sound of a trumpet spilled out of the town's one cantina, accompanied by laughter; a high-pitched trill from the women, and a deep guffaw from the men.

"Hey, Fargo, it's been a long, hard ride. What do you say we tie up here for a little while and let's get somethin' to drink," Dagen said.

"You got 'ny money?" Fargo asked.

"No, but you do."

"What makes you think I got 'ny money?"

"I know you took a whole packet of money out of the money pouch, 'cause I seen you do it."

"Yeah, I did, but for now, that's all we got left. We've got to make it last until we get our money back," Fargo said.

"What's the use of havin' it if we don't spend some of it?" Dagen asked.

"Come on, Fargo, Dagen's right," Casey said. "I gotta have me somethin' to drink to get the dust outta my throat. Hell, I'm that dry now that I can't even work up a good spit."

"Yeah, and I'd like somethin' to eat too," Monroe added. "Or was you maybe plannin' on starvin' us to death?"

"All right, all right, we'll stop and get us somethin' to eat and drink. Just quit your bellyachin'," Fargo said, heading toward the cantina. "I need to ask a few questions anyway."

The brightest building in town was clearly the cantina, with bright golden light shining through every window. The men tied their horses off in front of the cantina, then stepped up onto the little wooden porch and pushed through the curtain of hanging, clacking beads. It was easy to see why the inside was so brightly lit. It was accomplished by the expedient of using two wagon wheels suspended from the ceiling, each of which supported half-a-dozen lanterns. In addition to the overhead light, there were several lanterns placed on shelves around the walls. The result was a light that made the room almost daytime bright.

Mesquite was further north than Sassabi Flat, and whereas Sassabi Flat had been almost all Mexican, in this little town there appeared to be nearly as many Americans in the bar as there were Mexicans. Fargo found a table in the corner and then ordered a meal of beans, bacon, and cornbread.

"And beer," Dagen said. "Don't forget the beer."

"And whiskey," Casey added.

"And women," Monroe said. "Don't forget to send some of them women over."

"We ain't got time for no women," Fargo said. "You seen what happened to us the other night when we was messin' with the women."

"Yeah, but that don't count," Monroe said.

"Why don't it count?"

"'Cause it was one of us what done it to us. And there ain't none of us goin' to do somethin' like that to us again," Monroe said. "Not without I kill 'im first," he added determinedly.

Fargo shook his head and chuckled. "Monroe, I'm sure there must be some sense in what you just said, but damn if I can figure it out."

Evidently, Fargo's admonition to his men to avoid the women had not reached the women themselves. For as the men were eating, a couple of the bar girls came up to the table. Like the other girls in the cantina, and like Carmelita and Rosita from the other night, both of these soiled doves were Mexican. They had long black hair and smooth, clear skin that shined golden in the lantern light. One of the soiled doves was a little younger than the other, and she was considerably prettier than most bar girls any of the men had encountered. Somehow she sensed that Fargo was the leader of the group, and she sidled up to stand beside him.

"My, all of you are such handsome hombres," the

younger girl said, smiling seductively, not only at Fargo, but at every man around the table.

"We're more'n handsome, honey, we're . . ." Dagen started, but before he could finish his comment, Fargo interrupted.

"I'm looking for an American whore," he said.

"Oh, Señor, you do not want an American whore," the young one said. "The blood of American whores runs cold. The blood of the Mexican whores runs hot. I am Mexican," she added. "That means my blood runs hot for you."

She emphasized her comment by arching her back proudly and pushing her pelvis forward. "Don't you want me, Señor?"

"I told you, I am looking for an American whore. Do you know a whore named Suzie?"

"Suzie? *Sí, Señor,* we know Suzie," the older of the two girls responded. "But I think you will like Frederica and me better than Suzie."

"This one is Frederica," Dagen said, pointing to the young one. "What is your name?"

"I am Ava."

"Well, Ava, me'n my pards here has rid a long ways and we're hungry and thirsty," Dagen said. "But as soon as we eat 'n drink, why, I reckon we could show you and little Frederica here a thing or two."

"No, we cannot," Fargo said. "I told you boys, we ain't got time for none of this. Leastwise, not till we get back what's rightfully ours," he added, using the term "rightfully" in its broadest possible sense since they actually had no right to the money at all.

Fargo looked directly at Frederica. "I want Suzie," he said.

"Sorry, Señor, but Suzie is not here now," she answered.

"You don't have time for us, but you have time for a gringo girl?" Ava asked, pouting.

"Honey, I got time for you," Monroe said. "It don't take me very long a'tall. Hey, Fargo, come on, what do you say a few of us take a little time off and go upstairs with . . . ?"

"No!" Fargo said sharply. Then, turning to Frederica, he asked again. "Where is Suzie?"

As she realized that she was not making any progress with him, the smile left Frederica's face and she shrugged. "She is in her crib, Señor, but I know she will not see you now. She has a man with her, and I think he will stay the night."

"Who is he?" Fargo asked. "Who is the man with her?"

"It is someone," Frederica answered. "I do not know his name."

"What does he look like?"

"He is a gringo," Frederica said with a shrug of her shoulders. "How can I tell you what he looks like? All gringos are the same."

"You can't tell me anything about him at all?" Fargo asked. "Tall, short? Beard, no beard? Cowboy, miner?"

Frederica shrugged. "He is not tall and he is not short. He does not have a beard but he needs a shave."

Fargo took out two dollars and put the money on the table. "Are you sure that is all you can tell me?"

The woman shrugged. "Maybe I can tell you something more," she said. *"El gringo cojea."*

"What?"

"Son of a bitch!" Dagen said, slapping his hand on the table. "Fargo, it's him! Suzie is with Ponci!"

"What did she say?" Fargo asked.

"She said the gringo has a limp."

"A limp? The hell you say." Fargo smiled and nodded. "Yes, that's our boy Ponci," he said. "It has to be." Happily, he gave a dollar each to the two women.

"Gracias," they said, taking the money and putting it down into their exposed cleavage.

"I told you boys we would find him," Fargo said. "Come on, let's go see the son of a bitch."

"It will do you no good to go see the gringo, Señor. Suzie will not see you," Frederica said as the four men stood up from the table.

"Oh, I think she will," Fargo said.

"Don't you ladies go anywhere. We'll be back," Casey promised as they started toward the door.

"Don't count on it," Fargo said.

At a table in the back corner of the saloon, Billy Cates turned so that Fargo Ford wouldn't see his face. Billy had once ridden with Fargo, but they'd had a falling-out over some money. Billy and his friend Les Wilson accused Fargo of cheating them on their share of the money they'd stolen from a general store over in Cholla. They settled the argument with guns, and when it was over, Fargo rode away with all the money, leaving Billy wounded and Les dead on the floor.

Billy had been going straight ever since then, working now as a cowboy on a ranch just outside of Mesquite. He did not want to renew his acquaintance with Fargo Ford under any circumstances.

He stayed there, with his back turned, until Fargo and the others were gone.

"Do you know where to go?" Dagen asked after they stepped outside.

"Yeah, I know where to go. I know where her crib is."

"Listen, Fargo, uh, since you wouldn't let us have nothin' to do with Frederica or Ava, how about while you're dealing with Ponci, we . . . well, not you, but would you mind if the rest of us . . . uh . . . well, I mean, I know she is your sister, but if she is a whore and . . ."

Dagen let the sentence hang when he saw the way Fargo was looking at him.

"After we take care of Ponci, we ain't going to be staying around long enough for nothin' like that," Fargo said. "Besides, you think I'm just goin' to stand around and let you screw my sister?"

"Why the hell not? You said yourself she's a whore. Ain't that what whores do?"

"Yeah, Fargo, what do you say? I mean, you could come back here with one of them Mex girls whilst the rest of us screw your sister," Casey said.

"Unless you got a thing aginst us doin' what ever'one else is doin' to your sister."

"You could all three screw her at the same time as far as I'm concerned," Fargo answered. "That ain't got nothin' to do with it. But after we get finished with Ponci, I don't think it will be all that smart for us to be hangin' around here."

"Oh," Dagen said. "Oh, yeah, I reckon I see what you mean."

The four men mounted their horses and rode down to the far end of the street, stopping in front of a leather goods store.

A sign hung from an iron rod that protruded from the front of the store.

ARMBRUSTER'S LEATHER GOODS
SADDLES—BOOTS
HOLSTERS—BELTS—CHAPS
H. Armbruster, Prop.

The sign made a squeaking noise as a gentle breeze moved it back and forth on its hinges. Next door to the leather goods store was WHITE'S APOTHECARY. It didn't have an overhanging sign, but there was a painting on the window of a mortar and pestle.

Fargo dismounted, and handed the reins of his horse to Casey. "You boys wait here," he said. "And take care of the horses. When I come out of there, I don't want to be pickin' my nose and scratchin' my ass, lookin' for my horse like what happened to us back in Calabasas."

"You don't need to be worryin' none about that," Dagen said. "Your horse will be here when you come back, I promise."

Fargo smiled. "Oh, I ain't goin' to worry none, Dagen," he said. "If my horse is gone when I come back, I'll just kill you and take yours."

"Your horse will be here," Dagen said again.

"Hey, how come I don't seen Ponci's horse anywhere?" Monroe asked.

"The dumb son of a bitch ain't that dumb," Fargo answered. "He's not likely to leave his horse tied up out on the street where we could see it now, is he? I mean, you have to know he's figurin' on us comin' after him."

"Yeah, I guess you're right," Monroe said.

Fargo pulled his pistol, then started walking through the narrow passageway between the leather goods store and the apothecary. He continued on down the constricted path between the two buildings until he reached the alley. Then he saw it, his sister's crib. It was on the other side of the alley, a small, one-room shack made of unpainted wood. A very dim light, which Fargo supposed was a candle, glowed from inside the little crib.

Fargo walked very quietly to the front door, then slowly tried the door handle. The door was locked, but Fargo knew where Suzie kept a spare key. He reached up into the eaves and poked around with his fingers until he felt it. Then, putting the key in the lock, he turned it very carefully and pushed the door open. He stepped inside with his gun arm extended before him.

"What the hell?" a man's voice shouted as he rose up in the bed.

"Ponci, you son of a bitch!" Fargo shouted. "Did you think you would get away with it?"

Fargo pulled the trigger twice. The gun boomed, and the muzzle flash lit up the little room. The sound of the gunshots drowned out Suzie's screams.

Fargo hurried over to the bed and jerked the sheet down.

"Holy shit!" he said, looking down at the body of the man he had just killed.

It wasn't Ponci.

"Who is this?" he demanded.

By now, Suzie had recognized Fargo, and her screams stopped.

"Fargo, what the hell has gotten into you? What are you doing?" she shouted at him, hitting him angrily. "Why did you come in here shooting like that?"

"Stop it! Stop hitting me!" Fargo replied, covering up from her blows. He pushed her away, then using his still-smoking pistol, pointed it at the body of the man he had just shot.

"I thought that was Ponci."

By now several dogs were barking outside.

"That's it? You thought it was Ponci, so you came in here shooting?"

"I'm sorry," he said.

"You're sorry? You're sorry? You break into my crib, kill the man who is in my bed, scare me to death, and all you can say is you are sorry?"

"I told you, I thought it was Ponci. Where is Ponci anyway?" Fargo asked.

The dogs continued to bark, and now, from a nearby house, a baby added its crying to the noise.

"Why are you asking me where Ponci is? How the hell am I supposed to know?" she asked. "I haven't seen Ponci in nearly a year. I thought he was with you."

"No, Ponci isn't with me," Fargo said angrily. "If he was

with me, I would have already killed the son of a bitch, instead of coming here to do it."

"Yeah? Well, you didn't do it. You killed poor Mr. Thompson."

"Who is Mr. Thompson?"

"*That's* Mr. Thompson," Suzie said, pointing to the body in her bed. "He works in the general store. What made you think it was Ponci?"

"One of the Mex whores down at the cantina told me the man you were with has a limp. Does this man have a limp?"

"He doesn't have anything now, you ignorant bastard," Suzie said. "You just killed him."

"All right, before I killed him, did he have a limp?" Fargo asked.

"Yes, he did have a limp. One of his legs was deformed."

"Yeah, well, then you can see that it was an honest mistake. She said he had a limp, so I thought it was Ponci."

"What are you talking about? Ponci doesn't have a limp."

"He does now."

"What was that shooting?" a man's voice called from outside.

"I don't know, it come from down that way," a muffled voice answered. "And I think I heard a woman scream."

"Listen, you'd better get out of here," Suzie said, shoving him toward the door. "And if I were you, I would leave town."

"How are you going to handle this?" Fargo asked. "What are you going to tell the sheriff when he finds a dead man in your bed?"

Suzie sighed. "I don't know. I guess I'll just tell him what happened, that someone broke in here and shot him."

Fargo's eyes narrowed.

"Oh, don't worry, I won't tell him who did it. I'll just say I don't know who it was."

"What if they blame you?" Fargo asked.

"They aren't going to blame me," Suzie replied. "As soon as you are out of here, I'm going to start screaming bloody murder. And anyway, do you really give a shit if I get blamed for this?"

Fargo shook his head. "No," he said. "No, I don't give a shit."

"I didn't think you would. Now, get the hell out of here."

Fargo left the house, then ran back up between the two buildings.

"Hurry, there's some people comin'," Casey said, handing the reins back to Fargo. "I can see 'em comin' this way from the other end of the street."

"Did you get the money?" Monroe asked.

"No," Fargo answered, swinging into the saddle.

"What the hell, you killed the son of a bitch and you didn't even get the money?"

"Look, down there!" someone shouted from the darkness at the far end of the street. "There's riders in front of Armbruster's!"

"This is the sheriff!" a voice called. "You men hold it right there!"

"Throw a few shots their way, then let's get the hell out of here!" Fargo said.

Fargo, Casey, Monroe, and Dagen began shooting toward the approaching crowd. The muzzle-flame patterns lit up the building fronts like flashes of summer lightning, and the sounds of gunshots filled the street.

The shooting had the desired effect, because the crowd screamed and scattered, just as Fargo thought they would.

"Let's go!" Fargo shouted, and he and the other three galloped out of town.

"You didn't get the money?" Monroe shouted over the sound of the galloping horses. "Why did you kill him without getting the money?"

"It wasn't Ponci!" Fargo yelled back. "I killed the wrong man!"

CHAPTER 15

Falcon had seen scores of Army posts just like Fort Lowell all over the West. But unlike the forts of the Northwest, this one did not have a palisade. Instead, it had a low-lying rock fence, more as a means of marking out the property than providing any protection. But there was a front gate, from which hung a sign denoting this as the Fort Lowell Military Reservation, and the gate was manned by an armed guard.

As Falcon and Sheriff Corbin approached the gate, the guard, a young private, stepped out to meet them. He held his rifle at the high-port position.

"Halt!" he ordered.

Falcon and Sheriff Corbin complied.

"Dismount," the guard ordered.

Falcon and Corbin swung down from their horses and, holding the reins, approached the guard.

"Who are you, and what is the purpose of your visit?" the guard asked.

"Private, I'm Sheriff Corbin from Oro Blanco," Corbin said. He pointed to Falcon. "This is . . . my deputy," he added, cutting a quick glance toward Falcon and asking him silently to go along with the ruse.

Falcon said nothing to dispute the sheriff.

"What can I do for you, Sheriff?" the guard asked.

"We are here on official business. I need to speak with the fort commander."

"Wait here," the guard ordered. He stepped back a few paces, then turned his head to shout. "Corporal of the guard! Repair to post number one!"

His call was repeated by the next-nearest sentry to him.

"Corporal of the guard! Repair to post number one!"

They heard it repeated three more times, each call becoming less distinct than the preceding call as the relaying guards grew farther away. Then they heard the returning call, repeated several times until it reached the guard nearest this one.

"Corporal of the guard is repairing to post number one!"

"The corporal of the guard will be here shortly, sir," the private at the front gate said.

Falcon chuckled. "Yes, we heard."

A moment later, the corporal arrived. He was overage for his grade, and the corporal's corpulent body and patchy red face suggested that his lack of rank might be related to his love of drink. "What is it, Private Wilson? What's the problem?" he asked.

"These men are here to speak with Colonel Dixon," Private Wilson answered.

The corporal looked at Falcon and the sheriff. "I'm Sergeant . . ." he started, then corrected himself. "That is, I'm . . . Corporal . . . Gibson. You are here to see the colonel?"

"We are."

"What do you want to speak to the colonel about?"

"That's between us and the colonel," the sheriff said.

Corporal Gibson shook his head. "No, it ain't between you and the colonel. Not unless I say it is. I'm in charge here, so I'm the one you are going to have to deal with. Now, I'm goin' to ask you one more time, real nice. What do you want to see the colonel for?"

"And I'm going to tell you one more time . . . real

nice," the sheriff replied, emphasizing the "real nice," "that what we want to talk to your commanding officer about is none of your business. It is between the colonel and us."

With a dismissive wave of his hand, the corporal turned and started walking away. "In that case, the answer is no, you cannot see the colonel," he called back over his shoulder.

"How the hell are we going to get around this arrogant shit?" the sheriff asked, frustrated by the self-inflated ego of the corporal.

"Wait here for a moment, Sheriff, and let me talk to him," Falcon said. "I'm pretty sure I will be able to reason with him."

Sheriff Corbin shook his head. "No, I don't think you can. I've seen his kind before. He's probably been up and down the ranks a dozen times or more, and he wears what stripes he has managed to hang onto like a crown . . . lording it over anyone he can."

"Don't give up yet. Let me try," Falcon said, walking quickly toward the corporal. "Corporal," he called. "Wait a moment. Let's see if we can't work this out."

The corporal turned toward him with a smirk. "So, you goin' to tell me what you want to talk to the colonel about?" he asked. "I thought you might come around."

"No," Falcon said. "But I do believe we can work this out. You see, I'm going to give you one more opportunity to take us to see him. And I think you ought to take it, because otherwise I don't think you will care much for the consequences."

"*You* are going to give *me* one more opportunity?" the corporal asked. He laughed. "All right, you've given me my . . . opportunity . . . so what happens now if I don't take it? What consequences are you talking about?"

"It's a rather severe consequence, Corporal. Because

you see, if you don't take us to see the colonel, I am going to kill you," Falcon said easily.

"You'll what?" the corporal replied. Again he laughed, but this time the laughter was strained. "What did you just say to me?"

"I said, if you don't take us to see the colonel, I am going to kill you," Falcon repeated.

"How are you going to do that?" the corporal asked with a nervous, snorting type of laugh.

"Easy. You see, I'm wearing a gun and you aren't. I'll just pull my gun and I will kill you."

"Just like that?"

"Just like that."

"Are you crazy? You are in the middle of an Army post. Do you think you could just shoot me here and get away with it?"

"Oh, I don't just think I can. I know I can," Falcon said.

The corporal pointed to the gate. "Look, mister, in case you haven't noticed it, there is an armed guard not fifteen yards from here."

"Oh, that's all right. I'll kill him too," Falcon said. "Of course, I'd rather not shoot him unless I have to, because he hasn't pissed me off. But Corporal, you *have* pissed me off. So believe me when I say that I won't have any trouble killing you at all."

"Now . . . wait a minute," the corporal said, pointing at Falcon. "You can't . . . uh . . ." He stopped in mid-sentence. His pupils were dilated with fear, his nostrils were flared, sweat was popping out all over his face, and he started licking his lips nervously. "You . . . you are serious, aren't you? You really would kill me."

Falcon smiled. "Maybe you aren't quite as dumb as you look. It's time to get down to the nut-cutting, Corporal. Do we see the colonel, or do I kill you? It's up to you, and at this point I really don't give a shit which it is.

I believe I'd just as soon kill you as not." Falcon didn't pull his gun, but he did let his hand rest lightly on the handle of one of his pistols. "What's it going to be?"

"All right, all right!" the corporal said nervously. "I'll take you to see the colonel."

"Good. Oh, and Corporal, this conversation we just had? Let's keep it our little secret, shall we? I mean, we wouldn't want to be blabbing it to my friend the sheriff, or to the colonel, or anyone else, that I was going to kill you, would we?"

"No," the corporal answered in a muffled and choked voice.

"No, what?"

"No, I won't say nothin' to nobody about it," the corporal mumbled. Pulling a handkerchief from his pocket, he wiped at the big drops of sweat that had suddenly popped out on his face.

"I thought you might see it my way," Falcon said. He turned toward the sheriff and waved him on. "Come along, Sheriff. The corporal and I have worked things out."

"You have?"

"Tell him it's all right," Falcon said to the corporal.

"It's . . . all right," the corporal said. "I'll take you to see the colonel."

"Well, I'll be damned," Sheriff Corbin said, coming toward them, leading both horses. "You must have some kind of a silver tongue."

"Yeah," Falcon said. "I can be pretty damn persuasive when I want to be."

Still unmounted, Falcon and Sheriff Corbin followed the corporal from the front gate and out onto the post toward the headquarters building. The fort was laid out around a large, square parade ground, fronted on all four sides by the buildings of the garrison. Most of the buildings were two-story wooden barracks buildings. But next to every third barracks building were somewhat smaller structures. These, Falcon knew, were the individual company mess halls.

The parade ground was a large rectangle, with the barracks buildings and mess halls on each of the longer sides. The stables and corral occupied one end of the rectangle, while the post hospital and sutler's store sat at the opposite end. Midway down the far side of the parade ground, and situated right behind the flagpole, was a brick building. This was the only brick building on the entire fort, and it was to this building the three men were headed.

A white sign in front of the brick building featured crossed swords, in gold, while in black letters were the words:

FORT LOWELL MILITARY RESERVATION
Headquarters
Fifth Cavalry Regt.
United States Army
Post Commandant and Regimental Commander
Fred M. Dixon
Colonel of Cavalry

"This here is the orderly room. You can tie your horses off here," the corporal said, pointing to a hitching rail.

"Thanks," Sheriff Corbin said as he began wrapping his reins around the rail. Falcon did the same; then they followed the corporal up onto the little wooden porch and Corporal Gibson knocked on the door.

"Enter," a voice called from inside.

Inside the orderly room of the headquarters building, they saw a tall, impressive-looking, clean-shaven NCO who was sitting at a desk in front of a large wall map of Pima County, Arizona. A sign on the NCO's desk read:

Seamus O'Riley
Regimental Sergeant Major

"What is it, Corporal Gibson?" the sergeant major asked.

"Sergeant Major, these here men are the sheriff and his deputy. They want to speak to the colonel, but I don't know what it's about."

"I wouldn't think that you would. It's not your business to know," Sergeant Major O'Riley replied. "If they want to speak to the colonel, then their business is with him."

"Yeah, but don't you think . . ." Corporal Gibson started to say, but the sergeant major cut him off.

"Don't try to think, Gibson," he said. "You're not that good at thinking."

"Yes, Sergeant Major," Gibson replied, contritely.

The sergeant major, who actually did have some authority to exercise had he chosen to do so, did not try to impress Falcon and the sheriff with his position. Instead, he stepped up to the door of the colonel's office, knocked once lightly, then at a muffled voice from within, stepped inside. No more than a few seconds later, he was back outside.

"If you gentlemen will go on in, the colonel will see you," he said.

"Thanks, Sergeant Major," the sheriff said as he and Falcon entered the colonel's office.

Colonel Dixon, who had stood to meet them, was the perfect portrait of an Army officer, trim and fastidious about his dress and person.

"Gentlemen, welcome to Fort Lowell. I'm Colonel Dixon," he said, extending his hand.

"Colonel Dixon, I'm Sheriff Corbin from Oro Blanco," the sheriff said. "This is my deputy." He did not say Falcon's name.

"Well, Sheriff, what can I do for you?" Dixon asked.

"We have had an incident with the Indians," Sheriff Corbin said.

"Which group?" the colonel asked.

"The Cababi Mountain band."

"Ah, yes, the Cababi Mountain band," the colonel repeated. "I believe they are the ones under Keytano, are they not?"

"They are."

"The Cababi band would be mostly what . . . Chiricahua?"

"I wouldn't say that. As you know, most of the Chiricahua have been moved to Oklahoma," Sheriff Corbin answered. "There are some Chiricahua left, of course, and many of them are with the Cababi band. But Keytano's village is actually a mixture of Western Apache, Jicarilla, and, of course, those few remaining Chiricahua I mentioned."

Colonel Dixon picked his pipe up from the desk and began tapping tobacco into the bowl.

"You said there was an incident. Are you talking about the three prospectors who were killed? Because I already know about them. It's a bad thing, but the truth is, those men were on Indian land, so there's not a whole lot we can do about it," the colonel said.

Sheriff Corbin shook his head. "No, I wish that was what we was here about, but that ain't it. This here incident might wind up startin' a war with the Cababi, and if it does, I don't mind tellin' you, it'll be our fault."

"What do you mean, our fault?" Colonel Dixon asked as he lit his pipe.

"By our fault, I mean white men," Corbin said. "Or, to be more specific, Fargo Ford and his gang."

The colonel took several puffs; then, through a cloud of aromatic tobacco, he answered.

"Fargo Ford. Yes, I've heard of him. But he's an outlaw,

isn't he? What does he have to do with an Indian problem?"

"Ford held up a stagecoach and took one of the passengers off the stage. That passenger was Cloud Dancer."

"Cloud Dancer? Wait a minute, isn't that Keytano's daughter? I thought she was back East," Colonel Dixon said.

"She was. She was going to school, but she finished and was coming back home. It turns out that the coach was carrying a money shipment, so Ford waited at the top of Cerro Pass, held up the stage, and took her off the coach."

"Is he holding her somewhere?"

Corbin shook his head. "He killed her," Corbin said.

That information startled Colonel Dixon enough that he took the pipe from his mouth. "You say he killed her. Do you know that for a fact?"

"Yes, we found her body," Corbin answered. He nodded toward Falcon. "And my deputy took her back to her father."

Colonel Dixon looked at Falcon with an expression of shocked surprise. "Wait a minute, a white man killed Keytano's daughter, and you took her body back?"

"Yes," said Falcon.

Dixon preened his mustache with his finger. "I'll be damned. I don't know whether to praise you for your courage, or damn you for your foolhardiness. Maybe both. It's a wonder Keytano let you out alive."

"Not really," Falcon said. "Keytano is a man of honor, after all."

"How can you call an Indian a man of honor?" the colonel asked, punctuating his question by sticking his pipe back in his mouth.

"Colonel, do you doubt that Indians can have honor?" Falcon asked.

"That certainly hasn't been my experience."

"How long have you been dealing with Indians?"

"Well, I confess that I've only been out here for about six months," Colonel Dixon replied. "I . . . uh, haven't really had to deal with them at all yet."

"I see. So, where did you get the idea that Indians had no honor?"

"Just things that I've heard," Colonel Dixon replied, clearly uncomfortable now with the direction the conversation was going.

"Indians are like anyone else, Colonel. There are Indians of honor, and there are those who are dishonorable."

"I'll, uh, take your word for it," Dixon said. "So, Sheriff, if your deputy took the girl's body back and got out alive, why are you here to see me?"

"The other day a drummer left Oro Blanco, driving a buckboard up to Arivica. He was driving a rented team, and the next day the team brought the buckboard back to the livery stable. The drummer, a man named Arnold Johnson, was in the back, mutilated and scalped."

"And you think it was retaliation for the chief's daughter?" Colonel Dixon asked.

"I think it was in direct retaliation, yes," Sheriff Corbin replied.

Colonel Dixon sighed. "After that business with the prospectors, I was afraid it might come to this. All right, I'll ask General Miles for orders to put the Fifth Cavalry into the field."

Falcon held up his hand. "No, don't do that, Colonel," he said. "At least not yet. I don't think there's any need for you to call out anyone. I don't believe this is a war with the Cababi Band. I think this is nothing more than one ambitious Indian who has been able to talk three or four others into following him."

"Are you talking about Keytano?"

"No, I don't think it is Keytano. So far, Keytano is on our side, or at least he's keeping most of the warriors back on the reservation. The one who is causing all the trouble is Naiche's nephew, Chetopa."

Colonel Dixon stroked his chin. "Chetopa? I'm not sure I've ever even heard of him."

"Yes, and that's Chetopa's problem. Nobody has heard of him, and he's not real happy about that. He wants his name to be spoken in the same tone as Naiche, Geronimo, and Cochise. If you turn out the Army, you'll be giving him exactly what he wants. It will not only give him the notoriety he's looking for; it will give him the opportunity to recruit a lot more warriors."

"Then, if you don't mind my asking, how would you propose that we take care of him without turning out the Army?" Colonel Dixon asked.

"You don't need the Army to take care of him. I'll take care of him myself," Falcon said.

Colonel Dixon laughed. "You'll take care of him? All by yourself?"

"Yes."

"Aren't you afraid you might be biting off more than you can chew?"

"Colonel Dixon," Sheriff Corbin said. "Maybe it is time I introduced this fella to you."

"You already introduced him, didn't you?" Colonel Dixon replied. "You said he was your deputy."

"Yes, but I didn't give you his name. It's MacCallister," Sheriff Corbin said. "Falcon MacCallister."

"Falcon MacCallister?" the colonel said, clearly searching for where he had heard the name before. Then it came to him. "The hell you say. *The* Falcon MacCallister? The gunfighter? The one who killed Naiche?"

"Yes," Sheriff Corbin said. "*The* Falcon MacCallister."

"Well, I'll be damn," Colonel Dixon said. He stuck his hand out again as a big smile spread across his face. "I am pleased to meet you, Mr. MacCallister. General Miles says you are a one-man army. So I reckon if any one man could take care of this Chetopa person, you'd be that one. Is there anything you would like for the Army to do?"

Falcon nodded. "As a matter of fact, there is. You might send a few patrols out," he said. "And if you see any prospectors getting over onto Indian land, discourage them. Oh, and while you are at it, it would strengthen my hand greatly if you would open up that dam and let some of the Santa Cruz River water back onto the reservation."

Colonel Dixon shook his head. "I can't. I wish I could do that, Mr. MacCallister. Because, in fact, I do think the Indians are being cheated out of their rightful supply of water. And I know that the Indian agent has made an appeal to the territorial governor, but the governor hasn't made a decision yet. He figures there are too many white people who want the dam to stay closed, and if he does anything, they'll contact Washington and he'll wind up losing his job."

"The territorial governor is a feather merchant, a civilian appointee who is afraid to take a piss without first getting authorization from Washington. Never mind him, he's an asshole anyway. You make the decision," Falcon said. "You alone. That is what Army commanders do, isn't it? Good commanders make tough decisions."

Falcon had perceived that Colonel Dixon was an officer of honor, integrity, and pride, and he knew this approach would appeal to him. Dixon smiled and nodded.

"You're right," he said. "That is exactly what Army commanders do, and it is what I should have done a long time ago. All right, Mr. MacCallister, you can count on it. I will see to it that enough water begins flowing through that dam to provide for the Indians."

"You do that, Colonel, and I guarantee you you will have no trouble from Keytano."

"And Chetopa?" Colonel Dixon asked. "Will that stop Chetopa?"

"No," Falcon said. "I'll have to stop Chetopa."

"Damn if I don't believe you will," Colonel Dixon said. "I'm not sure just how legitimate this is, but I will make no effort to stop you. And, as you asked, I will have my own troops on patrol, keeping prospectors out of the Indian land. Good luck, Mr. MacCallister."

"Thanks," Falcon replied.

CHAPTER 16

Ponci had lain in the cave for two days, looking over at the rotting piece of meat that had been his leg. The stench of it was overpowering, but until now, he had not been able to move well enough to get rid of it.

His horse had found a little graze within hobble range, as well as a puddle of water from the last rain. The puddle had survived only because a rock overhang had shielded it from direct sunlight, thus keeping it from evaporating. But now, even it was beginning to dry up, and if Ponci didn't get out of here soon, he and the horse faced the possibility of dying of thirst.

The horse was actually faring better than Ponci, who had not eaten in two days. Oddly, though he knew he should be ravenously hungry, he had no appetite. He had taken a few sips of water, having filled his canteen from the catch pool . . . and he had taken a few sips of laudanum, just enough to make the pain manageable.

For the last two days Ponci had run a fever, but now, for the first time since his self-amputation, he felt that the fever was gone. The bleeding had also stopped, and the pain in his stub had subsided to a dull throb. If he was ever going to make it into Mesquite, now was the time to do it.

Painfully and laboriously, Ponci managed to get his horse saddled. Then, he tried to mount. Automatically he swung his right leg, or what should have been his right leg, over the horse's back for balance and to carry him on into the saddle.

But the leg wasn't there, and Ponci's attempt to get mounted left him badly off balance. He felt himself slipping, made a desperate grab for the saddle horn, missed, then fell hard onto his wounded stump.

"Ahhh!!!" he screamed as pain shot up through his body.

Ponci lay there for a long moment, getting his breath and trying to regain his composure. Then he tried to mount again, this time holding tightly onto the saddle horn until he was seated. The sensation of sitting in the saddle with only one leg in the stirrup was unsettling, but he knew it was something he would have to get used to. Clucking at the horse, he left the cave, then rode out into the bright sunlight, headed for Mesquite.

Mesquite was ten miles ahead, and he figured on making it in two hours, given that he had no intention of trying to hurry.

Corporal Gibson left the sergeant major's office, still seething over his run-in with the sheriff and his deputy. When he returned to the guardhouse, he saw Private Carter lying on the bunk, waiting for the next relief change. Carter would be posted as one of the guards of the next relief.

Like Corporal Gibson, Private Carter had been in the Army for many years, and like Gibson, Carter had been up and down the ranks. Last month he had been a sergeant, but he got into a drunken fight with a cowboy over a whore he met in a saloon in Papago. His thirty days in jail in Papago were counted as unauthorized absence from his duty post, so he was busted.

Now, as a private, Carter had to perform the post duties like any other private.

"Carter, what are you doing here?" Gibson asked.

"I'm on the next relief, remember?"

"Oh, yeah, I forgot. Hey, come on down to the sutler's store and have a drink with me. We've got time."

"I don't mind if I do," Carter said, hopping up from the bunk and following his friend out of the guardhouse. It never dawned on him to suggest that what they were doing was against army regulations.

As the two men sat in the sutler's store drinking whiskey, Gibson told about his run-in with the two civilians who had come onto the post this afternoon.

"The deputy was a real bastard," Gibson said. "I'd like to know just who he thinks he is, coming in here like he owns the place. Why, he marched in to see the colonel without so much as a fare-thee-well."

"Are you talking about the fella that was with Sheriff Corbin?" the sutler asked. It was easy enough for the sutler to overhear their conversation. It was right in the middle of duty hours, and nobody else was in the place.

"Yeah, the deputy," Gibson replied.

The sutler laughed. "He was no deputy."

"Sure he was. At least, that's what Sheriff Corbin said."

"Maybe that's what Corbin said and maybe, for some strange reason, he is acting as the deputy right now. But I'll tell you this. He sure as hell ain't no ordinary deputy. Don't you know who that was?"

"No."

"That was Falcon MacCallister."

"Falcon MacCallister? Are you sure?"

"Who is Falcon MacCallister?" Carter asked.

"He's a gunfighter," Gibson said.

"Do you know him?"

"I've never met him, but I've sure heard of him. How do you know that was Falcon MacCallister?" Gibson asked the sutler.

"I know because I used to live in Tombstone. I met

him when he was down there. He ran with the Earps and Doc Holliday then."

"I'll be damn," Gibson said in awe. Then, his awe turned to fear as he remembered that MacCallister had threatened to kill him. His hand started shaking and some of the whiskey in his glass splashed out.

"You all right, Gibson?" Carter asked.

"Yeah," Gibson said. "I'm all right. Sutler, bring us another round."

Nearly an hour after what should have been the changing of the guard, Lieutenant Kirby, the Officer of the Day, showed up and saw Gibson and Carter drunk. He had two men with him.

"Place these two men under arrest and take them to the guardhouse," Kirby demanded.

Under the escort of the two privates, Gibson and Carter returned to the guardhouse, not as part of the guard detail now . . . but as prisoners.

When Private Wilson came into the guardhouse a little later, he threw his hat onto the bunk in anger.

"What the hell is going on around here?" he shouted. "I was an hour late getting relieved."

"Ask those fellas," one of the other guards said, pointing to the cell at the back of the guardhouse.

Wilson walked to the back, then saw Corporal Gibson and Carter in jail.

"Corporal Gibson, Sergeant Carter, what are you two doing in here?" he asked in surprise.

"That's Private Carter," Gibson said.

"Oh, yeah, Private. But what are you doing in here?"

"I tell you what," Gibson said. "Wait until the others are asleep, then come back here and we'll tell you."

Wilson looked confused. "Why should I wait until the others are asleep?"

"Because I'm going to tell you where my money is," Gibson said, "and I don't want anyone else to hear it."

"Your money?"

"Shhh," Gibson said, putting his finger over his lips. I told you, I don't want anyone else to hear. Wait until the others are asleep, then come back."

"All right," Wilson agreed, nodding his head. He walked back up to the front of the guardhouse, then lay on his bunk with his hands laced behind his head. "What money?" he asked aloud.

"What?" Pettigrew asked. Pettigrew was in the bunk next to his. "What'd you say?"

"Uh, nothing," Wilson replied. "I was just thinking out loud, that's all."

Unlike Carter and Gibson, Wilson had been in the Army for less than a year, and had never been anything but a private. It was also likely that he would never be anything but a private, because he had not found Army life to his liking. Wilson had grown up on a farm in Missouri and left when a young girl on a neighboring farm got pregnant and told him he was the father.

Wilson knew that it was possible that he could be the father, but it was also possible for at least four others that he knew. He wasn't ready to get married yet, especially if he was going to be tricked into it, so he left in the middle of the night and went to St. Louis, where he enlisted at Jefferson Barracks.

He regretted it almost immediately, and wished many times that he was back home, even if he did have to get married. Besides which, Lou Ellen wasn't that bad-looking a girl. He could've done worse.

An hour later, when snores rent the darkened interior of the guardhouse, Wilson got up from his bunk and walked quietly back to the cell.

"You fellas asleep?" he called into the darkened cell.

"No, we're awake," Gibson said. He and Carter appeared just on the other side of the bars, barely visible in the little ambient light that was available.

"All right," Wilson whispered. "I'm here. What is this about your money?"

"It's not just my money," Gibson answered. "It's Carter's money, and your money too, if you have balls enough to come with me tonight to get it."

"Come with you tonight?" Wilson shook his head. "How am I going to go anywhere with you tonight? You are in jail."

"You noticed that, did you?" Gibson said.

"Well, yeah, I mean . . ."

"Get the keys to the cell," Gibson said. "They are on the corporal's desk."

"How'm I going to do that with him there?"

"He'll be posting the new relief soon," Gibson said. "When he does, all you have to do is get the keys and let us out."

"I don't know," Wilson said.

"Look, you been bitchin' and moanin' ever since you come in how much you hate the Army," Gibson said. "Haven't you?"

"Well, yes."

"Then this is your chance. Let us out, we'll go get the money, then we'll each go our own way."

"All right," Wilson said. "All right, soon as the new relief is posted, I'll get the key and let you two out."

Although Ponci reached Mesquite before dark, he decided to stop outside town and wait until the sun set, because he didn't want to ride in while it was still daylight. While he was waiting for nightfall, he utilized his time by finding a stout staff, cutting it to the right size, then crossing it at the top with a bar that would fit under his arm. The result was a usable crutch. It would have worked better if he had something with which to pad the armrest, but he had used his extra shirt and pants as bandages over the stump of his leg.

Eating a handful of grasshoppers and the fruit of a saguaro cactus, Ponci had his first food in three days. When night came, he waited outside town listening to the sounds of night creatures. He dozed off a couple of times, but woke himself up every time because he didn't want to sleep through the night out here.

Then, when he figured it was about midnight, or even a little later, he remounted and rode into town. He had purposely waited until it was this late because he didn't want to be seen. He knew that someone who came riding into town with only one leg would not only be noticed, he would also be remembered.

The town was very dark, with not a flicker of light from anywhere, not even from the cantina. But the bright full moon painted a soft silver halo around all the buildings and laid a shimmering path on the road before him. That provided him with enough illumination to ride down the familiar street until he reached the leather goods store. His horse didn't like going through the narrow passageway between the leather goods store and the apothecary, especially as the two buildings crowded out what little light there was from the moon. But Ponci cajoled the animal, and kicked with his one good leg until they were through and into the open area that lay between Suzie's crib and the rear of the leather goods store.

The inside of the crib, like every other building in town, was totally dark. Ponci took his horse around behind the crib and tied it off in the lean-to shed. The lean-to was less for the comfort of the animals, and more for the convenience of Suzie's customers, who might not want the presence of their horses to give away the fact that they were visiting a soiled dove.

With his horse secure and out of sight, Ponci used his

crutch to come around to the front of the little house. He reached up to the eave where he knew she kept an extra key.

It wasn't there.

He felt around a bit more, but still couldn't come up with the key. Where the hell was it? Finally, giving up on his search for the key, he knocked lightly on the door.

"Suzie," he called.

He knocked again.

"Suzie?"

"Go away," Suzie's muffled voice called back from inside. "It's too late to do any business."

"Suzie, it's me, Ponci. Will you open the damn door?"

"Ponci?"

"Yes. Open the door, will you? I can't find the key."

"I don't keep it out there anymore."

"Let me in."

"Just a minute."

Ponci heard her stirring around inside; then the door opened.

"The reason I don't keep the key out here anymore is because Fargo . . ." Then she gasped in mid-sentence when she saw him standing there on one leg and a crutch. "My God, Ponci! What happened to you?"

"Well, if you won't keep me standing out here on the stoop and let me come in, I'll tell you all about it," Ponci said.

"Yes, yes, come in," she said, stepping aside as he hobbled in.

Seeing the bed, Ponci hopped over to it, then sat down with a sigh of relief.

"Have you got anything to drink?"

"I've got some whiskey," she said.

"Water first," Ponci replied. "Then whiskey. And maybe something to eat."

"All I have in the house is a can of peaches if that'll do."

"That'll do fine. Open it. But first, I need a drink of water."

Suzie scooped a dipper of water from the water bucket and handed it to Ponci, who drank thirstily and with such abandon that some of it trickled down his chin and onto his shirt. He handed the empty dipper to her.

"More," he said.

"My, you are thirsty, aren't you?" she said as she handed him the refilled dipper.

"You said something about a can of peaches?" Ponci asked as he finished the water.

"Yes," Suzie said. Finding the can of peaches, she opened it, then handed it and a spoon to him.

"I don't need this," Ponci said, handing the spoon back to her. He turned the can up to his lips, drank the juice, then poured the peaches into his mouth directly from the can, gobbling them down ravenously.

"How long has it been since you ate?" Suzie asked.

"I had me some grasshoppers this mornin'," Ponci answered as he finished the last of the peaches.

"Grasshoppers?" Suzie shivered. "I can't imagine eating grasshoppers."

"You'll eat 'em if you're hungry enough," Ponci said.

"What happened to your leg?"

"I cut it off," Ponci replied, wiping his mouth with the sleeve of his dirty shirt. "Can you believe that shit? I cut off my own leg."

"My God! Why would you do that?"

"Because I had the gangrene," Ponci said. "And it was either cut off my leg or die." He giggled. "And since I'm rich, I wasn't particularly ready to die yet."

"What do you mean you're rich?"

"I'm rich, Suzie. I got more money than me or you has ever seen. After I lay up here for a few days, me'n you are going to leave this town. Maybe go back to St. Louis, or New Orleans, or even out to San Francisco. We'll go first-class by train, and when we get there, we'll live like a king and queen. What do you think of that?"

"Is this the same money that Fargo was talking about?"

The smile left Ponci's face, to be replaced by a quick flash of fear.

"Fargo? Is Fargo in town?"

"No," Suzie said. "He was here, lookin' for you. But he's not here now."

"You sure he's not here?"

"Yes, I'm sure."

Ponci gave a sigh of relief. "That's good," he said. "But you say he was here, looking for me?"

"Fargo come here lookin' for you, all right. He wants to kill you."

Unexpectedly, Ponci laughed. "Yeah, I reckon he does."

"What is all this about, Ponci? Where did all this money come from that you and Fargo are talking about? And how is it that you wound up with it?"

"We robbed us a stagecoach," Ponci said. "And we stole fifteen thousand dollars. Then I got hurt in the leg and caught me a case of the gangrene. Fargo wanted to leave me, without givin' me my share. So, I let on as I was in much worse shape than I was; then when Fargo and the others wasn't expectin' it, I stole all the money and lit out."

"What do you mean you was lettin' on like you wasn't hurt all that bad? It must've been pretty bad," Suzie said. "I mean, it had to be bad for you to cut off your own leg like you done."

"Yeah," Ponci said. "Well, it was bad, and over the next couple of days after I stole the money and started runnin', it started in gettin' a lot worse. Pretty soon, I know'd that if I didn't do somethin' soon, I was goin' to die. So, I didn't have me no choice but to cut off my leg, so, that's just what I done. I hacked her off, clean as a whistle."

Suzie shivered. "How in the world could you do such a thing?"

"It wasn't all that hard," Ponci said. "If you remember, before I took up to runnin' with your brother, I used to be a butcher. I was a good one too. I've carved up pork and beef lots of times, and I've cut a lot of legs off'n hogs 'n steers. And to tell you the truth, Suzie, cuttin' off a human leg was lots easier."

"But this ain't just any human leg you're talking about. That was your own leg you cut off! Didn't it hurt?"

"You're damn right it hurt. But hell, it was already hurtin'. And I had me some laudanum, so that helped. After that, I just waited till I healed up some, and here I am."

"So, where's the money now? Do you have it with you?"

Ponci shook his head. "No, I don't have it with me. I got it hid. I figured, if Fargo and the others happened to catch up with me, that might be 'bout the only thing that would keep 'em from killin' me soon as they seen me."

"Yeah," Suzie said, hiding her own disappointment that he didn't have the money with him. "Yeah, I see what you mean."

"Listen, Suzie, I'm goin' to need to stay here for a few days till I get stronger. Don't be bringin' no business in until then."

"You can't ask me to do that, Ponci. I've got to make a livin'," she said.

Ponci reached down into his pocket and pulled out one hundred dollars.

"No, you don't," he said. "This'll take care of you for the next few days. And once I'm on my feet again and we are out of here, there's lots more where that came from."

"What'll I tell my customers?"

"Tell 'em you're takin' care of a sick aunt, tell 'em anything. Just don't bring nobody here."

"All right."

Ponci lay back on the bed and closed his eyes.

"Don't wake me till breakfast time," he said.

CHAPTER 17

Two days later, Gibson, Carter, and Wilson found themselves on the west side of the Quigotoa Range, a good eighty miles from the post. The horses were now hobbled, while the men were poking around in one of the many washes that came down from the side of the mountain.

"They say these washes are the best place to look," Gibson said as he picked through the rocks. "The gold is flushed down after a rain, and collects in the washes."

"You lied to me, Gibson," Wilson said.

"How'd I lie to you?"

"You told me if I'd let you and Carter out, you'd take me to your money. You didn't tell me we'd have to look for gold to find it."

"Well, hell, boy, gold is money, ain't it?" Gibson replied.

"Are you sure there is gold out here?" Wilson asked.

"Hell, yes, there is gold," Gibson said. "Or, if not gold, there's silver. Why do you think the government is keeping the U.S. Army out here? It's to keep the Indians off the backs of the prospectors while they look for gold."

"That's the truth of it, Wilson," Carter added. "We're here to make it safe for the prospectors and the miners."

"And I'll be damned if I'm going to risk my neck for

someone else to get rich," Gibson said. "If I'm going to risk my neck, I'm going to risk it for me."

"Damn right," Carter said.

"I don't think I would'a let you two out of jail if I'd'a know'd you was just talkin' about maybe findin' some gold or silver."

"It's more'n just maybe. It's out here for real," Gibson insisted.

"So, what do you think, Corporal, do you have any idea where to look?" Wilson asked.

"You don't have to call me Corporal anymore," said Gibson. "We ain't in the Army right now."

"Yeah, well, far as the Army is concerned, we are still in the Army," Carter said. "I mean, it ain't like they give us papers cuttin' us loose or anything." Carter was the smallest of the three, with red, blotchy skin and a nose that was too big for his face.

"I sort of wish we was still in the Army," Wilson said. Wilson was tall and gangly, and by many years the youngest of the three. "One thing we did while we was in the Army was we got to eat. Which we ain't been doin' that much of since we deserted."

"We didn't desert," Gibson said. "We are absent without leave. There's a difference."

"What's the difference?" Wilson asked.

"Well, for one thing, deserters can be shot or hung," Gibson said. "But if we are just absent without leave, the most they can do is send us to Ft. Leavenworth for a couple of years."

"Yeah, but how do we convince the Army we are just absent without leave and not deserters?" Wilson asked.

"'Cause we are still carryin' a Army-issue pistol, that's why," Gibson said. "And as long as we got any part of the Army still with us, well, we ain't exactly deserted."

Carter laughed. "Don't listen to Gibson," he said. "He's

spoutin' off that barracks-law bullshit. Don't fool yourself, kid. If they find us, they're goin' to hang us."

"Even if we're carrying these pistols like Corporal Gibson said?" Wilson asked.

"Hell, yes, even if we're carryin' these pistols. Fact is, that'll make it worse. They'll hang us for desertin' the Army and for stealing Army property," Carter said, laughing.

"Shit," Wilson said. "I wish I was back in Missouri."

"Doin' what? Walkin' behind a plow horse?" Gibson asked. "Is that what you want to do for the rest of your life? Plow?"

"So if you don't want to plow, what do you want? To spend the rest of your life in the Army?"

"No, I don't really want to do that either. I wasn't exactly what you would call a good soldier," Wilson said.

Carter laughed. "I can't argue there. As a soldier, Wilson, you wasn't worth shit."

"Maybe not, but you was both good soldiers. Both of you have been sergeants."

"That's true," Carter said. "Fact is, we both been sergeants more'n a couple of times."

"I still can't believe that you both deserted."

"Unauthorized absence," Gibson said. "We didn't desert. You keep sayin' we deserted like that and you *will* wind up gettin' our asses hung."

"Yeah, well, I wouldn't worry none 'bout us gettin' hung, Gibson," Carter said, all the humor suddenly gone from his voice. "We prob'ly ain't goin' to live that long."

"What are you talkin' about?"

"Over there," Carter said, pointing to the next ridgeline. "Holy shit."

Six Apache Indians were coming toward them, riding fast and spread out in a long line.

"Hell, there's just six of 'em," Gibson said, pulling his pistol. "We'll take cover behind those rocks over there."

"Corporal, I only got about three bullets in my gun," Wilson said.

"I've got a box of ammunition in my saddlebag," Carter said.

"Forget it, Carter," Gibson said, holding out his hand to stop him. "You'll never make it to your horse."

The Apaches opened fire and bullets began frying the air around the three soldiers, hitting the rocks alongside, then whining off behind them.

The Indians began riding back and forth in front of them. They were excellent horsemen, and as they passed by in front, they would lean down behind their horses, always managing to keep their horses between them and the soldiers.

The three returned fire and for the next several seconds, the valley rang with the echo of gunfire.

"I'm out of shells!" Wilson screamed in panic.

Carter fired, then pulled the trigger to fire again. His hammer fell on an empty chamber.

"Damn! I am too!"

"I saved three bullets," Gibson said pointedly.

"Saved three bullets? What do you mean?" Wilson asked. "Three bullets ain't goin' to do us no good! There's six of them!"

"But there's only three of us," Gibson said pointedly.

"Three of us? What do you mean?"

"Let's do it," Carter said, understanding immediately what Gibson was talking about. He got down on his knees, crossed himself, then bowed his head.

Seeing him, Wilson realized what was about to happen.

"Oh, shit," Wilson said quietly, shaking his head. "Oh, shit, no. We can't do this!"

"Johnny, trust me, you don't want those heathens to take you alive," Gibson said. It was the first time he had ever called the young soldier by his first name.

"Do it, Mickey," Carter said to Gibson. "Do it before it's too late."

Gibson looked at Wilson.

Wilson's bottom lip was trembling, but he nodded his head in the affirmative. "Yes," he said. "Do it."

"God be with us, boys," Gibson said. He put the gun to Wilson's temple and pulled the trigger.

"Hurry, Mickey, hurry!" Carter said.

Gibson shot Carter. After that, he put the barrel in his mouth and squeezed the trigger.

The hammer fell on an empty chamber.

Nothing!

Had he miscounted?

He tried again, still nothing.

By now the Apache realized what he was doing and, incensed by being cheated of their prisoners, they rushed him.

"No!" Gibson screamed. He grabbed one of the pick-axes they had been working with and had the fleeting satisfaction of burying it halfway into the head of one of the Indians. But before he could pull it out, he was jumped on by three more, and despite his struggles, they were able to subdue him, tying his hands and feet with rawhide.

Falcon stood in the stirrups for a moment, just to stretch away his saddle ache, then urged his horse on. That was when he saw the vultures.

They were circling too warily, too cautiously, for it to be a small animal. And there were far too many for them to be attracted to one thing.

Falcon had seen them gather like this before, over the battlefields during the war in which he and his brothers had fought on opposite sides. He'd seen them since the war as well, during his wanderings through the West.

Slapping his legs against the side of his horse, he hurried it on for the next mile until he saw what was attracting the vulture's attention.

Three naked bodies lay white and bloating in the sun. Two of the bodies were just lying there, and one of those he recognized as Private Wilson, the young private who had challenged him and Sheriff Corbin at the gate when they visited Fort Lowell. Private Wilson and the man lying beside them were not mutilated in any way. Both had gunshot wounds in the temple, the bullet holes black with encrusted blood.

The third man was staked out on the ground, his arms and legs spread out. His penis had been cut off and, from the amount of blood that had pooled between his legs, it had happened while he was still alive. His eyes were cut out, and his scalp had been lifted, but Falcon was more than reasonably sure that this was Corporal Gibson, the corporal he had encountered on that same visit to Fort Lowell.

"What were you three doing out here?" he asked. "I'm sure Colonel Dixon did not send out a three-man patrol."

Looking around, Falcon saw a shovel, a pretty good-sized hole, and a few rocks that had been broken into smaller pieces. That told him all he needed to know.

"I'll be damn. You three men were deserters, weren't you?" he said. "Figured you'd come out here and dig yourself up some of that gold you heard people talking about." He sighed. "You should've thought about it a little more."

Picking up the shovel, Falcon enlarged the hole enough to be able to take all three bodies. Then he cut the corporal loose and dragged him and the others over to where he had been working. He pushed them down into the hole, covered them with dirt, then moved a few rocks over the top of the grave.

When he was finished, he looked down at the grave.

"Corporal Gibson, you were an asshole, but you deserved better than this. You others as well," he said aloud.

Then recalling a legend that brought comfort to
cavalrymen, he recited a poem:

> *Halfway down the trail to Hell,*
> *In a shady meadow green,*
> *Are the souls of all dead troopers camped,*
> *In a good old-time canteen.*
> *And this eternal resting place*
> *Is known as Fiddlers' Green.*

According to the legend, no man who had ever served
in the cavalry could have possibly lived a life that was
good enough to earn him a place in heaven. On the
other hand, the cavalrymen had all served enough
penance on earth to keep them from going to hell. The
alternative to heaven or hell was Fiddlers' Green, a place
where the water was cool, the beer was plentiful, there
was always bacon with the beans, and the dance-hall girls
were friendly.

"Save me a place, troopers," Falcon said, making a
half-salute. "It'll be a lifetime for me, but only a drink or
two for you."

Turning away from the hasty grave, Falcon mounted
his horse and started out in pursuit of the Indians who
had done this.

The Indian trail was surprisingly easy to follow. Falcon
was certain that the Indians he sought were being led by
Chetopa, and Chetopa either didn't think there were any
white men capable of trailing him . . . or he was so confi-
dent in the strength of his band that he didn't care if anyone trailed him or not.

Falcon caught up with them in late afternoon, then
stayed well back of them so that they were totally un-
aware of his presence. He stayed on their trail for the

rest of the day, actually enjoying the chase almost as if he were playing a game of chess—move and countermove. And what made this particularly enjoyable to Falcon was the fact that he was controlling all the moves.

When night fell, Falcon became much more careful in his tracking. That was because he knew that Chetopa would not travel at night, and he didn't want to suddenly ride in on them. In order to prevent that, Falcon decided to dismount. He led his horse through the darkness, picking his way very carefully so as not to dislodge any stones that would give him away.

Then, on the desert floor in the darkness ahead, he saw the glow of a campfire.

He smiled.

If they had known they were being trailed, they would have made a cold camp. So far, he still had the advantage of secrecy.

As Falcon ground-hobbled his horse, he thought of Diablo, who had served him faithfully for so many years. Diablo was old, and enjoying a well-earned retirement on Falcon's ranch back in Colorado. He found himself wishing he had Diablo with him now, rather than the horse furnished him by the sheriff in Oro Blanco. He and Diablo were simpatico. He could get the response he needed by just thinking things, and that had gotten him through some very tight spots over the years.

This horse was not Diablo, but Falcon had to admit that it had served him well, and he patted his mount affectionately on its face a couple of times.

"You've done a good job, and don't let anyone ever say otherwise. Now, what I want you to do is stay here and be quiet until I get back."

Falcon looked around, marking the position so that he could find his way back in the dark. Then, he started toward the Indian camp.

The moon was full, and there were a few clouds in the

sky. From time to time one of the clouds would pass over the moon, and when it did so, it would shine silver during its transit. At those times a shadow would fall across the desert floor, and Falcon utilized those opportunities to advance forward.

Whenever the moon was out, he would try to remain in the shadows of a saguaro cactus or a rock outcropping. Sometimes he would find a depression and move forward in defilade.

As he approached the camp, he could smell something cooking over the fire. He didn't know whether it was a rabbit, a snake, or some bird they had killed. Whatever it was, he was glad they were cooking, because the smell of cooking would mask any scent the Apache or one of their horses might get of Falcon as he approached.

He heard one of the Indians say something, and the others laughed. He was surprised by how close it sounded, and he stopped, remaining perfectly still, barely breathing, for a long moment.

Standing there, still and quiet, gave Falcon the opportunity to look around. That was when he picked out a shadow within a shadow, noticeable only because it was even blacker than the surrounding darkness.

The shadow moved, then coughed.

The shadow was an Indian, a guard perhaps, though Falcon knew that Indians rarely posted guards.

The Indian guard stood up and blew his nose onto the ground. That gave Falcon the opportunity to move forward several feet. He advanced through the night as silently as the clouds overhead. As he came closer to the Apache on guard, he pulled out his Arkansas toothpick.

The Indian shouted something toward the camp, and one of the ones around the fire lifted a chunk of cooking meat and looked at it, then shouted back. Evidently the Indian was hungry.

Well, Falcon would take care of that.

Falcon moved closer, ever closer, until he was but inches behind the rock the guard had chosen to use as his backrest. The guard sat back down, then leaned back against the rock.

The rock only came halfway up the Indian's back, which was very good for Falcon's purposes. Falcon raised up, put his arm around the Indian, and clamped his hand down on the Indian's mouth.

The Indian tried to shout something, but Falcon had him so clamped down that only a very muted sound escaped.

Falcon drew his knife across the Indian's neck in one quick slice, severing his jugular. Falcon jerked his hand away as blood gushed from the wound. The Indian fell back, flopped a few times like a fish out of water, then died.

Falcon cut around the base of the Indian's scalp, then turned him over on his belly. Putting his foot in the middle of the Indian's back, Falcon grabbed the Indian by his hair, then jerked. The scalp came off cleanly.

Falcon debated for a moment or two as to whether he should take the scalp with him. Then he decided against it. Instead, he cut a coup stick, put the scalp on the stick, then rolled the Indian over on his back and forced open the dead man's mouth. He then stuck the bottom of the coup stick into the open mouth, using it as a support mount for the stick.

Falcon left then, creeping away as quietly and as carefully as he had arrived.

Let them find their brother, neatly and expertly scalped, with no sign of who did it.

CHAPTER 18

The sun was high overhead, a brilliant white orb in a fixed blue sky. It beat down mercilessly on the four men who rode slowly across the desert floor.

"Hey, Fargo, are you sure you know where we are?" Casey asked.

"Yeah, I know."

"You sure? 'Cause I don't want to get lost out here, maybe have somebody find our bones about a hundred years from now."

Dagen laughed.

"What you think's so funny?" Casey asked.

"Somebody findin' our bones a hunnert years from now," Dagen said.

"I don't think that's funny. I don't think that's funny a'tall."

"Will you three shut the hell up? It's too damn hot to be listenin' to the three of you palaverin' all the damn time," Fargo said.

"Well, I'd like to know just where the hell we are. I mean, we was headin' north when we left town; next thing you know we started curvin' aroun', we was going west for a while; now damn me if it don't seem we're goin' south. If you ask me, we're just ridin' in circles. And when a fella starts ridin' in circles, that means we're lost."

"We ain't lost," Fargo said. "We're doublin' back is all."

"Doublin' back? Doublin' back for what? If you hadn't

shot that son of a bitch back in Mesquite, we wouldn't have to be out here and we wouldn't be hot. We'd still be sittin' in a nice, cool saloon," Dagen said. "Drinkin' beer and talkin' with the women . . ."

"And eating," Monroe said, interrupting Dagen.

"Yeah," Dagen agreed. "And eating."

"What the hell did you shoot that son of a bitch for anyway?" Casey asked.

"I told you why I shot him. I thought it was Ponci," Fargo said.

"What if it had been Ponci and he had hid the money somewhere?" Dagen asked. "Then he would be dead and we wouldn't have no money, or no idea where it was. Did you think of that?"

"No, I reckon I didn't," Fargo admitted. "All I could think of was that the son of a bitch stole money from us and I wanted to kill him." The four men rode on for a while longer before Dagen spoke again. "Hey, Casey, you got 'nything left to eat? Jerky or somethin'?"

"No."

"How 'bout you, Monroe? You got 'ny jerky? Anything to eat?"

"I ain't got nothin' a'tall left," Monroe said.

"Well, son of a bitch, I'm hungry."

"Yeah, me too," Casey said. "I could damn near eat this saddle."

"Quit your bellyachin', all of you," Fargo said. "Do you think I ain't hungry? But you don't hear me bitchin' about it, do you?"

"Well, what are you goin' to do about it?" Dagen asked.

"What do you mean, what am I going to do about it? What am I supposed to do about it?"

"You're the leader, ain't you? Leastwise, you been claimin' to be the leader. You the reason we had to hightail it out of Mesquite. So by my way of thinkin', that means it's up to you to find us somethin' to eat," Dagen said.

"Yeah," Casey agreed. "You're the leader. Do some leadin'. Get us somethin' to eat."

"All right, there's a ranch up ahead," Fargo said. "We'll get somethin' to eat there."

"How? Are we just going to walk up to the door and say, 'Excuse me, but we're awful hungry, and we was won-derin' iffen maybe you wouldn't feed us'?" Dagen said.

"Something like that," Fargo replied.

"Well, I ain't one for beggin'," Dagen said. "I like to earn my keep."

"Earn it?" Casey said with a laugh. "Dagen, what the hell do you mean earn it? You're a thief, for crying out loud. We're all thieves."

"Yeah, well, that's earnin' it," Dagen said. "Sort of."

The others laughed.

"Don't make me laugh no more," Monroe said. "I ain't got enough spit left to laugh."

"Where is this here ranch anyhow?" Casey asked. "'Cause, I sure don't see nothin' that looks like a ranch."

"It's just up ahead a little ways," Fargo said. "Another couple of miles is all."

"You sure about that?"

"Yes, I'm sure about that. I told you, I used to live around here. Fact is, I worked on this ranch once. It's the Double R Ranch."

"Double R," Dagen said.

"Double R for Raymond Reynolds," Fargo said. He tore off a chew of tobacco, settled it in his jaw, then put his plug away.

"How come you quit ranchin'?" Monroe asked.

"'Cause the only thing dumber'n a cow on a cattle ranch is the men who are dumb enough to punch 'em," Fargo said. "You are either too hot or too cold, too wet or too dry, and you ain't never got two nickels to rub together in your pocket. I had me a bellyful of it, so I just up and quit."

"I've always thought I'd kind of like to be a cowboy," Monroe said.

"You'd make a good cowboy," Fargo said.

"I would?"

Fargo leaned over and spit. "Yep. You're just exactly what all the ranchers is lookin' for. Someone who is dumb enough to do it."

"That ain't right for you to say," Monroe said. "I ain't all that dumb."

"You ain't?"

"No."

"You're ridin' with me, ain't you?" Fargo asked. He spit again, then wiped his mouth with the back of his hand. "Anyone who would ride with me is dumber'n shit."

"Hey," Dagen said. "When you say that, you're saying that about all of us."

"Yep."

"Includin' yourself," Casey pointed out.

Fargo spit the last of his chew. "I'm especially talkin' about myself," he said.

They rode on in silence for another few miles; then Fargo pointed toward a ranch house in the distance. "There it is," he said. "Just like I told you."

Dagen and the other two riders started sloping down a long hill toward the main house.

"Where you goin'?" Fargo asked.

"Toward the ranch house," Dagen replied. "Didn't you say we'd get something to eat here?"

"Yeah, but not there," Fargo replied. "Come this way." He cut his horse off to the left, at almost a right angle to the way they had been going.

"What are we goin' that way for? That's the house over there, ain't it?"

"Yeah, but I told you, we're not goin' to the house," Fargo said.

"Well, if we ain't goin' to the house, just where the hell are we goin'?"

"You'll see."

Fargo led them on for about two more miles, and though Dagen and the others were anxious to know what he had in mind, it seemed clear enough by his determination that he had something in mind. And at this point, there was nothing they could do but follow.

"There it is," Fargo said after a while. "That's where we'll get our next meal." He pointed to a small adobe cabin that rose, like a clump of dirt, from the desert floor.

"Yeah," Dagen said, smiling broadly and nodding his head. "Yeah, I see what you're up to now."

"Wait a minute! That's what we come all this way for? A little dirt hut like that? What the hell is it?" Monroe asked.

"Monroe, if you'd ever done one day's work in your life, you would recognize it," Dagen said. "It's a line shack."

"What's a line shack?"

"It's where the cowboys that watch over the herds in the field stay," Dagen said. "It's lonely work, but as I recall, most of the time the cowboys in the line shacks eat better'n the boys back in the bunkhouse."

"I've heard that my ownself," Casey said. "But I ain't never spent no time in a line shack."

"I have," Dagen said. "And believe me, whoever is in there now will have food."

"What if they do have food?" Monroe asked. "You don't really think they'll just share it with us, do you?"

"Oh, I don't intend to ask them to share it," Fargo said. "I intend to just take it. Dismount, pull your long guns, and follow me."

"What do we want with our rifles?" Dagen asked.

"You'll be needin' them," Fargo said without further explanation.

***

There were four cowboys inside the small adobe line shack. One was asleep on the bunk; the other three were sitting across a small table from each other, playing cards. They were playing for matches only, but that didn't lessen the intensity of their game. When one of them took the pot with a pair of aces, another one complained.

"Sandy, you son of a bitch! Where'd you get that ace?" His oath, however, was softened by a burst of laughter.

"Don't you know? I took it from Shorty's boot while he was asleep."

"Does Shorty keep an ace in his boot?"

"You think he don't? I never know'd him to do anythin' honest when he could cheat."

"That's the truth of it," Shorty admitted from his bunk, proving that he wasn't actually asleep. "Hell, it's the only way I can be sure to win. But Arnie is just as bad."

"I am not," the dealer replied.

"And so is Curley," Shorty added.

"Well, now you're right there," the third cardplayer said. "I will cheat if I think I can get away with it."

The others laughed.

The cards were raked in, the deck shuffled, then dealt again.

"Hey, do either one of you know Jennie?" Arnie asked as he dealt the cards.

"Jennie? Jennie who?" Sandy asked as he began picking up cards.

"You know Jennie who," Arnie insisted. "She's one of the whores down at the Desert Flower."

"Oh, yeah, that Jennie. What about her?"

"Well, here's the thing. Do you fellas think she likes me?" Arnie asked.

The others laughed. "Do we think she *likes* you?

Damn, Arnie, she likes anybody who has enough money to take her upstairs," Sandy said.

"You're just talkin'," Arnie said. "She won't go upstairs with just anybody."

"You may be right about that," Shorty said from the bunk. "She won't go upstairs with Curley. I mean, he's so damn ugly he can't come up with enough money to make any woman go upstairs with him."

Sandy added, teasing Curley, "How'd you get to be so ugly, Curley?"

Curley was short, round, freckled, and without a hair on his head.

"My mama says she was scairt by a bear when she was carryin' me, and some of that bear's ugly wore off," Curley replied.

The others laughed.

"But speakin' of Jennie," Curley continued, "better not nobody be messin' around with her unless they're wantin' to tangle with Tucker."

"Tangle with who?"

"Tucker Godfrey," Curley said. "You know, that bandy-legged little shit from the Flying J Spread? He's got his cap set for Jennie and he sees anyone sniffin' around her, why, he runs 'em off."

"Ha! You think I'm scared of Tucker? I could break that little pipsqueak over my knees like a piece of kindlin' wood," Arnie said.

"Hell, any of us could, if we could ever catch the little son of a bitch without his gun. But he's damn good with that gun, and he has it with 'im all the time. Folks say he even has it with him when he goes to take a shit."

The others laughed again.

At that moment, four riders stopped on a little hill overlooking the line shack. They ground-tied their mounts about thirty yards behind them, then moved to the edge of the hill at a crouch and looked down toward the little building.

"Can you see anybody inside the shack?" Fargo asked.

"Yeah, I can see three men sittin' at a table, just inside the window," Casey said.

"When I give the word, everyone start shooting at the same time," Fargo said, raising his rifle to his shoulder. The others raised their rifles as well, and waited for Fargo.

"Now! Shoot!" Fargo shouted, squeezing the trigger that sent out the first bullet.

Arnie died instantly, a bullet coming through the window to crash into the back of his head. Sandy and Curley heard the little tinkle of glass as the window broke; then they watched in surprise and shocked horror as blood and gore exploded out of the top of Arnie's head. By the time the sound of the shot reached them, other bullets were flying through the little cabin.

As Arnie flopped forward across the table, Curley felt a blow to his chest, as if he had just been kicked by a mule. His chair went over backward, and he fell to the floor.

Sandy went next, a bullet in his neck.

By now Shorty, who had remained on the bunk, had rolled onto the floor.

"Jesus!" he said. "What is it? What's happening?" Shorty called.

"Shorty!" the wounded man on the floor called. "Shorty, I'm hit bad!"

Shorty crawled over to Curley, then saw the blood on his chest. The wound was sucking air and Shorty knew it would soon be over for his friend. He put his hand on the wounded man's forehead. That gesture of comfort was Shorty's last mortal act because the next bullet hit him right between the eyes.

Less than a moment later, all four men were dead.

"Hold your fire," Fargo said, holding up his hand to stop the others.

The men quit firing.

"See any movement?"

"No," Casey said.

"Casey, how about you go up and see if anyone is still alive?" Fargo said.

"What do you mean go up and see if anyone is still alive?" Casey replied. "Hell, you go up."

Fargo glared at Casey, then got up and, upright and without caution, walked straight toward the shack.

"What's that dumb son of a bitch trying to do? Show off?" Casey asked with a growl.

Casey, Dagen, and Monroe watched as Fargo kicked the door open and went inside. They waited to hear some sign of a struggle or, barring that, for him to come out and tell them it was all right to come in.

A long minute went by.

"What do you think happened?" Casey asked.

"What do you mean?"

"You think Fargo's dead?"

"Did you hear anything?"

"No."

"Then he probably ain't dead."

"How come he hasn't come out and told us anything?"

"'Cause the son of a bitch has found the food and he's eatin' it all himself," Dagen said in a sudden realization.

Dagen started toward the line shack and after only a moment's hesitation, the others went with him. When they got to the shack they saw Fargo inside, eating beans straight from the pot. He was sitting at the table, totally oblivious of the dead man whose head was leaking blood and brains right beside the pot of beans.

There were three other men in the room and they lay dead on the floor.

"What the hell has been keeping you?" Fargo asked around a mouthful of beans. "Hurry up and eat. We're goin' back after our money."

"Going back? To Mesquite?" Casey asked. "You think that's the smart thing to do? I mean, seein' as you kilt that man an' all."

"Hell," Dagen said as he opened a biscuit and filled it with beans. "What are you worried about, Casey? You didn't kill that fella. Neither did Monroe or me. If the sheriff is goin' to be after somebody's ass, it's goin' to be Fargo's, right, Fargo?"

Fargo glared at Dagen across the top of the bean pot.

"So I figure," Dagen said, taking a bite of his biscuit and letting beans and juice dribble down either side of his mouth, "if there's a chance of getting the money back by goin' back to Mesquite, then let's go."

CHAPTER 19

"Natanke, there is food!" Kwazi called to his friend. Kwazi pulled a stick with skewered rabbit from the fire. It was roasted brown and from it curled a wisp of aromatic smoke. "Food!" he called again.

"Why does he not come?" one of the others asked. "Did he not say he was hungry?"

"Maybe he has fallen asleep," Kwazi called.

"Give the meat to me," Chetopa said. "I will take it to him, and if he has fallen asleep, I will send him back. We have no place for anyone who cannot remain awake when he is keeping watch."

Kwazi gave the meat to Chetopa, though he did so reluctantly because he did not want to be the cause of his friend getting in trouble.

"Natanke!" Chetopa called, holding the meat up. "Are you a child going to sleep when you should be awake? Natanke, answer me!"

Because it was dark, Chetopa didn't see Natanke until he almost tripped over him. Then, he was so shocked by what he saw, that he wasn't sure he was actually seeing it.

"Kwazi! Mensa! Turq! Everyone, come!" he called loudly, and the others, some of whom had just started eating, hurried through the dark toward their war chief.

Chetopa pointed.

"What do you see?" he asked.

"I see . . ." Kwazi began. Then, letting out a shout of

anger and grief, he dropped to his knees beside the prostrate form of his friend.

"Natanke!" he shouted.

But Natanke didn't hear him, because he was lying on his back, his head scalped. His mouth was open and a stick stood in his mouth. At the top of the stick was Natanke's scalp.

"Ayiieeee!" Chetopa shouted. He ran back to the encampment, followed by the others. There, he grabbed his rifle and fired into the desert; the others did as well, and for a long moment, the night was lit by the lightning-like flashes of the muzzle blasts.

Then, as if suddenly realizing what they were doing, Chetopa quit firing and held up his hands.

"No, no!" he shouted. "Do not shoot!"

The shooting ended raggedly with one or two late shots being fired, followed by echoes coming from the nearby hills and mountains.

"To shoot is to waste ammunition," Chetopa said.

"Chetopa, who did this thing?" Kwazi asked.

"I believe it was Dlo Binanta," Chetopa said.

"Dlo Binanta? Has the Bird Man come for us?" one of the others said, the fright in his tone obvious.

"Let him come for us," Chetopa said. "Yes, let Dlo Binanta come for us. We will kill him and then our medicine will be strong."

Chetopa stepped forward, then raised his rifle over his head.

"Dlo Binanta!" he shouted as loudly as he could. The words rolled back from the hills.

"Dlo Binanta!"

"Dlo Binanta, do you hear me when I say I am not afraid of you?" Chetopa shouted.

"Dlo Binanta, do you hear me when I say I want you to come for me?

"Dlo Binanta, do you hear me when I say I will kill you?"

". . . *kill you, kill you, kill you?*" the words echoed back.

Falcon MacCallister was some one hundred yards away from the Indian encampment, standing behind a saguaro cactus and hidden by the dark.

"Now you hear me, Chetopa!" he called back. "I, Dlo Binanta, will kill you and all who ride with you. I will kill Kwazi, Mensa, and Turq as I killed Natanke."

"Ayiee, he is a devil! He knows our names!" one of the Indians said, his voice quaking with fear.

"Before the sun rises, another of you will die!" Falcon shouted.

"Will die . . . will die . . . will die!"

The words echoed and reechoed from every corner of the desert, just as Falcon knew they would. Because of the echoes, Chetopa was unable to place him by sound. Nevertheless, Chetopa fired where he thought Falcon was, and again the night was lit by the muzzle flashes of discharging rifles.

The echoes had Chetopa so badly confused, however, that he didn't have the slightest idea where Falcon was. As a result, he and the others were firing in a totally different direction.

Falcon remained in the darkness, watching, until once more Chetopa realized that he was only wasting ammunition. Then, when the Indians quit firing, Falcon moved back through the darkness until he found his horse.

"Still here, I see," Falcon said to the horse. "Did you enjoy the show? I hope so, because it's just beginning."

"Seems to me like we should be to Mesquite by now," Dagen said. He twisted around on his horse and examined the countryside, trying to figure out where he was.

"Yeah," Monroe said. "We didn't ride this long from Mesquite before we decided to start back."

"I didn't say we was goin' back to Mesquite," Fargo said.

"The hell you didn't," Dagen replied. "That's exactly what you said when we was in that line shack having our supper."

"That's right," Monroe seconded.

"I said we was goin' back," Fargo said. "I didn't say we was goin' back to Mesquite."

"Well, if we ain't goin' to Mesquite, just where the hell are we goin'?"

"We're goin' to back-trail and see if we can find Ponci."

"Back-trail?"

"Yeah. Look, the truth is, I figure the son of a bitch is dead somewhere. And I figure to find him before someone else does. Because whoever finds him is going to find our money."

"How do you know he is dead?"

"You heard what the doctor said same as me," Fargo said. "He said if Ponci didn't get that leg cut off, he was goin' to die. Well, Ponci didn't get the leg cut off."

"But the doctor give him all that medicine," Monroe said.

Fargo snorted. "Laud'num ain't real medicine," he said. "It don't do nothin' to cure you; it just stops the pain for a while. No, sir, our Ponci boy is lyin' out here dead somewhere, and he's got our money with him."

"So, how are we goin' to find him? I mean, we come up the trail after him and we didn't see him nowhere," Dagen said.

"Like as not, when it got real bad he pulled off somewhere, figurin' to rest up some. Only he didn't get rested up. What he got was dead."

"You're sure he would'a come this way?" Casey asked.

"Where else would he go?" Fargo asked. "He lived in

Mesquite before he joined up with me. We went to the right place, all right. We just got there too fast is all."

"So, what are we lookin' for?"

"Anyplace that might make a good spot to hole up for a while," Fargo said. "A big rock stickin' out, maybe a gully, or a cave."

"A cave!" Dagen said, snapping his fingers.

"What?"

"I know where one is," Dagen said. "And Ponci knows it too, 'cause he pointed it out to me once."

"Where?"

"It's about ten miles south of Mesquite."

"All right, let's go there," Fargo said, urging his horse into a quicker pace.

It was about three o'clock in the morning and Falcon was downwind of the Indian encampment. He could smell them ahead: the body odor, the grease in their hair, and the pungent aroma of horseflesh gradually giving off the warmth of the sun from the day before.

Once again he had left his horse behind, and once again he had slipped forward through the night, his knife clamped in his teeth as he crawled, slithered, and moved from cactus to rock, from rock to mesquite bush, from mesquite bush back to cactus.

There had been some discussion among the Indians of posting a guard, but they finally decided that if the five of them stayed together, one man couldn't hurt them. And with that sense of security, they had thrown out their blankets and now slept in the cool night air.

Because he was moving with such caution, it took Falcon almost one hour to advance the last hundred yards. Now, he was less than ten feet away from where the five men were sleeping.

When Falcon issued his challenge just after supper

last night, he had called out the Indian names, doing so because he knew it would unnerve them. He knew the names only because he had heard all of them being used, but except for Chetopa, he did not know one Indian from another.

Falcon slithered on his belly for the last ten feet, then looked at the Indian nearest him. He didn't know who it was, but he knew who it wasn't. It wasn't Chetopa.

Falcon hesitated for just a moment, thinking it would be better for him to go to each of the sleeping Indians until he found Chetopa, then kill him. He finally decided that the risk was too great. Let Chetopa and the others awaken tomorrow to find still another of their number dead.

Falcon put his hand across the Indian's mouth and pressed hard, squeezing his nostrils closed as well. The Indian woke up, then looked up at Falcon with eyes that were wide with fear. Falcon plunged his knife into the Indian's heart and twisted it around, cutting vital arteries and chambers within that organ.

The bright look of fear in the Indian's eyes faded fast as he felt his life slipping away from him. Within a few seconds they were opaque and lifeless. Falcon looked at the others, to see if any of them had been disturbed by the action, but not one of them awakened.

Once again, Falcon took a scalp, and this time, using the knife of the Indian he had just killed, he pinned the scalp to the Indian's chest.

Falcon was awakened at sunrise the next morning by the screams of anger, grief, and terror from the Indians. They had found his calling card.

"There," Dagen said, pointing. "That's the cave I was talkin' about."

"Dismount here," Fargo said. "Monroe, you hang onto the horses. Dagen and Casey, come with me. We'll come up on both sides, so if he is in there looking out, he won't see us."

Pulling their pistols, the three men advanced toward the side of the hill, running forward at a crouch. Fargo went up to the right of the cave opening; Dagen and Casey went up to the left.

Fargo picked up a rock, and indicated by a sign that he was going to toss it into the mouth of the cave. Both Dagen and Casey cocked their pistols to be ready.

Fargo threw in the rock and they waited, but nothing happened. He indicated then that they should get closer to the cave opening.

"Son of a bitch! What is that smell?" Casey asked as they got closer.

"Fargo," Dagen called. "Do you smell that?"

Fargo nodded.

"You know what it is, don't you?," Dagen asked.

"I have an idea," Fargo answered.

"It means Ponci's dead and his body has got good'n ripe," Dagen said.

"You think he's dead?"

"Hell, yes, he's dead. What else would give off a stink like that?"

"Then why don't you go in and have a look around?" Fargo said.

Dagen started toward the cave, then stopped. "Hey, whyn't we throw a few rounds in there just to be sure?" he said.

Fargo nodded. "Not a bad idea."

The three men started firing then, the bullets screaming as they ricocheted through the cave, the gunshots echoing back from the hills.

The three emptied their pistols, then stood there as the echoes of the final shots returned from the hillsides.

Dagen poked out the empty shell casings, reloaded, then with his gun ready, stepped into the cave.

Fargo and Casey watched him disappear into the blackness and they waited for a long moment.

"Holy shit!" Dagen shouted from inside the cave and his words, amplified by the megaphone effect of the cave, boomed out.

"What is it?" Fargo called.

"Get in here," Dagen said. "You ain't goin' to believe this!"

Fargo and Casey started into the cave.

"Hope this don't take long," Casey said. "That stink's so bad I can't hardly breathe."

"Did you find him?" Fargo called.

"Partly," Dagen answered mysteriously.

"Partly? What the hell do you mean partly?"

"You'll see."

With their eyes accustomed to the darker interior of the cave, they saw Dagen standing about a quarter of the way back, looking down at something. Whatever he was looking at seemed to be the source of the smell.

"Holy shit, what is that?" Casey asked.

"It's a leg," Dagen said.

"What?"

"It's a leg. Ponci's leg."

"Where the hell did Ponci find a doctor out here to cut off his leg?" Casey asked.

"He didn't find no doctor," Fargo said.

"What do you mean he didn't? That's his leg, ain't it?"

"Yes."

"Well, how'd it get here if he didn't have no doctor with him?"

"He cut it off his ownself," Fargo said.

"Son of a bitch!" Casey said. "Who would do a thing like that?"

"Evidently Ponci did."

"Who would have figured that Ponci would have the guts?" Dagen said.

"Didn't nobody ever say he didn't have guts," Fargo

said. The three men stood there for a moment longer. Then, with a shout of disgust, Fargo kicked the leg. It came apart in stinking, rotting chunks of flesh.

"Let's go!" he said, storming out of the cave.

"Go where?"

"Back to Mesquite," he said. "The son of a bitch is there, I know he is."

"With your sister?"

"I'm sure of it."

"What if she is hiding him?"

"I'll kill the bitch," Fargo said.

CHAPTER 20

There had been five who followed Chetopa from the camp when he left to carry the war to the whites. Now only two, Mensa and Turq, remained.

"What type of man can come and go without being seen?" Mensa asked. "He is a spirit warrior."

"He is not a spirit warrior; he is just a man like any other man," Turq said.

"No," Chetopa said, holding up his hand. "He is not a devil, but he is not just like any other man. He is like an Apache. He can move like smoke through the night. He is very good, so we must be better."

"How can we be better?"

"When has he attacked us?" Chetopa asked.

"When we sleep," Tarq said.

"When we eat," Mensa said.

"Yes. He comes to us. I say, we will not wait for him to come to us. From now on we will go to him. We will find where he sleeps, and we will find where he eats, and we will kill him."

"Yes, we will kill him," Tarq agreed.

Like all Apache, Chetopa, Tarq, and Mensa were skilled trackers and ferocious warriors. But like many, they were used to white men who were badly deficient in those skills, so they had underestimated Falcon.

That underestimation had proven fatal. But Chetopa did not intend to underestimate Falcon again. He knew that Falcon was nearby, and might even now be watching them. So, working from that premise, he decided to turn back upon their own trail. If they did that, he would either have to retreat from them, or leave the trail and make a new one.

After backtracking for several hours, Chetopa saw a fresh horse dropping on the trail and, leaping down from his horse, he examined it. It was soft and odorous.

"Yes," he said to the others. "We have found him." Then, in English, he shouted at the top of his voice.

"Dlo Binanta! Dlo Binanta, do you hear me? We have found you! We have found you and we will kill you! And after you are dead, I will cut your heart out and feed it to the dogs in our village!"

"Ayieee!" the Indians yelled, holding their rifles over their heads.

"Dlo Binanta, do you hear me?" Chetopa yelled.

"Hear me . . . hear me . . . hear me?" the words echoed back.

"I hear you, Chetopa," Falcon said. Although he spoke quietly, Chetopa, Mensa, and Tarq heard him quite clearly, because he was standing less than ten yards behind them.

Chetopa and the others whirled toward the sound of the voice and, doing so, saw Falcon standing there, challenging them. Amazingly, his guns were in his holsters. Seeing this, Chetopa smiled.

"You dare to face us without your weapons?"

"I have my weapons," Falcon said easily.

"But they are not in your hands," Chetopa said. His smile grew broader as he brought his rifle around to bear.

Faster than Chetopa could blink, or even contemplate the action, the pistols were in Falcon's hands. He fired three times, killing all three Indians before even one of them could get off a shot.

He stood there for a moment after, smoke curling up

from the barrel, even as the sound of the three shots echoed and reechoed back from the mesa walls.

Falcon went about his gruesome task. He scalped Chetopa, Mensa, and Tarq. Then, he put each of the Indians belly-down on their ponies, tied their hands to their feet with strips of rawhide, and using their own knives, pinned their scalps to their bodies. That done, he slapped the ponies on the rear and threw up his hat to start them. They galloped away.

Fourteen-year-old Kinte was tending the herd of ponies as they grazed just outside the village. He was proud to be given such a responsibility, for this was part of his training in becoming a warrior.

Of course, being a warrior was not like it once was. Kinte had heard stories of bravery and wars well fought. He knew of great leaders and warriors such as Cochise, Victorio, Geronimo, Juh, Nana, Naiche, Chalipun, and Eskiminzin. Perhaps, one day, the name Kinte would join that list of brave Apache.

Kinte thought about Chetopa. He should have gone with Chetopa. Of course, because he was so young, Chetopa would not have let him go, at least not at first. But if he had followed Chetopa, then joined him later, Chetopa would have let him stay.

Kinte admired Chetopa. Keytano was their chief, and Kinte knew that all the people respected Keytano, but he thought Keytano was an old man and should not be their leader now. Their leader should be Chetopa.

Perhaps, when Chetopa returned with the scalp of Dlo Binanta, the others in the village would make him chief. And with a brave and ferocious leader like Chetopa, the Apache would no longer be farmers and old women. They would be warriors again, and Kinte would be there with them.

Kinte saw three ponies galloping toward him. At first he thought they were riderless; then he saw that each of the three was carrying a burden of some sort. As the ponies came closer, he ran toward them, holding up his arms to stop them.

The ponies, tired from their long run, and glad to be back to familiar territory, stopped their running and began peacefully grazing. They made no effort to move away as Kinte came closer to see what they were carrying.

"Ayieee!" he shouted in horror and grief as he saw the scalped body of his hero, Chetopa.

"We must go to war to avenge this!" Caiche, one of the warriors of the village, shouted in anger. Caiche, as well as every other man, woman, and child of the village, had come to the center circle to look down upon the bodies of Chetopa, Mensa, and Tarq.

"No!" Keytano said.

"But the whites have done this thing! Can we let this go unavenged?" Caiche asked.

"Do you see the scalps?" Keytano asked, pointing to the bodies. "This was not done by the whites. It was done by one white man."

"One white man? Five warriors were with Chetopa. And you say that one white man did this?"

"Yes."

"What one white man could best Chetopa and five warriors?"

"Falcon MacCallister," Keytano said. "The one we call Dlo Binanta."

"How do you know it was Dlo Binanta?" Caiche asked.

Keytano pulled the knife from Chetopa's body, then held out the scalp.

"Dlo Binanta has sent us a message," Keytano said.

"He has told us that, as he promised, he will take the scalps of his enemy."

"We should go after him," Caiche said. "Then, after we kill him, we will make war with the whites for what they have done."

"No," Keytano said sharply. "If more of our young men go after him, more of our young men will die. Falcon MacCallister has said that he will kill and scalp the evil ones who killed my daughter. I say we will let him do as he promised he would do."

"And I say we should go after him and kill him," Caiche insisted. He turned to face the others. "I will lead you! Who among you is not afraid to die? Who among you will ride with me to find and kill Dlo Binanta? Come with me, all who are brave of heart!"

Caiche stepped to one side in an invitation to the warriors of the village.

"Come with me if you would avenge the death of our brothers!" Caiche shouted.

He waited.

Kinte started toward him, but he was grabbed by his father and pulled back. Another, even younger boy started toward Caiche, and the Indians, seeing that only young boys were joining him, laughed.

Caiche glared at them for a long moment, then, in humiliation, stormed out of the circle.

"Go back to your wickiups," Keytano said to the others when he saw that the immediate crisis was over. "Go back to your wickiups and prepare for the burial of these brave but foolish men."

The sun was a red orb just above the eastern horizon when Fargo and the others arrived in Mesquite. Although the sun was producing light, its orange disk was not yet too bright to look at.

Although the smell of frying bacon and coffee indicated that a few people were awake and preparing breakfast, the streets were empty, except for an old red dog that was sleeping on the front porch of one of the buildings.

Seeing the riders come into town, the dog got up and ambled across the street in front of them, then took a position under another porch. Since the saloon was not open at this early hour, there was no question about anything getting in the way of the task at hand. The riders went directly to the house of Fargo's sister.

This time, Fargo checked the lean-to behind Suzie's house. There, tied to a hitching bar and nibbling contentedly on some hay, was a familiar horse.

Fargo got down from his own horse and patted the animal a few times.

"He's here!" Fargo said quietly to the others. "This here is his horse. The son of a bitch put one over on us!"

"You think he's in the house?" Casey asked.

"No, I think he's somewhere doin' the fandango dance on one leg," Fargo replied.

"I was just askin'."

"Hell, yes, the son of a bitch is in the house," Fargo said. "Where else would he be?"

Fargo went around to the front of the little house and felt for the key.

The key wasn't there.

"Damn!" he said.

"What is it?"

"The bitch has moved the key."

Stepping back, Fargo raised his leg, then kicked hard. The door popped open and Fargo, Dagen, Monroe, and Casey dashed in.

Two figures sat up in the bed, surprised by the sudden entry. This time there was no mistake. The man in bed with Suzie was Ponci.

"Fargo!" Ponci shouted in alarm.

"Give us our money, Ponci," Fargo said.

"It ain't here."

Fargo pulled the trigger, and a bullet slammed into the bedstead just beside Ponci's head.

"I said give us our money!"

"Damn it, stop that! I told you, it ain't here!"

"You, Dagen, jerk the cover offen their bed. I want to have a look."

"I'm naked, Fargo," Suzie said. "Are you going to let all these men see your own sister naked?"

"Hell, it ain't like you ain't never been seen naked before," Fargo responded with a sneer. "Back when you first started whorin', I used to charge my friends a nickel to see you getting your legs spread."

"You are a crazy bastard," Suzie said.

"Dagen, jerk the cover offen that bed like I told you to!"

"Sure enough, Fargo," Dagen said as he reached down to grab the top of the blanket. He smiled at Suzie. "Fact is, I'm goin' to enjoy this," he said.

Dagen jerked the cover off and as Suzie said, she was naked. Dagen and the others stared at her as she tried, without success, to cover her breasts with one arm, and the little dark spade of pubic hair with her other.

"Sum' bitch," Dagen said. "She wasn't tellin' no lie. She was naked, all right."

Ponci was naked as well.

"Holy shit," Fargo said as he looked at the discolored stump of Ponci's mangled leg. "You really did cut off your own leg, didn't you?"

"Yeah."

The money wasn't under the bedcovers.

"Where's the money?"

"I hid it," Ponci said.

"You hid it? Under the bed?" Fargo walked over to Suzie's side of the bed, then leaned down to look underneath.

That was when Suzie made her move. "Fargo! You son of a bitch!" she shouted as she made a grab for Fargo's gun. "Get the hell out of here!"

Fargo jerked back from her, and as he did, he automatically pulled the trigger. The bullet hit Suzie in the face, just under her left eye, and she fell back on the bed dead.

The muzzle flash lit up the little room, and the gun blast was so loud that it left everyone's ears ringing.

"Suzie!" Ponci shouted. "Suzie!"

He examined her, but by the way her head was thrown back and her eyes were open but sightless, he knew she was dead.

"Son of a bitch! You just killed your own sister," Ponci said, shocked by what he had just seen.

"Yeah, well, the bitch had no business going for my gun," he said. "Now I'm going to ask you just one more time. Where at is the money?"

"I hid it," Ponci said.

"Where did you hide it?"

"If I tell you that, you won't have any reason to keep me alive."

"I don't have any reason to keep you alive anyway," Fargo said. He cocked his pistol. "Now, you got until I count to three to tell me where you hid that money, or I'll kill you dead right here and we'll just go steal some more money somewhere else."

Ponci glared at him.

"One," Fargo started.

"I ain't tellin' you shit."

"Two."

Fargo cocked the pistol and aimed it directly at Ponci's head. Ponci started quivering.

"All right, all right, I'll tell you," Ponci said. "I buried it in a cave back between here and—"

That was as far as Ponci got before Fargo shot him.

The bullet crashed into Ponci's chest, and the black hole that appeared just over his heart started pumping blood. Because he was naked, his wound was clearly visible, and Ponci reached down to try and staunch the flow of blood. Bright crimson spilled through his fingers, and he looked up in surprise.

"You said if I told you, you wouldn't shoot," Ponci muttered, his words strained.

"I also said I would count to three," Fargo told him. "I lied both times."

With Chetopa and his band of followers taken care of, Falcon was now able to turn his attention to Fargo Ford. He had learned from Sheriff Ferrell that at least two of the men in the gang, Fargo Ford and Ponci Elliot, were from Mesquite, so that seemed to be the logical place for him to start.

It was mid-morning when Falcon rode into Mesquite, and as he came into town, he saw a crowd of people gathered around the front of the hardware store. Dismounting at the saloon, Falcon tied off his horse and started into the saloon. Then he heard something from the crowd that got his attention.

"This here was Fargo Ford's sister. I wouldn't want to be the person that done this when he finds out about it."

Falcon turned away from the saloon then, and walked across the street to see what everyone was looking at. That was when he saw the two coffins that were propped up just behind the front window of the hardware store.

That was when he saw too that the hardware store was also an undertaker's parlor.

The body in one of the coffins was a woman. Her blond hair was neatly combed, and she was wearing a lavender dress. Her arms were crossed in front of her chest, and she was holding an artificial rose. There was a bullet hole under her left eye.

The other body was wearing a pair of overalls, with the bottom of one leg tied in a knot, showing that one leg was missing. He too had his arms folded across his chest and he was clutching a Colt pistol in one of his hands. Although the undertaker had done what he could to clean the wound, it was easy to see how he died, because there was a purple hole in his chest.

Neatly lettered signs identified each of the bodies. Under the woman's body the sign said SUZIE FORD. Under the man's body the sign said PONCI ELLIOT.

Ponci Elliot was one of the men Falcon was looking for.

"Where is the sheriff's office?" Falcon asked a man standing next to him.

"It's right down there across from the bank," the man answered. "You need to see the sheriff?"

"Yes."

"Well, his name is Meeker. Sheriff Meeker, and if you go on down there, why, like as not you'll find him sittin' in his office reading dime novels."

"Thanks," Falcon said.

Falcon stayed on this same side of the street until he reached the bank, then crossed over to the sheriff's office. When he pushed the door open, the room was filled with the aromatic smoke of the sheriff's pipe tobacco. The sheriff, a middle-aged, overweight man, was sitting at his desk puffing on a pipe, and reading a dime novel.

"Sheriff Meeker?" Falcon said as he stepped inside.

The sheriff looked up. "That's me," he said. "Can I help you?"

"I hope you can. What can you tell me about the two bodies that are on display down at the hardware store?"

The sheriff put the book facedown on his desk, then stared at Falcon with eyes that showed some curiosity as to why Falcon might be interested. He put that curiosity into words.

"Why do you want to know about them?" he asked.

"Because the man, Ponci Elliot, was riding with Fargo Ford, and I've been after him. Well, I've been after all of them actually. Fargo Ford, Ethan Monroe, Casey Jackson, and Dagen Mendoza."

"What do you mean, you've been after them?"

"They robbed a money shipment back in Calabasas, killing the express agent. The sheriff caught them and put them in jail, but they broke out, killing four men as they did so. Later, they took a young Indian girl off a stagecoach and killed her."

Sheriff Meeker shook his head slowly and let out a low whistle.

"They've been busy, haven't they?"

"Yes, they have. But I intend to put them out of business."

"You intend to put them out of business? All by yourself, are you?" Sheriff Meeker said with a chuckle. "And just who might I be talking to? Wyatt Earp? Wild Bill Hickock? Doc Holliday? Or is it Falcon MacCallister perhaps?"

"Yes," Falcon answered.

"Yes, what?" Sheriff Meeker asked, not quite understanding Falcon's response.

"Yes, I'm Falcon MacCallister."

"What?"

"You just rattled off a bunch of names, asking if any of them fit me. As it turns out, one of them does. I'm Falcon MacCallister."

"The hell you say!" Sheriff Meeker said, standing very quickly. "Mister, you aren't just fooling with me, are you?" he asked. "You really are Falcon MacCallister?"

"Well, I'll be damned!" the sheriff said. Moving around the desk quickly and displaying a big smile, Sheriff Meeker reached out to grab Falcon's hand, then began pumping it fiercely. "I'll be damned," he said. "Imagine me meeting

Falcon MacCallister. Why, I'm reading about you right now, in fact."

"You don't say."

"Yes, it's all about how you, Jesse James, and Billy the Kid robbed a train back in Missouri. What was it you would always say when you was facin' down someone with a gun?" the sheriff asked, a puzzled expression on his face. "Oh, yes, I remember now. You would say, 'Get ready to eat supper in hell.'"

"Yes, something like that," Falcon replied. He had never used that line in his life, but Sheriff Meeker wasn't the first person to point out to him that the dime novels reported that he always said that just before shooting someone.

Falcon had long since stopped refuting it, nor did he point out now how unlikely it was for him, Billy the Kid, and Jesse James all to be participating in the same holdup.

"Damn," Sheriff Meeker said. He laughed. "I really like that line. 'Get ready to eat supper in hell.' I may use it someday."

"Be my guest," Falcon said.

"Oh!" Sheriff Meeker suddenly gasped. He stepped back from Falcon and his eyes grew wide with fear. "I've . . . I've got paper on you!"

Falcon chuckled. "Don't worry about it. That paper is very old. I'm not wanted by anyone now. You can send a wire back to the sheriff that issued that warrant on me, if you want to."

"No, no," Sheriff Meeker said quickly, obviously not wanting to get into any argument with Falcon MacCallister. He had read too much about the deadly gunfighter to want to have to face him down.

"So, back to my original question, Sheriff Meeker. What can you tell me about these two people who were killed?"

"Other than who they are, I can't tell you much,"

Sheriff Meeker said. "Some of Suzie's neighbors reported hearing gunshots this morning, around sunup."

"Did they look into it?"

"No, not at first," Meeker said.

"Why not?"

"Gunshots ain't all that unusual around here," Meeker said. "Most of the time it's just a rancher, or maybe a miner, who stayed in town all night. Nobody figured this was any different."

"When did you find out it was something different?"

"Well, sir, the undertaker lives in the back of the hardware store and when he went back to the privy first thing this mornin', why, he noticed that Miss Suzie's door was open. He stepped up onto her stoop to tell her about it, and that's when he seen 'em. They was both lyin' there in Miss Suzie's bed. Nekkid as jaybirds, both of 'em was."

"Do you know who did it?"

"No, not yet. But in case you don't know it, Miss Suzie was a soiled dove. So what some of us has figured out, it was probably someone who got jealous or something."

"Maybe," Falcon said. "But it could've also been Fargo Ford and his gang."

"What? No! Didn't I tell you? Miss Suzie was Fargo Ford's own sister. I don't think a body, even someone as evil as Fargo, would kill his own sister."

"Unless she got in the way of money Fargo figures is his," Falcon said.

"Well, I'll be damn," Sheriff Meeker said. "I never thought of that."

"Fargo is from Mesquite, isn't he? So, if he came into town recently, someone might have seen him who recognized him?"

"If he came into town and somebody saw him, yes, they would have recognized him," Meeker admitted.

"Then, if you don't mind, I think I'll ask a few questions around town to see what I can find out."

"No," Sheriff Meeker said. "No, I don't mind at all. If fact, I'll go with you and help you out. If people see me with you, why, they might be a little more willin' to talk to you."

"Good idea," Falcon agreed.

The two men started at the saloon. Falcon, who had eaten nothing but trail food for the last several days, had a meal of spiced beef, beans, and rolled tortillas. He sat at a table in the back of the room while Meeker, with great fanfare, called people over, one at a time, to ask if any of them had seen Fargo Ford.

"Yeah, I seen him a few days ago," one of the men said.

"You seen him, Billy?" Sheriff Meeker asked.

"Yes."

"Come on over here. Billy Cates, this here is my friend Falcon MacCallister," Sheriff Meeker said. "I reckon you have heard of Falcon MacCallister, haven't you?"

"I reckon I have," Billy answered.

"Where did you see him?" Falcon asked, looking up from his meal.

"He come in here with three other men. They was all talkin' to Frederica and Ava, but I don't know what they was talkin' about. I was too far away to hear 'em."

"Did he say anything to you?" Falcon asked.

"To me? No, sir." Billy Cates cleared his throat. "Look, this here ain't somethin' I'm very proud of, but I used to ride some with Ford. Me'n Ponci Elliot and Les Wilson. But that was a long time ago and I've been on the up and up ever since then. Why, you can ask the sheriff about that."

"Billy's tellin' you the truth," Sheriff Meeker said. "He's rode the straight and narrow for a long time now."

"I believe him," Falcon said.

Billy looked relieved. "If you want, I'll send Frederica and Ava over so's you can talk to them. Maybe they can tell you what they was talkin' about."

A moment later the two bar girls stood in front of the table looking with admiration at the tall, handsome man who was asking so many questions.

"I know nothing about them," Frederica said. "I know only that they asked for Suzie."

"Suzie?"

"Fargo Ford's sister," Sheriff Meeker said.

"Oh, yes, I remember the sign in front of the coffin."

At the mention of the coffin, Frederica and Ava suddenly remembered that Suzie was dead, and both of them made the sign of the cross very quickly.

"Thank you, ladies, you have both been very helpful," Falcon said.

After learning that Fargo Ford had been in town recently, Falcon spent the rest of the day talking to everyone who knew him in order to get as good a picture as he could get of the man's habits. By nightfall, he had gathered enough information to give him an educated guess on the best way to track him down.

Falcon took a room in the hotel, spending the night in bed, his first night in bed in several nights.

It was still dark when Falcon left town the next morning. When the sun came up and the undertaker came up front to close the caskets of the two bodies, he noticed that Ponci Elliot was wearing a hat. That seemed strange. He hadn't put a hat on Ponci's head. He wondered where the hat came from.

Removing the hat, he gasped.

Ponci had been scalped.

CHAPTER 21

"It stinks in here," Dagen complained as he, Monroe, Casey, and Fargo looked through the cave where Ponci had done his self-amputation to see if they could find the money.

"You can put up with a little stink," Fargo said.

"A little stink? We could be up to our bottom lip in shit and it wouldn't stink anymore," Dagen said.

The others laughed.

"What the hell are we lookin' for?" Monroe asked.

"What are we looking for? We're looking for the money," Fargo replied.

"Yeah, I know that. But is it in a bag or what?"

"It could be," Fargo said. "But like as not it's . . ." He stopped in mid-sentence, then leaned over and started tossing a few rocks aside.

"Have you found something?" Casey asked.

Fargo pulled out a set of saddlebags, then opened the flap and looked inside. A broad smile spread across his face.

"Here it is, boys."

"Is the money there?" Dagen asked.

"It's here."

"Let's divide it up," Dagen said.

"Not here."

Dagen looked at the other two men and, sensing that they were behind him, he looked back at Fargo. Fargo was holding the saddlebags and looking down inside. He didn't notice that Dagen had pulled his gun.

"Yeah, let's do it here," Dagen said.

"I'm in charge here," Fargo said. "And I'll decide when and where we divide the money."

Dagen pulled the trigger and the gun flashed and boomed loudly inside the cave. A little puff of dust flew up from the front of Fargo's shirt and his eyes opened wide in pain and surprise. He dropped the saddlebags and put his hand over the wound.

"You son of a bitch," he said. "You killed me."

"Yeah," Dagen said easily. He pulled the trigger a second time, and Fargo went down.

Monroe and Casey looked on with shock.

"What the hell did you do that for?" Casey asked.

"Because I don't believe the son of a bitch had any intention of dividing up that money," Dagen said. "I think he was planning on just stringin' us along for a while, then, first chance he got, he was going to run out on us."

"When do you plan on dividing the money?" Monroe asked.

"Right now," Dagen said. He smiled. "That is, as soon as we get out of this stink."

Leaving Fargo dead inside the cave, the three bandits walked outside into the bright sunlight. Dagen took a deep breath.

"Damn, it feels good to be able to breathe again," he said.

"Yeah," Monroe said. "I don't know how much longer I could've stayed in there."

"Ha," Casey said. "If you think it stinks in there now, what's it goin' to be like when ole Fargo gets ripe?"

"Ain't goin' to be that much worse," Dagen said. "Fargo always did have a stink about him anyhow."

The others laughed, even though they knew that they probably smelled just as bad.

Dagen dumped the money out onto the ground; then the three men squatted down around it and began counting it out. It totaled fourteen thousand, two hundred dollars.

"Looks to me like it's a couple hundred dollars short," Monroe said.

"Ponci must've taken some of it," Dagen said.

"Maybe, but don't forget, Fargo had some too. We ought to go back in and see how much he has," Casey suggested.

"You want it, you can go in and get it," Dagen said, picking up his share of the money. "I doubt he has a hundred dollars on him, and for me, it ain't worth goin' back into that stink for no more'n thirty dollars, which is about what we would each get."

"Yeah," Casey said as he stuck the money inside his shirt. "Yeah, that's what I think too. So, where do we go now?"

"Anywhere we want to go," Dagen said. "We don't even have to stay together no more if we don't want to."

"Yeah," Monroe said. "But till we get back to town it might be better if we stayed together."

"Why's that?"

"I've heard talk of some renegade Indians. I don't want to run into any all by myself."

"Monroe's right," Casey said. "I say we stay together till we get back to Sassabi Flat."

Dagen shook his head. "We can't go back there."

"Why not?" Monroe asked. "They got whiskey, whores, and food there."

"Fargo killed one of the whores, remember? And he killed the bartender too."

"Oh, yeah," Casey said. "Damn, where can we go?"

"How about Providence Wells?" Dagen suggested. "They got whiskey, whores, and food there too. And there ain't none of us ever been there, so there won't be nobody there that know us."

"Yeah, good idea," Casey said.

The three men mounted. Then Casey looked over at Fargo's horse.

"What about Fargo's horse? Should we take him with us?" Casey asked.

"Why?" asked Dagen.

"We can sell 'im."

"We got enough money, we don't need to be bothered with tryin' to sell no damn horse."

"Well, it wouldn't be right just to leave him here," Casey said.

Dagen pulled his pistol and shot Fargo's horse in the head. The animal dropped without a sound.

"Son of a bitch!" Casey shouted in surprise.

"Now it won't bother him to stay here," Dagen said. "Let's go."

Falcon saw the vultures first, from at least a mile away. Then, as he drew closer, he saw a large brown form on the ground, and knew that it was a horse.

It looked as if one of the horses had gone down, leaving the outlaws with four men and three horses. Although he felt bad about the horse, he knew it would slow the men down somewhat and make it easier for him to track them.

Something didn't look quite right when Falcon finally reached the horse. He couldn't put his finger on what was bothering him . . . maybe it was just intuition. Whatever it was, Falcon decided it was worth a closer look, so he dismounted, then walked over to examine the horse. Kneeling beside it, he ran his hand across the legs of the horse, but he couldn't find any sign of a broken bone.

"What happened here?" he asked aloud. "If you didn't

go down on them, why would they shoot you and leave themselves one horse short?"

Falcon lifted the head, then let it drop. There was still some flexibility in the animal, so it hadn't been dead long.

Sighing, Falcon stood up, then removed his hat and ran his hand through his hair. Looking around, he saw a set of saddlebags lying open near a boulder. Looking back at the dead horse, he saw the horse had its own saddlebags.

Falcon walked over for a closer look at the saddlebags near the boulder, and when he stuck his hand down inside, he pulled out a little paper band, the kind of paper band that is wrapped around stacks of money. He read the printing on the band.

$100
WESTERN EXPRESS COMPANY

Looking around the area, Falcon saw the opening to a cave. Pulling his pistol, he moved up to one side of the opening, then cautiously looked inside.

That was when he became aware of two things: the overwhelming stench coming from inside the cave, and the fact that Fargo Ford was lying dead on the floor of the cave.

Holstering his pistol, Falcon pulled his knife and went into the cave.

"Two down and three to go," he said aloud. "You men just keep killing each other off. That makes my job real easy."

It was after dark when Falcon got to Providence Wells. Dismounting in front of the saloon, he walked along all the horses that were tied to the hitching rail, then saw one that he had seen before. It was one of the horses Pete Tucker had been holding during the botched holdup attempt back in Calabasas. That meant that the men he was looking for were here.

Going inside the saloon, Falcon looked around, but didn't see anyone he recognized.

"Yes, sir, what will it be?" the bartender asked.

"A beer," Falcon said. He decided against asking for any specific information, believing he could find out more just by being quiet and observing.

Falcon had just about finished when a girl came down the stairs and stepped up to the bar. One eye was red and swollen.

"Good Lord, girl, what happened to you?" the bartender asked.

"Nothing," the girl said, putting her hand up to cover the eye.

"Don't tell me 'nothing.' You've got as big a shiner there as I've ever seen on anyone."

"He . . . he wants a bottle of whiskey," the girl said, nodding back toward the bar and putting some money on the bar.

"What happened to you? Did that fella hit you?" The bartender reached up to touch the girl's eye, but she pulled away from him.

"No, please," she said. "I don't want any trouble."

"Honey, it looks to me like you've already got it. What's going on up there? Listen, you want me to go tell him his time is up?" The bartender started toward the end of the bar.

"No, don't!" she said. "It's all right, nothing is going on." She reached out to grab him. "Nothing, honest. Please, don't start anything. There are three of them."

That caught Falcon's attention. "Three of them, you say?" he asked.

"Don't get me wrong, they aren't all three with me," the girl said. "The other two are with other girls."

"Why are you interested?" the bartender asked. "Do you know these three men?"

"I'm not sure. When did they get into town?"

"No more'n a couple of hours ago," the bartender said. "At first, we was glad to see 'em 'cause they're spendin' money like water. But the drunker they got, the meaner they got, and right now I'd like to see 'em be on their way, money or no money." Then, to the bar girl, he said, "Honey, you don't have to go back up there. Not if he's beating you."

"It'll be all right," the girl insisted, taking the whiskey. "I just don't want any more trouble, that's all."

She started for the stairs, but by the time she reached the bottom step, Dagen, wearing only his trousers and gun belt, appeared at the railing on the upper balcony.

Falcon recognized him at once as one of the men he had seen back in Calabasas, and he turned toward the bar and pulled his hat down. Because Dagen was standing on the landing above, Falcon's hat had the effect of preventing the outlaw from getting a clear view.

"Hey, you! Bitch!" Dagen called down to the girl. "I sent you down there to get a bottle of whiskey, not to have a quilting bee. You've been down there long enough. Get back up here!"

"Mister, she's already been up there long enough," the bartender said.

"What do you mean, she's been up here long enough? I decide when she's been up here long enough."

"Well, you know how it is," the bartender replied, forcing a laugh. "I mean, she is a working girl. There's other gents in here wantin' her time too. I can't let one man just have all her time. Why, how'd it be if you was waitin' on her right now?"

"Yeah? Well, I ain't waitin' on her," Dagen said. "But I want to be fair about it," he added with a mirthless smile. He looked down over the floor of the saloon. "Who's waitin'?" he asked. "Who else wants her?"

The bar girl looked out over the floor, her eyes showing an expression of desperate hope that someone would back up the bartender. There was absolute silence. The other men, who didn't want any trouble, managed to avoid the girl's pleading look.

"Well, now, that's just what I thought," Dagen said. The smile left his face. "They don't nobody but me want her, 'cause she's nothin' but a worthless slut. Now, you get back up here."

The girl shut her eyes tightly, squeezing out a tear. She started up the stairs, then stopped. Clenching her hands into fists, she shook her head resolutely.

"No," she said. "No, I'm not coming back up."

"What do you mean you ain't comin' back up? I paid for you! Do you hear me, girl? I paid for you! You belong to me."

The girl put her hand down in a dress pocket, then pulled out two crumpled bills.

"Here is your money," she said. "I'll give it back to you."

Dagen pulled his pistol and pointed it toward the girl.

"I don't want my money, bitch. I want you. Now you get back up here or else I'm goin' to put a bullet right between your eyes."

The room was now deathly quiet, so quiet that the loudest sound to be heard was the steady tick-tock of the clock that hung from the back wall. And because of the silence, Falcon's quiet words resonated loudly.

"Miss, if you're not busy now, I'd like a little of your time," he said.

Dagen looked toward Falcon, then, recognizing him, gasped.

"You!" he said. "You're Falcon MacCallister, ain't you?"

"I am," Falcon said.

There was a gasp of recognition among many in the saloon, for though none had met him, all knew about him.

"I thought we killed you."

"You thought wrong," Falcon said.

"Yeah, well, I guess I did. What are you doing here?"

"I thought I might have a drink," Falcon said. "And maybe spend a little time with a woman." He looked pointedly at the girl. "That woman," he said.

Dagen shook his head. "Huh-uh. Better pick yourself another one. This one's comin' back up to me."

"I don't think she wants to do that, and as a matter of fact, I don't want her to do it either."

"What the hell do I care what she wants?" Dagen said. "She's got no choice. Neither do you, mister. Or haven't you noticed that I happen to be holding a gun in my hand."

"Oh, yeah, I see the gun," Falcon said. "But what are you going to do with it?"

"What do you mean what am I going to do with it?" Dagen answered, obviously exasperated by Falcon's question.

"Well, here's the thing," Falcon said as if patiently explaining something to a child. "You see, you are pointing that gun at the girl. But she's not your problem . . . I am. If you move it toward me, I'm going to kill you. If you shoot her, I'm going to kill you. If you so much as twitch, I'm going to kill you. The only way you are going to get out of this alive is to drop your gun right now."

"What? Are you crazy? Your guns are still in your holster," Dagen said.

"What'll it be, mister? Are you going to drop the gun, or are you going to die?"

"Mister, if you don't get out of here right now, I'm going to kill this girl," Dagen said.

"Go ahead."

"What?"

"Go ahead," Falcon said. "While you are shooting her, I'll be shooting you."

With a shout of rage, Dagen swung his gun toward

Falcon and fired. The bullet slammed into the bar just alongside him. In one motion, Falcon had his own gun out and he fired back just as Dagen loosed a second shot.

Dagen's second shot smashed into the mirror behind the bar, scattering shards of glass but doing no further damage. Dagen didn't get off a third shot because Falcon made his only shot count.

Dagen dropped his gun over the rail and it fell with a clatter to the bar floor, twelve feet below. He grabbed his chest, then turned his hand out and looked down in surprise and disbelief as his palm began filling with his own blood. His eyes rolled back in his head and he pitched forward, crashing through the railing, then turning over once in midair before he landed heavily on his back alongside his dropped gun.

Dagen lay motionless on the floor with open but sightless eyes staring toward the ceiling. The saloon patrons, who had scattered when the first shot was fired, now began to edge toward the body. Up on the second-floor landing, a half-dozen girls and their customers, in various stages of undress, moved to the smashed railing to look down on the scene.

Gun smoke from the three shots merged to form a large, acrid cloud that drifted slowly toward the door.

Upstairs, Monroe had opened the door from his room to tell Dagen to have his whore get an extra bottle of whiskey. Before he could say anything to Dagen, he heard Dagen call Falcon MacCallister by name.

"Son of a bitch!" Monroe said under his breath. He stepped back inside and grabbed his pants, then dashed back into the hall. He started to stop at Casey's door just long enough to warn him, and he got as far as putting his hand on the doorknob.

He hesitated. Why the hell should he warn Casey? Let

Casey look out for himself. In fact, the longer Dagen and Casey could delay Falcon, the better it would be for him.

Monroe ran down to the end of the hall, lifted the window, climbed out onto the mansard roof just below; then, even as he heard the shooting, he dropped down to the alley. He moved around quickly to the front of the saloon, mounted, and rode away, fighting the urge to put his horse into a gallop.

When Casey heard the shooting, he jumped from the bed and grabbed his gun, then ran out into the hall, where he was joined by at least three other whores and two other customers. He ran to the head of the stairs and looked down to the saloon below. That was when he saw Dagen lying on his back, his gun on the floor beside him. A tall man with a smoking gun in his hand was standing over Dagen, looking down at him.

"Oh, shit!" Casey said. He fired at the tall man, but missed. Those around him screamed and started running.

The bullet from Casey's gun buzzed by Falcon's ear and plunged into the floor beside him. Falcon looked up, but couldn't return fire because of the people around Casey.

Casey turned and ran back down the hall, and Falcon ran up the stairs, taking them two at a time. Just as he reached the top of the stairs, he saw the second door down on the right side closing. He looked at one of the women, who was cowering in fear on the opposite side of the hall. Silently, he used his pistol to indicate the door he had just seen shut, and with a quick nod she verified it was where Casey had gone.

At that moment Falcon heard glass crashing. The son of a bitch was escaping through the back window!

Falcon kicked open the door, then ran inside. The

back window was smashed out and he stepped over to look through it, then sensed someone moving up behind him.

Falcon turned, just as Casey was bringing his gun down to smash him on the head. Falcon managed to deflect the blow, moving it away from his head. It did crash down on his shoulder, however, and a numbing, shooting pain caused him to drop his pistol.

Unarmed now, Falcon had no recourse but to wrap his arms around his assailant in a bear hug. It had the effect of pinning Casey's arms by his sides, so he could not raise his pistol. Falcon threw Casey to the floor and he heard Casey gasp as they went down. Then he felt all the strength leave Casey's body.

Carefully, Falcon raised up from him, and saw a bloody shard of glass sticking up through Casey's neck. Casey flopped a few times; then he died.

When Falcon stepped back out into the hallway, the same girl who had indicated which room Casey went into, now pointed to the open window at the end of the hall.

"The other one went out that way," she said.

"Thanks."

By the time Falcon got back downstairs, the sheriff had arrived.

"Mister, you've got some explaining to do," he said.

Falcon wished now that he had taken a badge from Sheriff Corbin.

"My name is Falcon MacCallister. Get in touch with Sheriff Corbin at Oro Blanco; he'll tell you what this is all about."

The sheriff smiled. "I don't have to get in touch with him, Mr. MacCallister. He's already sent me a letter. Fact is, he sent ever' sheriff in this part of the territory a letter, explaining what you are doing."

"Did he tell you everything I'm doing?" Falcon asked.

He nodded toward Dagen's body. "What I need to do to stop an Indian war?"

"Don't do it here," the sheriff said cryptically. "I'll have the bodies taken down to the undertaker's office. You can do what has to be done there."

Jane Stockdale was taking clothes down from the line. She removed the pins from a large bedsheet, then took it down.

"Oh!" she gasped.

Removing the bedsheet exposed a man standing behind it. He was holding a pistol.

"Where at is your man?" he asked.

"He's in the house," she said. "And if he sees you here, he will shoot you."

In fact her husband was not here. He and Timmy had gone into town to buy some supplies. But Jane was afraid to tell the man she was alone.

"Is that a fact?"

"Yes."

"I don't believe you. If your man was here he'd be out here right now, wantin' to know what is goin' on. That is, if he was a man."

"He's here," Jane said, though her declaration sounded weak even to her own ears.

"Uh-huh. Then who was that man and kid I seen leavin' in the buckboard about fifteen minutes ago?"

"Who are you?" Jane asked. "What do you want?"

"The name is Monroe. And what I want is a little food, that's all. Just a little food and I'll be on my way."

"All right," Jane said, fighting to keep her voice calm. "I would never like it said that I turned away a hungry man." She started toward the house.

"Hey, you, wait a minute," Monroe said. He pointed at

Jane. "I know who you are now. You was on that stage, wasn't you?"

Jane gasped. She had realized, almost from the moment she first saw him, that he was one of the men who had robbed the stage, killed the shotgun guard, and later killed Cloud Dancer. But she had thought it might be dangerous to let him know that she recognized him, so she had not challenged him.

"I don't know what you are talking about," she said, still trying to pretend he'd made a mistake.

"The hell you don't. You was on that stage all right. You, your kid, a drummer, an Injun girl, and MacCallister."

"Why did you kill her?" Jane asked, no longer trying to keep up the pretense of not knowing him. "Why did you kill Cloud Dancer?"

"Cloud Dancer? That was her name?"

"Why did you kill her?" Jane asked again.

Monroe started to tell her that it was Ponci who killed her, that he didn't have anything to do with it. But he changed his mind, deciding it might be better if she feared him.

"I killed her because she wouldn't do what I wanted her to do." He leered at Jane. "Do you get my meanin'?"

"I . . . I suppose I do," Jane admitted.

"Good, good, I'm glad we understand each other. So, just to show me that you do understand, I want you to take off your clothes."

"What?"

"You heard me. I said take off your clothes," Monroe said.

"I . . . I thought you were hungry. Let me get you something for you to eat."

"There will be plenty of time for food later," Monroe said. "Take off them clothes."

"Please," Jane said in a pleading voice. "Don't make me do this thing."

"I ain't goin' to ask you again," Monroe said, pointing his pistol at her head and cocking it.

Slowly, reluctantly, and fearfully, Jane began unbuttoning her dress.

She pulled the dress over her head, then began unlacing the camisole. When she had it completely unlaced, she looked at him pleadingly.

"Please," she said. "Don't make me do this."

Monroe's eyes were clouded with lust, and Jane thought she could see something red deep down inside them. She opened the camisole and felt the effect of the air on her bare nipples.

Then, to her shock and surprise, the side of Monroe's head seemed to explode as blood, brain matter, and bits of bone spewed out from his temple. Monroe's eyes rolled back, showing all white. Not until he was falling did she hear the distant report of a rifle.

Jane gasped, but she didn't scream. Instead, she just looked down at Monroe's body as she dispassionately relaced the front of her camisole. She had herself covered by the time the man who shot Monroe came strolling up.

"Mr. MacCallister," she said. "I might have guessed it was you."

"Yes, ma'am," Falcon said. "Are you hurt?"

"I'm all right," Jane replied. She turned her back to him as she continued to lace up the camisole. "If you'll forgive me, I'll try and recover my modesty, if not my dignity."

"You don't need to worry about that, Mrs. Stockdale," Falcon said. "Your dignity was never compromised."

"Five," Keytano said, counting the scalps Falcon laid on the ground before him. "You have killed five of your white brothers."

"They were white," Falcon said. "But they were not my brothers."

"You also killed six Apache," Keytano said.

Falcon shook his head. "I killed only five. One of your brothers was killed by another."

Keytano shook his head. "They were Apache," he said. But they were not my brothers."

Keytano put his hand on Falcon's shoulder, and Falcon did the same.

"You and I are brothers," Keytano said.

Falcon smiled. "It's good to hear you say that, Keytano," he said. "Because I've got a silver mine that needs to be worked. And as it turns out, it's pretty close to your territory."

"Hear me," Keytano called out, loud enough that the many who had gathered in the center circle could hear his words.

"This is Dlo Binanta. From this day forward, he is my brother. For him, I will be a white man, and for me, he will be an Apache."

"Well, I thank you for that," Falcon said.

"It is okay," Keytano said. He smiled. "For I know you will share twenty percent of your silver mine with me."

"You want twenty percent of my silver mine?"

"Is it not the way of the white man to take what is not his?" Keytano asked innocently.

Falcon laughed out loud. "Keytano," he said. "All I've got to say is, you are one hell of a fast learner."

AFTERWORD

Notes from the Old West

In the small town where I grew up, there were two movie theaters. The Pavilion was one of those old-timey movie show palaces, built in the heyday of the Mary Pickford and Charlie Chaplin silent era of the 1920s. By the 1950s, when I was a kid, the Pavilion was a little worn around the edges, but it was still the premier theater in town. They played all those big Technicolor biblical Cecil B. DeMille epics and the corny MGM musicals. In Cinemascope, of course.

On the other side of town was the Gem, a somewhat shabby and rundown grindhouse with sticky floors and torn seats. Admission was a quarter. The Gem booked low-budget B pictures (remember the Bowery Boys?), war movies, horror flicks, and Westerns. I liked the Westerns best. I could usually be found every Saturday at the Gem, along with my best friend, Newton Trout, watching Westerns from 10 AM until my father came looking for me around suppertime. (Sometimes Newton's dad was dispatched to come fetch us.) One time, my dad came to get me, right in the middle of *Abilene Trail*, which featured the now-forgotten Whip Wilson. My father became so engrossed in the action, he sat down and watched the rest of it with us. We didn't get home until after dark, and my mother's meatloaf was a pan of gray ashes by the time we did. Though my father and I were both in the doghouse the next day, this remains one of my fondest childhood memories. There was Wild Bill Elliot, and Gene Autry, and Roy Rogers, and Tim Holt, and, a little later, Rod Cameron and Audie Murphy. Of these newcomers, I never missed an Audie Murphy Western, because Audie was sort of an anti-hero. Sure, he stood for law and order and was an honest man, but sometimes he had to go around the law to uphold it. If he didn't play fair, it was only because he felt hamstrung by the laws of the land. Whatever it took to get the bad guys, Audie did it. There were no finer points of law, no splitting of legal hairs. It was instant justice, devoid of long-winded lawyers, bored or biased jurors, or black-robed, often corrupt judges.

Steal a man's horse and you were the guest of honor at a necktie party.

Molesting a good woman meant a bullet in your heart or a rope around your gullet. Or at the very least, getting the crap beat out of you. Rob a bank and face a hail of bullets or the hangman's noose.

Saved a lot of time and money, did frontier justice.

That's all gone now, I'm sad to say. Now you hear, "Oh, but he had a bad childhood" or, "His mother didn't give him enough love" or, "The homecoming queen wouldn't give him a second look and he has an inferiority complex." Or cultural rage, as the politically correct bright boys refer to it. How many times have you heard some self-important defense attorney moan, "The poor kids were only venting their hostilities toward an uncaring society"?

Mule fritters, I say. Nowadays, you can't even call a punk a punk anymore. But don't get me started.

It was "howdy ma'am" time, too. The good guys, anti-hero or not, were always respectful to the ladies. They might shoot a bad guy five seconds after tipping their hat to a woman, but the code of the West demanded you be respectful to a lady.

Lots of things have changed since the heyday of the Wild West, haven't they? Some for the good, some for the bad.

I didn't have any idea at the time that I would someday write about the West. I just knew that I was captivated by the Old West.

When I first got the itch to write, back in the early 1970s, I didn't write Westerns. I started by writing horror and action adventure novels. After more than two dozen novels, I began thinking about developing a western character. From those initial musings came the novel *The Last Mountain Man: Smoke Jensen*. That was followed by *Preacher: The First Mountain Man*. A few years later, I began developing the *Last Gunfighter* series. Frank Morgan is a legend in his own time, the fastest gun west of the Mississippi . . . a title and a reputation he never wanted, but can't get rid of.

For me, and for thousands—probably millions—of other people (although many will never publicly admit it), the old Wild West will always be a magic, mysterious place: a place we love to visit through the pages of books; characters we would like to know . . . from a safe distance; events we would love to take part in—again, from a safe distance. For the old Wild West was not a place for the faint of heart. It was a hard, tough, physically demanding time. There were no police to call if one faced adversity. One faced trouble alone, and handled it alone. It was rugged individualism: something that appeals to many of us.

I am certain that is something that appeals to most readers of Westerns.

I still do on-site research (whenever possible) before

starting a Western novel. I have wandered over much of the West, prowling what is left of ghost towns. Stand in the midst of the ruins of these old towns, use a little bit of imagination, and one can conjure up life as it used to be in the Wild West. The rowdy Saturday nights, the tinkling of a piano in a saloon, the laughter of cowboys and miners letting off steam after a week of hard work. Use a little more imagination and one can envision two men standing in the street, facing one another, seconds before the hook and draw of a gunfight. A moment later, one is dead and the other rides away.

The old wild untamed West.

There are still some ghost towns to visit, but they are rapidly vanishing as time and the elements take their toll. If you want to see them, make plans to do so as soon as possible, for in a few years, they will all be gone.

And so will we.

Stand in what is left of the Big Thicket country of east Texas and try to imagine how in the world the pioneers managed to get through that wild tangle. I have wondered that many times and marveled at the courage of the men and women who slowly pushed westward, facing dangers that we can only imagine.

Let me touch briefly on a subject that is very close to me: firearms. There are some so-called historians who are now claiming that firearms played only a very insignificant part in the settlers' lives. They claim that only a few were armed. What utter, stupid nonsense! What do these so-called historians think the pioneers did for food? Do they think the early settlers rode down to the nearest supermarket and bought their meat? Or maybe they think the settlers chased down deer or buffalo on foot and beat the animals to death with a club. I have a news flash for you so-called historians: the settlers used guns to shoot their game. They used guns to defend hearth and home against Indians on the warpath. They used guns to protect themselves from outlaws. Guns are a part of Americana. And always will be.

The mountains of the West and the remains of the ghost towns that dot these areas are some of my favorite subjects to write about. I have done extensive research on the various mountain ranges of the West and go back whenever time permits. I sometimes stand surrounded by the towering mountains and wonder how in the world the pioneers ever made it through. As hard as I try and as often as I try, I simply cannot imagine the hardships those men and women endured over the hard months of their incredible journey. None of us can. It is said that on the Oregon Trail alone, there are at least two bodies in lonely unmarked graves for every mile of that journey. Some students of the West say the number of dead is at least twice that. And nobody knows the exact number of wagons that impatiently started out alone and simply vanished on the way, along with their occupants, never to be seen or heard from again.

Just vanished.

The one-hundred-and-fifty-year-old ruts of the wagon wheels can still be seen in various places along the Oregon Trail. But if you plan to visit those places, do so quickly, for they are slowly disappearing. And when they are gone, they will be lost forever, except in the words of Western writers.

The West will live on as long as there are writers willing to write about it, and publishers willing to publish it. Writing about the West is wide open, just like the old Wild West. Characters abound, as plentiful as the wide-open spaces, as colorful as a sunset on the Painted Desert, as restless as the ever-sighing winds. All one has to do is use a bit of imagination. Take a stroll through the cemetery at Tombstone, Arizona; read the inscriptions. Then walk the main street of that once infamous town around midnight and you might catch a glimpse of the ghosts that still wander the town. They really do.

Just ask anyone who lives there. But don't be afraid of the apparitions—they won't hurt you. They're just out for a quiet stroll.

The West lives on. And as long as I am alive, it always will.

Turn the page for a preview of

THE LAST GUNFIGHTER: RENEGADES,

the new Frank Morgan Western from master storyteller

William W. Johnstone with Fred Austin

Coming in October 2005

wherever Pinnacle Books are sold

CHAPTER 1

Brown County, Texas, and all the violence that had taken place there were a long way behind Frank Morgan now. He was riding southward toward the Rio Grande, taking his time, in no hurry to get where he was going . . . wherever that was. Someplace where his past might not catch up to him. A haven where he could go unrecognized.

But as idyllic as that sounded, Frank Morgan knew there wasn't much chance that he would ever find such a sanctuary.

It was hard to blend in when you were the last of the really fast guns.

Some of the others were still alive—Wyatt Earp, Bat Masterson, and Smoke Jensen were three that Frank could think of right off the top of his head. Somehow they had managed to settle down. John Wesley Hardin was still alive too, but he was in prison. Bill Hickok, Ben Thompson, Doc Holliday, Luke Short . . . They were all dead, along with most of the other shootists and pistoleers who had made a name for themselves at one time or another on the frontier.

It was a sad time, in a way. A dying time. But a man couldn't stop the march of progress and so-called civilization. Nor was Frank Morgan the sort of hombre to brood about it and cling to the fading shadows of what once had been. He looked to the future, not the past.

Now the future meant finding a warm, hospitable place

to spend the winter. It was November, and up north the snow and the frigid winds were already roaring down out of Canada to sweep across the mountains and the plains, all the way down to the Texas Panhandle. Hundreds of miles south of the Panhandle, however, here in the Rio Grande Valley of south Texas, the sky was blue, the sun was shining, and the temperature was quite pleasant. Frank even had the sleeves of his blue work shirt rolled up a couple of turns on his muscular forearms.

He was a lean, well-built man of middle years, with gray streaking the thick dark hair under his Stetson. His range clothes were of good quality, as was his saddle. A Colt .45 was holstered on his hip, and the stock of a Winchester stuck up from a saddle sheath under his right leg. He rode a fine-looking Appaloosa called Stormy and led a dun-colored packhorse. The big shaggy cur known as Dog padded alongside him as Frank rode down a trail that cut its way through the thick chaparral covering the mostly flat landscape.

Frank didn't know exactly where he was, but he thought he must be getting close to the Rio Grande. Some sleepy little border village would be a good spot to pass the winter, he mused. Cool beer, some tortillas and beans and chili, maybe a pretty señorita or two to keep him company . . . It sounded fine to Frank. Maybe not heaven, but likely as close as a gunfighter like him would ever get.

Into every heavenly vision, though, a little hell had to intrude. The distant popping of gunfire suddenly came to Frank's ears.

He reined in and frowned. The shots continued, coming fast and furious. They were still a ways off, but they were getting closer, without a doubt. He heard the rumble of hoofbeats too. Some sort of running gun battle, Frank decided.

And it was running straight toward him.

He had never been one to dodge trouble. There just wasn't any backing down in his nature. Instead he nudged his heels into Stormy's sides and sent the Appaloosa trotting forward. Whatever was coming at him, Frank Morgan would go right out to meet it.

Now he could see dust clouds boiling in the air ahead of him, kicked up by all the horses he heard. A moment later, the trail he was following intersected a road at a sharp angle. The pursuit was on the road itself, which was wide enough for a couple of wagons and a half-dozen or so riders.

Only one wagon came toward Frank, a buckboard that swayed and bounced as it careened along the road. The dust from the hooves of the team pulling it obscured the occupants to a certain extent, but Frank thought he saw two men on the buckboard, one handling the reins while the other twisted around on the seat and fired a rifle back at the men giving chase.

There were more than a dozen of those, Frank saw. He estimated the number at twenty. They rode bunched up, the ones in the lead banging away at the fleeing buckboard with six-guns. The gap between hunter and hunted was about fifty yards, too far for accurate handgun fire, especially from the saddle of a racing horse. But the rifleman on the buckboard didn't seem to be having much better luck. The group of riders surged on without slowing.

Frank had no idea who any of these men were and didn't know which side he ought to take in this fight. But he'd always had a natural sympathy for the underdog, so he didn't like the idea of two against twenty.

He liked it even less when one of the horses in the team suddenly went down, probably the result of stepping in a prairie-dog hole. The horse screamed in pain, a shrill sound that Frank heard even over the rattle of gunfire and the pounding of hoofbeats. Probably a broken leg, he thought in the instant before the fallen horse pulled down the other members of the team and caused the buckboard to overturn violently. The two men who had been in it flew through the air like rag dolls.

Frank sent Stormy surging forward at a gallop. He didn't know if the men had survived the wreck or not, but it was a cinch they were out of the fight, at least for the moment, and wouldn't survive the next few seconds unless somebody helped them. He drew the Winchester and guided Stormy with his knees as he brought the rifle to his shoulder and blazed away, firing as fast as he could work the repeater's lever.

He put the first couple of bullets over the heads of the pursuers to see if they would give up the chase. When they didn't but kept attacking instead, sending a couple of bullets whizzing past him, Frank had no choice but to lower his aim. Stormy's smooth gait and Frank's years of experience meant that he was a good shot even from the hurricane deck. His bullets laced into the crowd of gunmen in the road.

Frank was close enough now to see that most of the pursuers wore high-crowned, broad-brimmed sombreros. *Bandidos* from below the border, he thought. A few men in American range garb were mixed in the group, but that came as no surprise. Gringo outlaws sometimes crossed the Rio Grande and fell in with gangs of Mexican raiders. A man who was tough enough and ruthless enough—and good enough with a gun—could usually find a home for himself with others of his kind, no matter where he was.

Two of the bandits plunged off their horses as Frank's shots ripped through them, and a couple of others sagged in their saddles and dropped out of the fight, obviously wounded. The other men reined their mounts to skidding, sliding halts that made even more dust billow up from the hard-packed caliche surface of the road. Clearly, they hadn't expected to run into opposition like that which Frank was putting up now.

But the odds were still on their side, and after a moment of hesitation they attacked again, yelling curses and firing as they came toward the overturned wagon.

Both of the men who had been thrown from the wreck staggered to their feet as Frank came closer. He didn't know how badly they were hurt, but at least they were conscious and able to move around. They stumbled toward the shelter of the buckboard as bullets flew around them.

While Stormy was still galloping, Frank swung down from the saddle, as good a running dismount as anyone could make. He had the Winchester in his left hand. With his right, he slapped the Appaloosa on the rump and ordered, "Stormy, get out of here! You too, Dog!"

The horse veered off into the chaparral at the side of the road, finding an opening in the thorny stuff. The big cur was more reluctant, obviously hesitant to abandon his master in the middle of a fight. Frank didn't want to have to worry about him while he was battling for his life, though, so he added, "Dog, go!"

With a growl, Dog disappeared into the brush.

Frank ran to the wagon and joined the two men who were already crouched behind it, firing revolvers at the charging *bandidos.* The man who had been using the rifle earlier had lost the weapon when the buckboard flipped over. Both of them had managed to hang on to their handguns, though.

The buckboard was on its side, turned crossways in the road. The horses had struggled back to their feet, except for the one with the broken leg, and they lunged and reared in their traces, maddened by the gunfire and the reeking clouds of powder smoke that drifted through the air. A couple of them had been wounded by flying lead.

Frank rested his Winchester on the buckboard and opened fire again, placing his shots carefully now that he had a chance to aim. One of the raiders flipped backward out of the saddle as if he had been swatted by a giant hand, and another fell forward over his mount's neck before slipping off and landing under the horse's slashing hooves.

Bullets pounded into the buckboard like a deadly hailstorm of lead. The thick boards stopped most of them, but a few of the rounds punched through, luckily missing Frank and his two companions. The shots from the men fighting alongside him were taking a toll on the attackers as well. Less than half of the *bandidos* were unscathed so far. The others had been either killed or wounded.

The Winchester ran dry. Frank dropped it and drew his Colt. The range was plenty close enough now for an expert pistol shot like The Drifter. He triggered twice and was rewarded by the sight of another rider plummeting from the saddle.

The gang of *bandidos* had had enough. They wheeled their horses, still snapping shots at the buckboard as they did so, and then lit a shuck out of there. Frank and the two men threw a few shots after them to hurry them on their way, but the riders were out of pistol range in a matter of moments.

Frank holstered the Colt and picked up the Winchester, then proceeded to reload the rifle with cartridges from his pocket in case the raiders turned around and tried again. From the looks of it, though, the bandits had no intention of returning. The dust cloud their horses kicked up dwindled in the distance.

"Keep riding, you bastards!" growled the older of the two men from the buckboard as he shook a fist after the *bandidos*. "Don't stop until you get back across the border to hell, as far as I'm concerned!"

The man was stocky and grizzled, with a graying, close-cropped beard. Most of his head was bald. His hands and face had a weathered, leathery look, an indication that he had spent most of his life outdoors.

The second man was younger, taller, and clean-shaven,

but he bore a resemblance to the older man that Frank recognized right away. He pegged them as father and son, or perhaps uncle and nephew. Both men were dressed in well-kept range clothes that would have looked better if they hadn't been covered in trail dust. They had the appearance of successful cattlemen about them.

Frank spotted the other rifle lying on the ground about twenty feet away. He nodded toward it and said, "Better pick up that repeater, just in case they come back."

The older man snorted contemptuously. "They won't be back! Bunch of no-good, cowardly dogs! They travel in a pack and won't attack unless the odds are ten to one in their favor."

"And we cut those odds down in a hurry," the younger man said. He hurried over to retrieve the rifle anyway, Frank noted.

The riders had disappeared in the distance now, without even any dust showing. Deciding that they were truly gone, Frank walked out from behind the buckboard and went to check on the men who had fallen from their horses during the fight. He counted seven of them. Six were already dead, and the seventh was unconscious and badly wounded. Blood bubbled from his mouth in a crimson froth with every ragged breath he took, and Frank heard the air whistling through bullet-punctured lungs. The man dragged in one last breath and then let it out in a shuddery sigh, dying without regaining consciousness.

Frank's expression didn't change as he watched the man pass over the divide. *Any man's death diminishes me,* John Donne had written, and in a philosophical way Frank supposed there might be some truth to that. Donne, however, had never swapped lead with a *bandido.*

Five of the men were Mexicans, typical south-of-the-border hardcases. The other two were Americans of the same sort. Frank checked their pockets, found nothing but spare shells for their guns and some coins.

A pistol shot made him look around. The younger man had just put the injured horse out of its misery.

Frank walked back to the buckboard. The younger man began unhitching the team and trying to calm the horses. The older man met Frank with a suspicious look. He asked, "Who are you, mister? Why'd you jump into that fracas on our side?"

"My name's Morgan," Frank said, "and I just thought it looked like you could use a hand. I never have liked an unfair fight."

The man nodded and wiped the back of his hand across his nose, which was bleeding a little. That seemed to be the only injury either of them had suffered in the wreck of the buckboard. They had been mighty lucky.

"Well, the boy an' me are much obliged. My name's Cecil Tolliver. That's my son Ben."

Ben Tolliver paused in what he was doing to look over at Frank and nod. "Howdy." He turned back to the horses and then paused and looked at Frank again. "Wouldn't be Frank Morgan, would it? The one they call The Drifter?"

Frank tried not to sigh. Just once, he thought, he would like to ride in somewhere and not have somebody recognize him almost right away.

And it would have been nice too if nobody shot at him.

CHAPTER 2

"Yes, I'm Frank Morgan," he admitted.

Cecil Tolliver frowned. "I don't mean to sound ignorant, mister, but I don't reckon I've heard of you."

Ben came over and held out his hand to Frank. "That's because you never read any dime novels," he explained to his father. "Mr. Morgan here is a famous gunfighter."

Tolliver grunted. "I never had time for such foolishness, boy. I was too busy tryin' to build the Rockin' T into a decent spread. You was the one who always had your nose in the *Police Gazette.*"

Frank shook hands with both of them and said to Ben, "Most of what's been written about me in those dime novels and the illustrated weeklies was a pack of lies made up by gents who don't know much about the real West."

"You can't deny, though, that you've had your share of gunfights," Ben said.

Frank inclined his head in acknowledgment of that point. "More than my share," he allowed.

"Well, we're much obliged for the help, whether you're famous or not," Tolliver said. "If you hadn't come along when you did, I reckon Almanzar's boys would've done in me and Ben."

"Almanzar," Frank repeated. "I'm not familiar with the name. Is he the leader of that gang of *bandidos?*"

"You could call him that. He runs the rancho where those gunnies work."

Now it was Frank's turn to frown. He waved his left hand toward the sprawled bodies of the raiders and said, "Those don't look like vaqueros or cowhands to me."

"That's because Almanzar's a low-down skunk who hires killers rather than decent hombres."

"Sounds like you don't care for the man."

"I got no use for him," Tolliver said stiffly. "Him and me been feudin' ever since I came to this part of the country, nigh on to thirty years ago. Almanzar specializes in wet cattle, if you know what I mean."

Frank understood the term, all right. It referred to stock rustled from one side of the river and driven to the other. Down here in this border country, a lot of cattle had gotten their bellies wet over the past few decades, going in both directions across the Rio Grande.

Young Ben spoke up. "You don't know that Don Felipe has been rustling our cows, Pa."

"I know all I need to know," Tolliver replied with a disgusted snort. "Almanzar's a thief and a bloody-handed reiver, and this ain't the first time he's tried to have me killed!"

Obviously, there was trouble going on around here, Frank thought. Just as obviously, it was none of his business. But by taking a hand in this gun battle, he had probably dealt himself into the game, whether he wanted that or not. If Cecil Tolliver was correct about Don Felipe Almanzar sending those gunmen after him and his son, then Almanzar would be likely to want vengeance on Frank for killing several of his men.

"Another thing," Tolliver went on angrily to Ben. "I don't want to hear you callin' that bastard by his Christian name again. He ain't our friend and never has been."

"What about when you first settled here, before I was born?" Ben asked. "I've heard you say more than once, Pa, that without Señor Almanzar's help, the Comanches would have lifted your hair back in those days."

"That was a long time ago," Tolliver growled. "Things change."

Frank wasn't really interested in the history of the feud between Tolliver and Don Felipe Almanzar. He said, "Where were you men headed?"

"Back to the Rockin' T," Tolliver replied. "We'd been to San Rosa for supplies." He shook his head in disgust. "All the boxes done bounced out back along the road, when that bunch jumped us and we had to take off so fast. We're lucky the damn buckboard didn't rattle itself to pieces."

"San Rosa's the nearest town?"

"Yep, right on the river about five miles upstream from here. The name's fouled up—it ought to be Santa Rosa— but the fella who stuck the name on it didn't savvy Mex talk. Still a pretty nice place."

"I'll pay it a visit," Frank said. "I was looking for a place to get something to eat and somewhere to stay."

"You don't have to go to San Rosa for that." Tolliver jerked a thumb at the buckboard. "Help us set that wagon up, and then you can ride on to the Rockin' T with us. You'll be our guest for as long as you want to stay, Mr. Morgan."

"Call me Frank. And I wouldn't want to impose—"

"Impose, hell!" Tolliver had picked up his hat and now he slapped it against his leg to get some of the dust off. As he settled it on his head, he went on. "After what you done to help us, I'll consider it a personal insult if you don't let us feed you and put you up for a spell."

Frank smiled. "In that case, I accept."

He whistled and Stormy came out of the chaparral, followed by Dog. Tolliver and Ben looked with admiration at the big Appaloosa, but were more wary where Dog was concerned. "That critter looks a mite like a cross between a wolf and a grizzly bear," Tolliver commented.

"He's all dog," Frank said with a grin. "Just be sure

you've been introduced properly before you go to pet him. Unless you're a little kid," he added. "He'll let kids wool him around like he's still a pup."

Frank took his rope from the saddle and tied one end to the buckboard. Ben saw what he was doing and brought over the surviving three members of the team. The rope was tied to their harness, and the horses did the work as the buckboard was soon pulled upright again. Frank hitched Stormy into the empty spot in the team. The Appaloosa didn't care much for that, but he was willing to tolerate it if that was what Frank wanted him to do. Stormy turned a baleful eye on his master for a moment, though.

"I'd watch out for that horse if I was you, Mr. Morgan," Ben said. "He looks like he might sneak up on you sometime and take a nip out of your hide."

"I fully expect that he will," Frank agreed with a chuckle. He grew more sober as he gestured toward the bodies again. "What about them?"

"I'll be damned if I'm gonna get their blood all over my buckboard," Cecil Tolliver said. "When we get to the ranch, I'll send a rider to San Rosa to notify the law. In the meantime, a couple o' my hands can come back out with a work wagon to load up the carcasses. The undertaker can come to the ranch to get 'em for plantin'."

"There's law in San Rosa?"

"Yeah, a town marshal who don't amount to much. But there's a company of Rangers that's been usin' the town as their headquarters for a spell, while they try to track down some bandits who've been raisin' hell around here."

Frank's interest perked up at the mention of Texas Rangers. Over the past year or so he had shared several adventures with a young Ranger named Tyler Beaumont. Beaumont was back home with his wife in Weatherford now, recuperating from injuries he had received in that fence-cutting dustup in Brown County. Frank respected the Rangers a great deal as a force for law and

order, even though his reputation as a gunfighter sometimes made the Rangers look on him with suspicion.

He wasn't looking for trouble down here along the
border, though, so it was unlikely he would clash with
the lawmen.

Tolliver and Ben climbed onto the seat of the buckboard. Frank tied his packhorse on at the back of the vehicle, then sat down with his legs dangling off the rear.
When he snapped his fingers, Dog jumped onto the buckboard and settled down beside him. Tolliver got the team
moving and drove on toward his ranch, the Rocking T.

Frank saw cattle in the chaparral as the buckboard
rolled along. They were longhorns, the sort of tough,
hardy breed that was required in this brushy country.
Longhorns seemed to survive, even to thrive, in it where
other breeds had fallen by the wayside. The ugly, dangerous brutes had been the beginning of the cattle in-
dustry in Texas, back in the days immediately following
the Civil War. Animals that had been valuable only for
their hide and tallow had suddenly become beef on the
hoof, the source of a small fortune for the men daring
enough and tough enough to round them up and make
the long drive over the trails to the railhead in Kansas.

As a young cowboy, Frank had ridden along on more
than one of those drives, pushing the balky cattle through
dust and rain, heat and cold, and danger from Indians
and outlaws. Since the railroads had reached Texas, the
days of such cattle drives were over. Now a man seldom
had to move his herds more than a hundred miles or so
before reaching a shipping point. As much as he lamented
some things about the settling of the West, Frank didn't
miss those cattle drives. They had been long, arduous,
perilous work.

With an arm looped around Dog's shaggy neck, he
turned his head and asked the Tollivers, "How much
stock have you been losing lately?"

"Not that much," Ben said.

His father snorted. "Not that much at one time, you mean. Half a dozen here, a dozen there. But it sure as hell adds up."

Frank knew what Tolliver meant. Rustlers could make a big raid on a ranch, or they could bleed it dry over time. Either method could prove devastating to a cattleman.

"The Rangers haven't been able to get a line on the wide-loopers?"

"They're too busy lookin' for the Black Scorpion."

"The Black Scorpion?" Frank repeated. "What's that?"

"You mean who's that. You recollect what I said about the Rangers huntin' for a gang of owlhoots? Well, the Black Scorpion is the boss outlaw, the son of a bitch who heads up that gang."

Ben laughed. "Now you're talking like the one who's been reading dime novels, Pa."

"The Black Scorpion's real, damn it," Tolliver said with a scowl. "Folks have seen him, dressed all in black and wearin' a mask, leadin' that bloodthirsty bunch o' desperadoes."

That sounded pretty far-fetched to Frank too, like the creation of one of those ink-stained wretches who made up stories about him. There might be some truth to it, though. The West had seen mysterious masked bandits before, such as Black Bart out in California. Frank was going to have to see this so-called Black Scorpion for himself, though, before he would really believe in such an individual.

Ben was equally skeptical, saying, "I'll believe it when I see it. It seems to me that Captain Wedge and the Rangers are wasting their time looking for phantoms when they ought to be hunting down rustlers."

"Well, I ain't gonna argue about that," his father said. "I wish they'd do something about the damn rustlers too."

Frank sat in the back of the buckboard and mulled over what he had heard. He had come down here to the border country looking for someplace warm and peaceful. It was warm, all right, but evidently far from peaceful, what with the feud between Cecil Tolliver and Don Felipe Almanzar, the rustlers plaguing the Rocking T, and another gang of bandits led by a mysterious masked figure. With all that going on, it seemed like trouble could crop up from any direction with little or no warning—or from several directions at once.

"Is it possible the Black Scorpion could be responsible for the rustling?" Frank asked.

"Folks have thought about that," Tolliver replied, "but me and some o' the other ranchers around here have lost stock on the same nights that the Black Scorpion's gang was reported to be maraudin' on the other side of the border. The varmint can't be in two places at the same time."

"No, I reckon not," Frank said, but he wasn't completely convinced. His instincts told him that there was even more going on around here than was readily apparent.

His instincts also told him that the smart thing to do would be to unhitch Stormy from the team, mount up, and light a shuck out of here. The troubles had nothing to do with him, and if he stayed around and was drawn deeper into them, his hopes for a quiet, relaxing winter might well be shattered.

On the other hand, he had never turned his back on trouble just to make it easier on himself, and he was a mite too old to start now. A leopard couldn't change its spots, nor a tiger its stripes.

The sun was low in the sky by the time the buckboard reached the headquarters of the Rocking T. Frank saw a large, whitewashed house sitting in the shade of several cottonwood trees. Behind it were a couple of barns, several corrals, a bunkhouse, a cookshack, a blacksmith shop, a chicken coop, and some storage buildings. There was a vegetable garden off to one side of the house and beyond it a small orchard filled with fruit trees. It was a mighty nice layout, Frank thought, the sort of spread that required years of hard work and dedication to build. He admired a man like Cecil Tolliver who could put down roots and create something lasting and worthwhile like this. For all of his accomplishments, Frank had never been able to achieve that. True, he had quite a few business interests scattered across the West, business interests that had made him a wealthy man, at least on paper, but he had inherited those things, not worked for them and built them himself. Most of the time, he felt as if all he truly owned were his guns and not much else. Stormy and Dog were friends, not possessions. And most of the time, that was all right. Frank didn't miss the rest of it except at moments such as this, when he looked at the Rocking T and wondered what his life would have been like if things had been different, if he hadn't been blessed—or cursed—with such blinding speed and uncanny accuracy with a gun.

Tolliver hauled back on the reins and brought the buckboard to a halt. "This is it," he said. "Welcome to the Rocking T, Mr. Morgan."

CHAPTER 3

Their arrival hadn't gone unnoticed. A small black, brown, and tan dog came racing around the house, barking sharply at the buckboard. The dog stopped abruptly, however, when it spotted the big cur sitting next to Frank in the back of the vehicle. A growl rumbled deeply in Dog's throat and was echoed by the smaller animal, even though Dog was more than ten times his size.

"Don't get your back fur in an uproar there, Dobie," Tolliver called to the little dog. "This here's a friend."

"Behave yourself, Dog," Frank said firmly to the cur.

Dog jumped down from the buckboard. He and Dobie sniffed warily at each other, but neither of them snapped. After a moment, Dog strolled over to a clump of grass and hiked his leg to relieve himself on it. Dobie followed suit, establishing himself as the boss around here. Dog seemed to accept that, and if he'd been a human he would have shrugged, Frank thought as he watched the byplay between the two animals.

Dobie wasn't the only one to greet the newcomers. Several men walked out of one of the barns and came toward the buckboard. At the same time, the front door of the ranch house opened and four women emerged. Two of them were fairly young and had the same sandy-colored hair that Ben did. One of the older women had gray hair, while the other was a stunning brunette.

"Come on," Tolliver said as he climbed down from the wagon. "I'll introduce you to the womenfolk."

Frank slid off the back of the buckboard and followed Tolliver and Ben to the house. When he reached the bottom of the three steps that led up to the porch, he took off his hat.

"Ladies, this here is Mr. Frank Morgan," Tolliver said. With rough-hewn gallantry, he went on, "Mr. Morgan, allow me to present my wife Pegeen and our daughters Debra and Jessie. And this is Pegeen's sister Roanne."

Frank held his hat in front of him and nodded politely. "Ladies," he said. "The honor and the pleasure are mine."

"We're pleased to meet you, Mr. Morgan," Pegeen Tolliver said. She was oldest of the four women, the one with gray hair. She was still a handsome woman, though, and the same lines of timeless beauty to be found in her face were also present in the faces of her sister and her daughters. Roanne, who was around thirty, Frank estimated, was especially lovely. There wasn't that much age difference between her and her nieces, who were both between twenty and twenty-five, fine-looking young frontier women. And both already married too, judging by the rings on their fingers.

Frank noted that Roanne wore no ring at all, for whatever that was worth.

The men who had come out of the barn reached the house. Two of them stepped up onto the porch and moved next to Debra and Jessie. "My sons-in-law," Cecil Tolliver said, then introduced them. "That's Darrell Forrest with Jessie, and Nick Holmes with Debra. They're both top hands."

Frank shook hands with Darrell and Nick and said, "Glad to meet you, boys."

Darrell Forrest looked intently at Frank and said, "Frank Morgan . . . that was the name, sir?"

Before Frank could say anything, Ben Tolliver said, "That's right, Darrell. He's The Drifter."

Pegeen put a hand on her husband's arm and said, "Cecil, you went to town for supplies, but I don't see any in the buckboard. And one of the horses is missing. Does that spotted horse belong to Mr. Morgan?"

"That's right," Tolliver told her. His bearded face grew grim as he continued. "The supplies are scattered up and down the road this side o' San Rosa, where they got jolted out when we had to run from a bunch o' gunmen."

Pegeen's hand tightened on Tolliver's arm. "Are you or Ben hurt?"

"I reckon we'll have some bruises tomorrow. We got throwed off the buckboard when it turned over durin' the chase. But Mr. Morgan come along right about then and helped us fight off those bast—those no-good skunks." Tolliver looked at Nick Holmes. "Nick, send a rider to San Rosa to tell Flem Jarvis that we've got the bodies of seven o' them owlhoots out here waitin' for the undertaker."

"Seven bodies!" Nick exclaimed. "But I don't see—"

"That's because they're still out on the road right now. Once you've sent a man to town, you and Darrell take a couple of hands and a work wagon and go out to get the corpses."

The ladies all looked a little shaken by this casual discussion of corpses and an attack by a gang of outlaws. Being good frontier women, though, they remained calm and didn't waste time with a bunch of chattering questions. It took more than a little trouble to rattle a true woman of the West. And these were Texas women, which meant they had backbone second to none.

Pegeen turned to Frank and said, "Thank you for helping my husband and my son, Mr. Morgan. I hope you plan to stay for supper and spend the night with us. A little hospitality is the least we can do for you."

"Yes, ma'am," Frank said with a smile. "Your husband

already told me I'd be staying a while, and I sure appreciate the kindness."

"You're very welcome. Come on inside. I'll bet you could use a cup of coffee."

"Ma'am, coffee is one of my biggest weaknesses," Frank said, his smile widening into a grin. He went into the house with Tolliver, Ben, and the women, while Darrell and Nick hurried off to carry out Tolliver's orders.

The house was well appointed, with thick rugs on the floors and heavy, overstuffed furniture. A massive stone fireplace dominated one wall of the parlor. A tremendous spread of longhorns adorned the wall above the fireplace. Several sets of deer antlers were attached to the wall as well, and rifles and shotguns hung on pegs. A cavalry saber was also on display, and when Cecil Tolliver noticed Frank's interest in it, the rancher said, "I carried that when I rode with Jeb Stuart, Fitz Lee, and Mac Brannon during the war, Mr. Morgan. That was before I came out here to Texas."

"I thought I detected a hint of Virginia in your voice, sir," Frank said.

"Were you in the war?"

"I was . . . but that was a long time ago."

Tolliver clapped a hand on his shoulder. "Indeed it was. After supper, I'll break out a bottle of brandy I've been savin', and we'll drink to old times. They weren't the best of times, but they made us what we are."

"I reckon that's true enough," Frank agreed. Almost three decades had passed since the end of the war, but it remained the single biggest event in most men's lives.

A man couldn't spend all his time looking backward, though. As the women left Frank, Tolliver, and Ben in the parlor, Frank steered the conversation back to the here and now by saying, "I suppose you've had your hands riding patrol at night, trying to stop the rustling."

Tolliver nodded. "Damn right I have. All it's gotten me

is one puncher shot dead and another laid up with a bullet-busted shoulder."

"So the rustlers don't hesitate to shoot?"

"Not at all. Anyway, this is a big spread. It'd take an army to cover all of it at night." The frustration was easy to hear in Tolliver's voice. "But I can't just call in my men and throw the ranch wide open to the damn wide-loopers."

Frank shook his head. "No, you can't do that," he agreed.

"If you have any ideas, Mr. Morgan," Ben said, "we'd be glad to hear 'em."

Tolliver got a cigar from a box on a table next to a heavy divan and jabbed it toward Frank. "What I ought to do is hire some gunmen and ride across the Rio to wipe out Almanzar. I'll bet our rustlin' troubles would stop then!"

Ben frowned darkly, and Frank got the feeling that the young man didn't care for his father's idea at all. Ben wasn't the only one. Pegeen had come back into the room with her sister in time to hear her husband's angry pronouncement, and she said, "You'll do no such thing, Cecil Tolliver! You can't take the law into your own hands, and besides, you don't know that Don Felipe is behind the rustling."

Tolliver stuck the cigar in his mouth and chewed savagely on it for a moment before he said, "When we first come out here, Peg, there wasn't no law but what a man could carry in his own fist. We did all right in those days."

"We all nearly got killed more than once, fighting off Comanches and outlaws," she snapped. "You leave such things to the Rangers."

Tolliver just made a sound of disgust. He took another cigar from the box and offered it to Frank, who slipped it into his shirt pocket. "I'll save it for later, with that brandy," he said.

"Good idea. I got to gnaw on this one now, though,

to keep from sayin' things I hadn't ought to say." Tolliver crossed his arms and glared at the world in general.

His wife dared his wrath by saying, "I still need those supplies. Come morning, Cecil, you'll have to go back to town to replace the ones you lost."

"All right, all right," Tolliver muttered around the cigar. "But I'm takin' more of the boys with me next time, and if Almanzar sends his gun wolves after us again, they'll get even more of a fight than they got this time!"

Debra and Jessie came out of the kitchen carrying trays with cups and saucers on them. Steam lifted from the coffee in the cups, and Frank smiled in appreciation of the delicious aroma.

The coffee tasted as good as it smelled. Frank sat in a comfortable armchair and sipped from his cup. A time or two, he caught Roanne watching him with undisguised interest. He wondered if she was married or a widow or had never been hitched. An unmarried woman of her age was considered an old maid out here, but there was nothing old about her. To be honest, the boldness of her gaze wasn't very maidenly either. Frank returned her looks with an interest of his own. She was a mighty attractive lady.

They hadn't been sitting around the parlor for very long when a sudden rataplan of hoofbeats welled up outside. A large group of riders was approaching the ranch. Tolliver and Ben set their cups aside and stood up quickly. So did Frank. No shouts of alarm had sounded from the ranch hands, but these days, no one was taking a chance. With his hand on the butt of the Colt at his hip, Tolliver strode to the front door. Ben and Frank were right behind him.

As the three men stepped out onto the porch, they saw a group of about twenty-five men entering the ranch yard. The rider in the lead was a big, barrel-chested man with a raw-boned, hawklike face and a shock of white hair under a black Stetson. The last of the fading light revealed a badge pinned to his coat. Frank recognized it as a star set inside a circle, the emblem of the Texas Rangers.

"Captain Wedge!" Tolliver called out as the newcomers reined in, confirming the guess Frank had just made. "Good to see you and your boys. Could have used you around a little while ago."

The Ranger captain swung down from his saddle and curtly motioned for his men to dismount as well. "Why's that, Tolliver?" he asked as he turned to face the rancher.

"Because my boy an' me were jumped by a gang o' Almanzar's gunmen from across the border. If it wasn't for Frank Morgan here, Ben an' me would probably be buzzard bait by now."

Captain Wedge turned his dark eyes toward The Drifter and repeated the name. "Frank Morgan, eh?"

Frank knew there was no point in denying anything. It came as no surprise to him that a lawman had recognized his name. He said, "That's right."

"Heard of you," Wedge said with a curt nod. "Don't think there's any paper out on you right now, though."

"There never has been except on trumped-up charges that were proven false," Frank said.

Wedge nodded again. "Pretty much what I figured. Heard too that you've given the Rangers a hand now and then."

"I'm a law-abiding man," Frank explained. "I do what I can to help when I'm called on."

"Good to know." Wedge turned back to Cecil Tolliver. "What's this about you and the boy being attacked by Almanzar's riders?"

"They jumped us while we were comin' back to the ranch from San Rosa," Tolliver said. "We'd been to town to pick up some supplies. A whole bunch of 'em came on us suddenlike, yellin' and shootin'. We tried to get away and make a fight of it at the same time, but our buckboard turned over. Then Mr. Morgan rode up and took a hand in the game. We knocked down enough of the bastards so that the rest of 'em turned tail."

"Sounds like you're lucky to be alive," Wedge said.

"That's the way I figure it too."

The Ranger captain frowned. "How do you know the men who jumped you work for Almanzar?"

"Who else would have it in for me?" Tolliver demanded. "Almanzar and me been crossways with each other for a long time."

"What about the Black Scorpion?"

Tolliver looked surprised at Wedge's question. "What about him?"

"Could the men who attacked you have been part of the Scorpion's gang?"

Ben put in, "That thought crossed my mind too, even though I'm not sure I believe in the Black Scorpion."

"He's real enough," Wedge said.

Tolliver shook his head stubbornly. "I didn't see no sign of any masked man leadin' the gang. They were just a bunch of border toughs, the sort of hardcases Almanzar hires to make life miserable for me."

"The reason I ask is, the men and I have been trailing the Black Scorpion since yesterday. He and his gang raided a ranch on the other side of San Rosa. They were coming in this direction and it seems logical to me that they could have run into you and your son."

"Nope. Those gunnies worked for Almanzar."

Frank read the skepticism on Captain Wedge's face, and to tell the truth, he was beginning to have his doubts about Tolliver's belief too. From the looks of things, Tolliver's hatred of Don Felipe Almanzar was so deep-seated that the cattleman was quick to blame Almanzar for everything bad that happened, whether Almanzar had anything to do with it or not.

It appeared that Wedge might have argued the matter

further, but at that moment the women came out of the house onto the porch. The light was behind them and shone on their hair. Wedge took his hat off and nodded politely to them, saying, "Ladies. After a long day on the trail, you are sure a sight for sore eyes, if I may be so bold as to say so."

"You may," Pegeen Tolliver told him with a smile. "Hello, Captain. Will you and your men be staying to supper?"

"That sounds mighty nice, ma'am, but we're on the trail of some bad men—"

"You can't follow a trail very well at night," Tolliver put in. "Join us for supper, Captain. Your men can eat in the bunkhouse with the hands."

Wedge chuckled. "That Chinaman who cooks for you probably won't be very happy about having that many extra mouths to feed."

"He'll get over it. There's plenty of room for your men to bunk in the barn too, and we'll find a bed for you in the house."

The captain returned his black Stetson to his head. "I'm much obliged, Tolliver, and on behalf of my men, I accept." He turned and said to his troop of Rangers, "Light for a spell, boys. We're spending the night here on the Rocking T."

A grin creased Tolliver's leathery face. "I'd like to see Almanzar's nighthawks come a-raidin' now, with a couple dozen Rangers on the place! They'd get a mighty warm welcome if they did!"